TAPI.

TORN

Godwill Tsvamuno

LOVE
KUDA

GPS CREATIVE BOOKS & PUBLISHING

GPS CREATIVE BOOKS & PUBLISHING
Published by GPS Creative Books :

29 Greenside Way,
Walsall, West Midlands,
WS5 4BT

EMAIL: gpscreative@gmail.com
FACEBOOK Username: @tornbookseries
WEBSITE: www.tornbookseries.com

This is the first book by the author and first publication
by GPS Creative Books

Published in The United Kingdom
through Amazon KDP ® and Createspace®

Published 2018

ISBN-13: 978-1722039479

ACKNOWLEDGMENTS

When you embark on a journey you need God on your side and the support of your loved ones to set you off. I feel that the reason why this book even exists is because of that support my family gives me, my wife Patience and my kids, Samantha & Casey, who sat and listened as I talked about it and read to them, EVERYDAY! They were and will always remain, my source of inspiration.

To V.L, thank you for the hours you put into going through my book and the wonderful edits you made. You refined and enhanced it and I will forever be grateful.

To my extended family, vast network of friends, acquaints and colleagues, thank you for being part of what makes me who I am. Your combined support for me throughout the years is what has kept me going.

To my new family; readers of my book, my audience, I am excited about this journey we are about to embark on together. May this book, and many more to come, give you something to enjoy, get you thinking and fulfil you in whatever way possible. Never underestimate your support, not just to me, but to many others who might also be starting out in their life ventures.

Thank you

TORN

VOLUME 1

Chapter 1

She sat alone in the Mug & Bean, a coffee cafe on the mezzanine floor of the Eastgate Plaza, nursing a mug of steamy milky coffee. As she cautiously sipped her beverage waiting, she perused the pages of the latest edition of the Marie Claire magazine she had picked up from a vendor earlier on. The coffee shop was reasonably busy, people mostly in pairs chatting, with the odd few sat alone typing away on their laptops or swiping at their smartphones. Harare had changed so much that from inside the cafe you felt like you could have been anywhere in the western world.

Eastgate was one such building that was testament to this new affluence Africa was enjoying. It was situated on the corner of Robert Mugabe Avenue and Second Street and had aided in raising the profile the city as one of the best metropolitan places in all of the Southern African hemisphere.

She sat up away from the fashion and beauty stories, and pulled back the sleeve of her woolen jumper to reveal an extravagant gold ladies watch studded with diamonds. It had been an engagement present from her boyfriend, now her fiancé, Justin. It was one of her most cherished possessions as she knew he had worked hard and saved hard to get it for her. She checked the time. It was a quarter past three. She covered it up again. She had to be careful because as much as Harare was evolving, changing to match up to the modern world, a fraction of its populace hadn't. Crime in the city was still so rampant, blatant at times and usually from ordinary looking people that you wouldn't even suspect. There were still a lot of wolves in sheep's clothing.

Harriet glanced out at the city below from the large window she sat next to. She was grateful that it was tinted, as the blazing African sun could sometimes be unforgiving. From her vantage point, she watched the people below as they went about their daily lives. The street was a myriad of varying activities and personalities. Most were young smart office types, clutching filofaxes and briefcases, walking purposefully and looking busy. Others were more casual, walking slower and seemed to have time to stop and admire shop front window displays.

In amongst them and also walking quickly and purposeful towards somewhere were women with large baskets full of fruit and vegetable produce skillfully balanced on their heads. Some even had babies strapped onto their backs, held tightly by a single large towel or cloth. They may have seemed inappropriately dressed for the city or for the office but they were definitely confident of their position within this urban ecosystem.

As she continued to look out at the life on the street below, Harriet noticed a group of young boys coming into view from the neighbouring street. There were about six in total and all looked barely past the age of ten. The boys wore very old and torn clothes, but that seemed to be the least of their worries. As they walked up the street they would approach people, begging for anything from money to food, or anything the person was holding.

They had developed quite a skill for it because almost everyone ended up giving them something, even if they had tried to ignore them initially. Their tactic involved following and nagging the person until he or she had no option but to give them something to shake them off. They were relentless, and brazen to a greater extent, taking on adults much bigger and stronger than they were, but no one dared to try anything physical to get them off; they walked in groups for a reason. Any moment one was in danger, the rest would flock to the scene in support, and suddenly the adult would become the victim of verbal and even at times physical abuse.

For many who lived in the city these groups of kids, 'street kids' as they were referred to, were now a menace. They were a pest, eating at the image of the city, harassing innocent citizens. Harriet agreed to some extent that there was an issue of kids on the street but she believed that the issue was not the kids themselves, but more the city that had turned a blind eye to their needs.

Turning away from the scene, Harriet looked towards the cafe entrance, hoping her date had arrived; there was no one she recognised. It seemed that her expected visitor was running late. She was just about to turn her focus away from the direction of the entrance when she caught sight of a familiar figure walk in. She smiled as the person noticed her too and began advancing towards her table. More smiles were exchanged as they drew closer towards each other.

"Hi, Sandy!" Harriet said, greeting her friend Sandra, who had now reached the table. Harriet got up from her seat and leaned over the table for a short embrace.

"Hi!" Sandra answered," So sorry shaz, got stuck at work; couldn't leave. Jeff swamped me with so much work this morning and said he had to have it back before lunch. Can you believe that man?"

"I know," Harriet laughed." All bosses are alike. They give you loads of work to do and expect it to be done yesterday."

"You can say that again," Sandra agreed, annoyance etched across her face.

By this time, they were both sitting down.

"Shall I get you some coffee?" Harriet offered.

"Hot chocolate please," Sandra replied.

Harriet got up from her chair and walked to the counter to buy the hot beverage her friend had requested.

They had been friends from as far as high school, and Sandra had been there when the first seeds of Harriet and Justin's relationship had been sown. She was the friend that Harriet often spoke to about her feelings towards Justin and Sandra was the one who often reminded them of how good they were together, especially those times when they fell out.

After high school Harriet and Sandra's lives had taken different paths. Harriet had been able to continue to her A Levels and then later went to the University of Central Africa to study for an Environmental Science Degree. At the end of her degree programme she had taken a few months off whilst she planned her next move, and as she met up with Sandra on this day, Harriet had big news to share.

Sandra, however, upon leaving high school had enrolled at the City College where she had gone on to achieve a secretarial qualification and now worked as a personal assistant to Jeff Munyai, an infamous local lawyer known for defending not-so-reputable characters. She had never been bothered by her boss's questionable reputation as he had always treated her well, at least most of the time.

Harriet returned to the table with a tall see-through glass mug of hot chocolate and placed it in front of Sandra. It looked inviting with a dollop of whipped cream and sprinkled dry chocolate on top.

"Oh wow, thanks sha. This looks yummy," Sandra remarked.

"Not a problem," Harriet answered as she went to take her seat on the opposite side. They both picked up their drinks, took sips and gently placed them back on the table. There was almost a synchronicity to the way they did this.

"So?" Sandra began." Tell me, I'm dying to know, what's the big news?"

Harriet smiled, evidently excited about what she was about to tell her friend, but she was also uncertain how Sandra was going to take the news. This was going to affect her and their friendship;

but it was a good thing. Surely she would be pleased for her once she knew.

"Well," Harriet began," You know how I've always wanted to do my Masters Degree? Well, I'm going to Europe for 2 years to study. My place at the Brunel University in London came through!"

Sandra had leaned in to listen.

"Oh my God!" She exclaimed excitedly," That is awesome Harriet! Oh my God; when did that happen? When do you have to leave?"

"Only got the news yesterday and I have to try and be in London by the end of March. The semester starts in September but I thought I might work a little before starting."

"Wow, that's in two months. Oh my God, I can't believe it. So happy for you sha. It's finally happening! This is what we have always talked about."

"I know!" Harriet agreed, "I'm so thrilled about it."

"Gosh, remember how we used to talk about how nice it would be to leave Zimbabwe for a while and experience something new, a new life, new cultures, new people." Sandra reminisced, as she gazed upwards, feeling quite envious of Harriet.

"Ye, we did. It's really a dream come true for me, especially that I also get to do my Masters. I am over the moon; it's going to be so good."

"What did your mum and dad say?" Sandra asked.

"They were so pleased; my dad is really proud. My mum cried later though, after it dawned on her that she might not be seeing me for 2 years, although I do intend to come back halfway through."

"And Justin? How is he going to manage for a whole two years without you?"

They both sniggered.

"I don't think he's really pleased about me leaving, but he's happy for me," Harriet replied. "I'm seriously going to miss him though. We've rarely been apart for more than two days and the thought that I might not see him for more than a year or two scares me. I never imagined I'd ever have to think about a situation like this."

"You're definitely planning on coming back in between, right?" Sandra asked, seeking reassurance from her friend that this was definitely on her mind.

"I will try, well, that's my intention but if I can't, maybe Justin could fly up to see me. You should come too," Harriet added, leaning in on her friend and reaching out to hold her hand that was on the table.

"E-ee sha, that would be so nice, but the UK isn't that easy to get into these days I've been told. Their immigration is ruthless. You will have to come back and see us. Can't do 2 years without you."

Harriet smiled, "I will."

She sat back in her chair and took another sip of her drink.

"He's going to miss you though," Sandra pointed out about Justin," But time flies and you'll be back before the two of you even know it."

"Ye, you're right. But it might be a good thing for the both of us I guess, having some time apart to work on our careers. When I finish I'll come back, get me a good job and then we can start to think about getting married and raising our family."

"That sounds like a brilliant plan; you should definitely do that.... But I'm also going to miss you even more, Harriet. What am I going to do without you?"

"Awww, babe, I know. We'll have to call each other every night," Harriet said, smiling fondly at her best friend, even though she knew in her mind that this was not going to always be possible. "You'll have to do something for me though while I'm away," Harriet continued, looking at Sandra quite intently. "When I return there are going to be two weddings that year; mine and yours. Your job, while I'm away, is to find a man, OK?"

They looked at each other for a second, Harriet looking at Sandra from above her sunglasses like a teacher eyeing a delinquent school pupil, whilst Sandra smiled sheepishly from across the table like a shy schoolgirl caught snogging a boy behind the school bicycle shed. Straight after they both burst out laughing.

"I think you might have to bring one for me on your way back," Sandra managed to say between their feats of laughter.

"I just might have to," Harriet agreed." Can't trust you to find a decent one for yourself."

They both fell back into another short laugh.

They had spent the rest of that afternoon together and even though they had both enjoyed each other's company, Harriet had not managed to pick out that Sandra was struggling with the idea of her friend's departure. Sandra had never been strong on her own. Harriet had always been her rock. Sandra could not bear to think how the rest of the year would go, let alone two. Who would she turn to if she needed someone? She was not about to

Harriet know though how she truly felt. What friend would she be if she was not encouraging and supportive? As far as she was concerned, this was Harriet's time and her own feelings were irrelevant, at least for now.

Chapter 2

Justin sat at his desk in his 20-foot square cubicle and studied the company's annual report that had just been published and distributed to all employees. The whole second floor was buzzing. Publishing day of the annual report was like the day school examination results came out. Every department wanted to know how well they had done but above all, everyone wanted to know who had managed to make it into the report. Making it into the report meant you had been exceptional at something and the top bosses would get to hear about you. Justin had been in the report the previous year for 'Best in Sales & Marketing'. He was good at his job, more of a natural, and he knew it would not be long before he moved up the ranks at Glenson & Glenson.

As he flipped to the next page of the fresh smelling, gloss printed report, Justin's face lit up like an African summer's afternoon. He had made it into the report yet again for the second year running, and underneath his picture were those words he had now grown to love 'Best - Sales & Marketing 2012 - 2013'.

As he read through that section of the report, Ken Langa, his friend and work colleague, came into view around Justin's cubicle and sat on a chair opposite him. Ken was a very crude comedic character, often making everyone on the sales floor laugh with his jokes. He was the resident clown of the second-floor marketing offices. Ken and Justin had started at Glenson & Glenson five years earlier, on the same day and had been friends since.

"You're in man," Ken began, with a half-smile on his boyish looking face," Two years running, no contest. This time you getting 'The Call' man", he said gesturing quotation marks with his fingers.

Every employee of Glenson & Glenson knew what 'The Call' meant. 'The Call' involved being called up to the top floor, to the company bosses, which usually also then meant a promotion. But 'The Call' now also held some sort of mythical symbolism amongst staff. It epitomised the crossing of that threshold, that line which separated the 'Top Brass' from everyone else. It was like moving from total obscurity and straight into the promised land.

"Ye man, about time too," Justin agreed, calmly and sarcastically.

Ignoring the sarcasm Ken leaned forward and spoke quieter. "But seriously Jussy, it's time one of us moves out of here. You have been top of this department for two years man, they have to do something now. Let me tell you something, you should actually be running this department. You'd do far better than Sonders."

Ken, like everyone in their department, held deep feelings of resentment towards their boss, Director of Sales and Marketing, Albert Sonderai. He was a leech, gaining praise from the board of directors off ideas he usually pilfered from junior staff in his department.

Justin smiled and continued to explore the annual report, trying not to pay too much attention to Ken. He agreed with him though; he potentially could run the department far better than Sonderai but he was not prepared to say it out loud. He knew sooner or later his skills would take him to where he needed to be.

As they sat and Ken talked, the phone on Justin's desk suddenly began to ring. They both stared at it and then stared at each other. The ringtone was internal and they both wondered if this was it. Justin leaned forward in his chair and picked it up.

" Hello, Justin speaking?" He answered.

"Singala, can you come to my office please?"

It was Sonderai's unmistakable husky voice. Justin was not sure whether to be pleased or worried. He put the phone down and whispered to Ken as he got up from his chair.

"It's Sonders, he wants me upstairs. Wonder what that's about?"

"Sonder's?" Ken said, slightly puzzled," Maybe he's getting pressure from up top to promote you. You do know that the Assistant Director of

Marketing post hasn't been filled since Fombe left six months ago."

"Nah, he probably just wants to know what I'm thinking today," Justin said with a casual smile, as he walked past Ken and towards the end of the office floor, where the elevators lived.

Albert Sonderai's office was on the fourth floor of the Glenson building, a floor shy of the company owners, brothers Mark and John Glenson. A few other executives sat on the top floor as well. The business was a very successful family-run company, started by Mark and John's grandfather and had occupied the same site since its launch in the 1940s; in what was then Salisbury, capital city of Southern Rhodesia.

As years passed and Zimbabwe received its independence from British colonial rule, the city had grown and now much taller skyscrapers towered over its streets. The Glenson building had seen a few renovations over the years to modernise it but on the whole, it remained one building that still carried a small portion of the country's history.

The elevator 'pinged' to announce arrival on the fourth floor. Justin walked out towards the reception desk. The fourth floor covered as much surface as all the other floors below it but it was so spacious. The offices on this floor were so much bigger than the cubicles Justin and his colleagues occupied.

"Hi Flo," Justin said as he approached the reception desk. Florence, the fourth-floor receptionist and personal assistant to the directors, looked up from her computer and smiled.

"Oh hi, Justin. What brings you up here?"

"I have been summoned by the powers that

be," he replied jokingly.

Florence smiled again," Well, good luck with that then, whatever it is. Go ahead, he's in."

Justin whispered a 'thank you' and strolled down a wide corridor towards Sonderai's office. As he walked past the other office doors in the corridor, he read each door plaque. There was Adam West, Human Resources Director, Rose Phiri, Acquisitions, William Wright, Communications and Public Relations, and at the very end was Albert Sonderai. Justin had done this all the time he came up to fourth floor. It was some kind of a ritual now for him. He believed strongly that one day it would be his name that graced one of these doors.

He reached Sonderai's office and knocked on the door lightly.

"Come!" sounded the husky voice from behind it.

Justin opened the door and walked in; it was quite a heavy fire door. Once inside, Justin noticed that Albert's office had changed a little. It was still as big as it had always been, with a large window looking out at the city, but the furnishings had recently been upgraded. His large mahogany desk still sat in the middle of the room, but two new, heavily padded single chairs, now sat in front of it. Even Sonderai's chair was new, a large black leather executive chair.

"Oh yes, come, sit, sit!" He said, gesturing Justin to one of the two new chairs in front of the desk.

"Thank you, sir," Justin said, as he went round and took one of the seats. He sat back in the chair, crossed his legs and looked up at Sonderai, waiting. Justin knew how to act important. He had learnt earlier on in his career that a tough, confident image said more than any words could. He always wanted his bosses, and customers, to have an image of him as a serious businessman who could get things done.

"So Young man," Sonderai began," Best Sales and Marketing yet again." He had a big confusing grin on his face. Justin could not tell whether he was genuinely complimenting him or mocking him.

"Thank you, Sir," Justin replied, unsure whether the statement required an answer.

He knew Sonderai rarely gave out compliments and usually being summoned to his office was never a good thing. Today though Justin was certain this would be a positive meeting. There had not been anything that had gone wrong that he could attach his name to, and besides, he was in the annual report; the least he expected from his department head was appreciation.

"You are proving to be a great asset for this company, young man," Sonderai continued.

"Thank you, Sir."

"U-mm," Sonderai mumbled in agreement, still studying the annual report.

Justin could not tell where all this was going. Although Sonderai seemed to be complimenting him, Justin could not help but sense that it felt insincere. Sonderai was taking his time and was certainly in no hurry to get to the point.

He spoke again. "You obviously know Fombe left a few months ago and his job as my Deputy Director has not been filled yet. I have been informed by Human Resources that you have shown interest in it and from what they tell me, they think you are the right man for the job."

Justin nodded to show understanding and tried to smile as little as possible. He did not want to appear desperate. He was smiling so much inside that he found it hard to contain himself. It was happening he thought to himself. Finally!

"I wasn't aware myself that you were interested in this job," Sonderai continued, "Do you really think you could take on such a demanding role?"

Justin was surprised by the question and vexed as to why his boss would even think to ask. It was not only the question that puzzled him but it was also the mixed messages he was picking up from Sonderai's demeanour. For a man who was about to deliver good news to someone, he was being extremely evasive.

"Definitely sir," Justin replied confidently. He was sensing doubt on his abilities in the man's words and wanted to prove himself.

Sonderai nodded, as if he were agreeing with him, but Justin could see through him.
Something was afoot and Sonderai was playing games with him. It now began to dawn on Justin that his boss had no intention of delivering any good news today.

"Look," Sonderai continued," You are good at what you do young man, I'll give you that, and the company could do with a lot more creative young people like yourself, but I think we should not get ahead of ourselves here. You need to build more experience before you can take on the massive responsibilities of a job such as Assistant Director. Do you understand what I mean young man?"

Justin could not believe what he was

hearing. His excitement transformed instantly into fury. Sonderai was like a snake, very slithery in his approach, and Justin knew this was nothing to do with his capabilities of managing the post. There had to be something else at play. Justin would have had a few choice words to say about the matter but Sonderai was still his boss and he did not want to jeopardise his position. He decided to argue the matter as delicately as he could.

"But sir, I think I am ready. I have been ready for far too long now. I've been top of the department for two years. That's got to show for something."

Sonderai knew what Justin was saying to be true but he just smiled at him and pretended to be understanding.

"And you are almost there," he answered patronisingly," Give it another year or so and you could be in my shoes running this department. I was where you are right now and I understand how it may feel, like you are being held back. Trust me, you will thank me when you do get to sit in this chair and see things from my perspective."

Justin had not expected this, especially today of all days. He had put himself out there, worked so hard, believing that his efforts would be rewarded. The fruits of his labour were evident for all to see and what was happening now was not part of his vision. To have to wait another year would be a set back and he was not sure how to handle this unexpected situation.

"Sir, I'm asking you to reconsider. I believe HR is right, I am the right man for the job."
Justin was desperate and he did not like anyone putting him in that position. He had to try and

convince his department head that he was about to make the biggest mistake ever but somehow he sensed that no amount of effort would change Sonderai's mind. The man seemed to have made his decision on the matter way before Justin walked into the room and had left no room for negotiation.

"OK son, we will take this up again another time. Just keep up the good work and have patience, OK?"

At this juncture, Justin had grown tired of Sonderai's demeaning tones. He had not referred to Justin by name since walking into his office.
It appeared to be some psychological tactic he was playing. Either way, Justin had had enough and before he could be excused, he thanked his boss and quickly exited the office.

He stomped down the corridor to the lifts and in his anger even forgot to acknowledge
Florence as he stepped into the lift. He banged the second-floor
button and slowly the doors closed.

"He said WHAT!" Harriet exclaimed in disgust," That is the worst pile of dog shit I have ever heard. The nerve of that man."

"I know," Justin replied, lazily," I can do his job with my eyes closed and he has the audacity to tell me he doesn't think I am ready for the deputy post. I was offended to my core."

"And you ought to be!" Sandra joined in," You have worked your arse off for that company."

All three had met up that evening at Pizza Palace, to celebrate Harriet's big news. Ken was joining them but was yet to show up. Justin had tried to keep his earlier encounter with Sonderai to himself, so as not to spoil Harriet's evening, but she had sensed that something was not quite right and had managed to get him to talk.

"I have said it time and time again Jussy, you are too valuable for that place. They have failed to acknowledge your worth." Harriet continued. "You need to leave. Find somewhere, where your talent will be appreciated more."

Harriet believed in Justin so much. She had watched him grow to be the man he was today. His upbringing had not been as privileged as hers. He was the eldest of three children, a brother to twin sisters, now teenagers themselves.

Harriet was a deeply ambitious person and had always wanted Justin to achieve as high as he could. She believed that someday they would be a high profile power couple, two highly successful people running highly successful business ventures. Her going abroad to study was part of that dream and she was going to encourage Justin to progress in his own path, whilst she was away.

Harriet and Justin had known each other for years, growing up in Greendale, a medium density suburb in Harare's western district. They knew each other as kids but it was only in high school that they had finally got together. It was not that they never liked each other before then but Harriet's brother had been so protective of her that no boys dared go near her. Unfortunately, he had passed away in a car accident some years later, which totally devastated Harriet's family. Harriet and Justin had eventually grown closer after that and had then proceeded to see each other more.

Justin was a couple of years older than Harriet and came from an average, low-class family. He was very bright growing up, doing exceptionally well at school. He had shown remarkable potential and his teachers had tipped him as one to come out with best grades in his 'O' level year group. No one could have guessed what went on to happen next.

With only a year to go to complete high school, Justin dropped out of school and never returned. At the time, Harriet and many others, especially most of his teachers, could not understand how he could have made such a terrible decision. It seemed a sad loss of such a talented young mind.

Only Justin knew the real reason for his decision and later, he had opened up to Harriet and told her what had happened.

John Sangala, Justin's father, was a haulage trucker who travelled all across Africa delivering cargo of all sorts. Many that knew him knew that his job kept him away for weeks, sometimes months. Many admired the Sangala's as a private family but no one knew the big secret that the family kept. John Sangala was not the hard working loving father that many thought of him to be. He was, in actual fact, quite a selfish and egotistical man, who was quite abusive to his wife and children. The whole family feared and loathed him.

He was a heavily built man who would frighten anyone, and had chosen to target his own family and subject them to fear and terror.

Sometime later, the abuse became more intense and John also began to spend many months away from home. Eventually, the family would learn that their father had actually established another life in Botswana, a neighbouring country to Zimbabwe and one of his many destinations. He had started a whole new life, a new family and was enjoying the pleasures of that double life. Soon after, any financial support from their father dried up and as Justin's mother was not employed, bills began to mount up.

Justin loved his mother and could not bear to see how she now struggled to raise him and his sisters. With so much anger towards his father, Justin vowed that he would do all he could to prove to him that they did not need him.

Justin had made the decision to leave school, despite strong objections from his mother, and for the rest of that year he worked as hard as his body could let him, sometimes working two to three jobs at a time, to support his family.

When Harriet heard what had happened to Justin, she felt sorry for him. She stayed with him and supported him through it all. She loved him and she resented his father for what he had done to him. She was as bitter as Justin was and she wished for the day Justin made a name for himself. She would marvel at the sight of the shame across his father's face upon realising that even though he had not been there for his family, Justin had turned out well.

Back in the pizza restaurant, the discussion continued.

"It will sort itself out," Justin added, a while later after having listened to Harriet hummer on about how he needed to 'grow a pair' and 'ditch the bastards'.

"Sort itself out!? sort itself out? It will never sort itself out Jussy. YOU need to sort it out."

Harriet did not like bullies, especially those that targeted her own. She was not one to just stand by and be rolled over; she was the kind that would risk anything to right any injustice.

"Harriet, there are ways to do these things," Justin tried to reason with her," Sonderai will get what's coming to him one way or another."

"That's typical of you Justin," she challenged him," never one for confrontation. If you don't stick up for yourself, especially against the likes of Sonderai, you'll never get anywhere."

"You are too confrontational sometimes Harriet," Justin remarked calmly, so as not to aggravate his already apoplectic fiancé further. "You need to let diplomacy take precedence. What's to be gained from making a big scene of it. It will only make the situation worse than it already is."

"I'm not confrontational. I'm just saying it as it is. That bastard should not be allowed to treat people like that!"

Sandra had decided not to get involved as the two lovers battled it out. She sat opposite them with her elbows on the table, taking sips of her Coca-Cola and occasionally picking up a fry from the small basket between them and nibbling at it.

As the exchange continued, Ken walked into the diner. He quickly located them and progressed swiftly towards them.

"Evening, evening people!" He began as he reached them and tacked himself on the bench next to Sandra.

"Hey, Mr Langa, nice of you to join us" Justin addressed his friend jokingly.

"Mr Langa? That's my father man, I am not that old," Ken replied, with a slight pretend annoyance in his voice.

They all sniggered. They enjoyed watching him get worked up over trivial things.

"So how are my favourite ladies doing tonight, especially you my dear?" Ken said as he turned towards Sandra, his mood making a sudden change. He slowly tried to put his arm around her back to cuddle her.

"Ken, keep your hands to yourself if you still want them," Sandra snarled viciously. She appreciated Ken for being Justin's friend but she did not particularly enjoy his comedic overtones.

Justin and Harriet chuckled at Sandra's reaction.

"OK, OK, my pretty one. I'll leave that for later," he continued, disregarding her disgust for him.

"Later! You wish," she snared again and sucked her teeth as she turned away from him. If there was anyone Ken enjoyed annoying it was Sandra. It was not that they totally disliked each other but it was just that one did not find the other amusing at all. Sandra made it worse for herself though, by always allowing herself to be affected by Ken's mischief. If she ignored him he probably would have stopped a long while ago.

Food and more drinks were ordered and as they waited, they continued to converse.

"So you leaving for Europe Harriet?" Ken asked.

Harriet just smiled and nodded casually. She

was enjoying Beyoncé's "If you like it put a ring on it" that was belting out of the Pizza Palace ceiling speakers.

"There you go Jussy, a whole year of freedom my friend," Ken said cheekily, maintaining sight of Harriet from the corner of his eye. He knew there was a risk his skit could miss the mark but he was willing to go with it.

Harriet knew Ken was just being Ken, always trying to wind her up, so she gave him a long stare which would have stopped anyone dead in their tracks but not Ken. He caught sight of her annoyed look and he burst out laughing.

"You have a death wish my friend, don't you?" Justin said laughing. Ken carried on laughing too.

"If I come back and he's shacked up with some other girl, I'll know it's your fault," Harriet said pointing viciously at Ken.

"Me?" Ken replied, with a shifty innocence," How will that be my fault?"

"Everything is always your fault Ken, even when you are not there, "Sandra added.

Harriet and Justine laughed again.

Some moments later the food arrived and they all tucked in. As they ate they talked about the wonderful opportunity Harriet had received and at some point, the conversation had gone back to touch on Justin's encounter with Sonderai, earlier that day.

Ken was as equally disgusted by Justin's story as much as Harriet was and he had advised his friend, as Harriet had done, not to stand for it. Justin remained calm about it, sticking to his reasoning that things would work themselves out, much to the annoyance of everyone.

The evening had naturally come to an end, sometime after ten o'clock. It had turned out to be an enjoyable night after all. Ken and Sandra wished Harriet all the success in her upcoming trip and they separated.

Justin flagged a taxi and as they sat in the back, driving out of the city centre, they realised that this was the only time in the day that they had managed to be alone. They had not really spoken much about the pending trip but one thing they knew for sure, was that it was not going to be easy for either of them.

Chapter 3

Harriet sat back in her seat aboard the giant Airbus 747 and closed her eyes. A plethora of emotions flooded her mind. It was excitement that mostly consumed her; the thought of a new life ahead, a totally new world to explore, new people, new experiences. But hiding in the shadows of all this anticipation were thoughts of sadness, guilt and fear. She had left home to travel so far, for the first time in her life, and she had no idea what she would be stepping into.

Before the day of her departure, it had all seemed easy. It had been easy to make the plans, easy to speak about it, and it had all seemed normal until the day to depart began to draw nearer. Suddenly, the realisation that it was all happening had begun to sink in; she was going to be leaving behind all she knew, everything she was used to, and above all, everyone she loved. Justin was, of course, on top of that list.

They were together that morning and it had been such an emotional scene that anyone watching would have been drawn to tears. Justin had arrived at her parent's house early to help with last minute preparations and the send-off at the airport. They were both in her bedroom, as she put the last few pieces of clothing into the large suitcase that sat ajar on her bed.

"I thought this would be easy," Justin said, as he handed her the black silk blouse that he had pulled out of the wardrobe.

"I know babe," she replied as she took the blouse, neatly folded it and placed it in the suitcase, on top of a mountain of already packed clothes.

"We're going to be fine," she continued, as she drew closer to him and took his hands. Their bodies touched and they stared into each other's eyes for a brief moment. "I will be back before you even know it. Two years isn't that long and besides, we will be talking to each other pretty much every day. Don't forget I'll be back to visit many times as well."

Justin just tilted his head to indicate that he understood and gave a half-hearted smile. He was not going to pretend he was happy. In as much as he wanted to show his support and knew how this was a perfect opportunity for her, he still wished it was not happening.

"This is a good thing for us," Harriet continued to comfort her fiancé. "You know our plans. It's going to be good when I come back. I'll be able to get a very good job, you'll have things sorted at work and you'll be where you are supposed to be. We'll then get married and have the biggest wedding Harare has ever seen."

She was smiling up at him and he managed a smile back. Justin knew the plan; they had laid it out together and it was going to be good. He just needed to be patient and work on his side of things. On her return, he wanted to have moved up in his career and there was no doubt in both their minds that this would happen; it was all just a matter of time.

There was a light knock on the door and Beatrice, Harriet's much younger sister, popped her head through the door. Beatrice was 17, slender in stature and unmistakable in her resemblance to her older sister.

"U-uh!" she said with a mischievous tone, as she walked in on the two lovers hand in hand. Her voice was lowered as she did not want their parents to catch on to what was happening. The fact remained that Harriet and Justin were not a married couple, yet.

"Shut up you," Harriet said jokingly, dismissing her sibling's impishness. She looked down at her watch and moved away from Justin.

"Have mum and dad finished. Are they ready?"

"Dad has but mum's doing her hair," Beatrice replied as she jumped to sit on the bed.

"I better get dressed. Don't want dad to start shouting. You know how he gets when he's ready and everyone else isn't." Harriet said. She turned to Justin. "You need to go. Come on, out, out, out!"

She had marched him out of the room and closing the door behind him so as to finish getting ready. The final goodbyes at the airport had been far more emotive than everything else they had been through that day. She remembered saying goodbye to her parents, who were full of the usual words of wisdom. Mum had not been able to hold back the tears, as she always did, no matter how far you were going. This time though she had a good reason to and both sisters had joined her.

Justin had his moment at the end and had made sure he said everything.

"Guess this is it," he had begun. "In eleven hours from now, you'll be on the other side of the world. Guess you are excited?"

"A little. More nervous really. Just seen the size of the aeroplane and I wish I could stop wondering how that big thing stays in the sky for all that time."

They both smiled. Harriet, in all her preparations, had not stopped to think about how she felt about flying. She was a virgin to the sky's and hoped she would enjoy the experience. It was too late anyway now, to think too much about it. The point of no return had already been crossed.

"Call me as soon as you land. I'll be waiting."

"Of course I will. That's the first thing I'll do once I get to Freda's place."

Freda was an old friend of Harriet's, who now lived and worked in London. Although they had not maintained much contact over the years, Freda had been excited to hear that her old friend was travelling to England, and she was happy to host her until she was ready to settle at her university.

The call had come over the airport intercom announcing that Harriet's flight was ready for boarding. Within minutes she was giving her last wave by the departure gate and as she stepped into the passenger lounge, with all other travellers, she had felt this sudden whelming feeling that now she truly was all on her own.

"Ladies and gentlemen, this is your captain speaking. I would like to inform you that in 20 mins we will be making our landing at London Heathrow airport. The time in London is 8:45 am and we have been advised that the weather is mild with a few showers. In a few minutes, we will be making our descend and the city will be visible from both sides. We hope you have enjoyed your flight with Kenya Airways and hope you will fly with us again soon."

The flight intercom bleeped as the captain finished his announcement and the whole plane came alive in a hive of activity. Some passengers got up from their seats and stood in the aisle for a little stretch, whilst others folded and packed away their flight blankets, books, gadgets and everything else they had been using during the flight.

Harriet had been awake for a while now and she sat looking out the little oval window hoping to catch a glimpse of what would be her home for the next 2 years. As they were still above the cloud line and it was overcast, she could make out bits of the city lights from gaps between the clouds. A few moments later, as if emerging from behind a large theatre curtain, the plane had descended below cloud level and there it was, spread out as far as the eye could see, the great city of London.

Harriet scanned and absorbed every inch with fascination and excitement. She could not believe that she had finally made it. Right there, below her, was the renowned city of London she had always heard about growing up. To her, back then when she was a little girl, London seemed like some sort of magical place, mythical almost. She remembered some of the old books she had read, 'The Great Expectations', books that illuminated the affluence of the lifestyle back then and even in today's world, London still clung on to the reputation of the 'must-see' cities of the world.

She was here now, Harriet thought to herself, and it was going to be good. This was the start of good things and she could feel it. Coming to London felt like an achievement on its own and a sign that they were on the right track.

As the plane made its final approach, Harriet could see more of the buildings below and the long stretches of roads, with moving lights from the cars like ant trails, a whitish glow in one direction and a reddish one going the opposite. So many cars she thought to herself, that's got to be many people.

She wondered a little more about them. Where they were off to so early in the morning? They would most probably be driving to work, she thought, who knew? Weirdly, for a further moment, another thought came into her mind. It was an even stranger thought, where she felt as though she were arriving on an alien planet, a place with a different species altogether. In a round about way this thought held some truth. They were different people down there obviously, being of another country and all, so she began to wonder whether she would fit in, accepted even.

The ground got closer and as the captain made what could have only been described as a perfect landing, the whole plane erupted into a roar of applause. Harriet had not expected this but joined in. She felt a bit at a disadvantage not being familiar with this ritual. How is it that almost everyone knew to do this? Was she the only one flying for the first time?

Harriet could not help but feel a little disappointment with herself. This little insignificant event, at the end of her journey, just reminded her of how sheltered her life had been. Whilst she thought she had been living quite a fulfilled lifestyle, others, like those clapping around her, where living far more involved lives that included frequent travels around the world; how else would they all know to do this. Where had she been?

The giant Airbus 747 slowly taxied to the entrance of the main terminal and came to a halt. As everyone prepared to leave the plane, Harriet began to think about the next leg of her journey. She had not thought much about it throughout the eleven-hour flight. She still had customs to deal with and then try to find her way to Freda's.

It was unfortunate that her friend had not been able to come out to receive her at the airport. Freda had said something to the effect that she had a 'shift' at work that she could not cancel. Harriet did not understand how her employers could not afford her a few hours to pick up a visitor from the airport. She expected them to be a bit more understanding. It would be much later after a few months living in the UK that Harriet would realise why Freda had not picked her up from the airport. It was nothing to do with her not getting permission to go off work but Harriet would realise that life in the UK revolved around work.

Most foreigners worked far too hard to either maintain some kind of lifestyle or in the case of most, to send money home to family. Unless you were in full-time work, most foreigners worked for employment agencies on a temporary basis, which meant that if you did not work, you did not eat, to put it simply. Work was sometimes hard to come by, 'shifts' as they called them, and when you got one you did not cancel it for anyone, not even for a friend travelling from thousands of miles away.

The plane was getting empty as the passengers alighted. Harriet picked up her small bag and walked into the aisle when her turn arrived. At a snail's pace, the queue advanced towards the exit door where two very cheerful air hostesses, smartly dressed in their red and navy uniforms, thanked everyone as they stepped into the tunnel leading to the terminal.

Harriet was envious of these two ladies. They looked so confident, so much in control. She thought of all the countries they had been to, all the places they had seen. She thought about how excited she was feeling, arriving in London for the first time. To these ladies, this probably meant nothing to them now; they had been there, done it and now just part of their normal life.

Harriet moved on quickly from her thoughts; there was no time to dwell on anything as there was so much to take in. Everything seemed to be moving much faster again as she moved into the tunnel and then into the first part of the main building. Harriet knew the significance of that short walk she was now making through the terminal. She was walking into a whole new life, a world she had only dreamt of, and seen in films. She wondered whether it would be how she had always imagined it.

The first part of the terminal was quieter

than Harriet thought it would be. There were some people mostly in uniforms and a few others who wore armless fluorescent jackets over their uniforms. They reminded Harriet of the police back home, whom she had seen wearing these sometimes. She wondered if they were the local police but she also wondered why they were not wearing their black rounded hats, the ones she had often seen in books and magazines.

Soon enough she realised who they were because they began to move into the crowd of passengers, randomly pulling out a few people to the side and asking them to stand in a small holding area to the side of the walkway. Harriet was one of those singled out.

She was puzzled by the sudden turn of events. Is this how they check in passengers, she wondered? How was it that only a few had been stopped though? She watched as the rest of the passengers walked on, past two large doors into the next part of the terminal. Harriet sensed that something wasn't quite right and she felt as though there was some force determined to deny her of this experience.

A couple of people in the group began to whisper, "It's the immigration people," one said to the other. " They are looking for illegals."

It began to make sense to Harriet. She had often heard stories of many Zimbabweans travelling to London, only to be turned back at the airport. There had been an influx of foreigners coming to the UK and the British government, as a preventative measure, was tightening its borders. Harriet felt a build up of anxiety within her. She was not coming in illegally as all her paperwork checked out but she had also heard that British Immigration sometimes just denied you entry for very minute issues. She hoped that this was not what was happening in that moment.

One thing that she had also begun to notice was that although the passenger pollution on her flight had been quite evenly multiracial, this group that she now belonged to seemed to comprise only of black Africans. Was this some racial bias to suggest that only blacks were likely to travel illegally or was it just a coincidence, she wondered? Harriet would soon realise that her feelings were not hers alone.

"It's unfair!" one woman in the group began to speak "They do this all the time, pick on black people. They are very racist."

The woman was very outspoken and she appeared to have been in this situation before. She was over confident and seemed not to be affected by this sudden interval in any way. And as the two British Immigration officers approached the group, she was the first one to speak.

"Excuse me sir, but why have we been stopped here?" she asked, with obvious displeasure etched across her chubby face.

Everyone in the group remained silent and were very worried for her. She was bringing unwanted attention to herself and this would surely have her put on the next plane back to Africa. The woman, however, had a bone to pick. It appeared that she had either been in this situation before or had seen it on previous flights, and had not been amused by it in any way. She knew something that no one in the group did and that gave her so much bravado. Harriet was in awe. She had already begun to amass a few feelings of rebellion of her own inside but she knew she would not have had the same intrepidness as this woman dared to show.

"Please bear with us madam," one of the officers answered with a hint of patronising politeness. "We will get you moving soon."

"Can we please take a look at your passports," the other said.

Harriet ruffled through her handbag and pulled out her passport. All the others did the same except for the woman who now focused all her attention on the first officer who had dared to answer her.

The poor man looked overwhelmed as the woman laid into him.

"I know what you are doing here," she continued, with a heavy Shona accent," This is purely racial discrimination. You never stop whites here, why? We never do this to you when you come to Zimbabwe."

"Madam," the officer attempted to interrupt her," Madam we are only trying to do our job. If your papers are in order then there is nothing to worry about."

This statement by the officer did not help the situation in the slightest.

"Why wouldn't my papers be in order. Are you trying to say black people can never be trusted to have their paperwork in order? Why would I travel all this way with no proper paperwork? This is not right."

"Madam please!" The officer again tried to stop her, this time genuine frustration beginning to show on his face.

There were more exchanges between the

woman and the officer and Harriet was beginning to get concerned that the woman was indeed digging a large hole for herself, one that she would not be able to climb out off. She genuinely had an important and crucial case for them to answer but Harriet knew nothing would be resolved at that moment. Harriet did not find fault in what the woman was trying to do; this was an issue that needed addressing.

Harriet handed her papers to the second officer, who scanned over the documents, asked why she had travelled to the UK and when he was satisfied, he gestured for her to proceed through a set of two large doors into the main terminal. Walking through those doors felt even more of a triumph for Harriet. For some reason, this little episode with the immigration officers and the courageous attempt by the woman to defy the supposed bias of the British immigration service, had empowered her somehow. She could smell London and could hear her calling to her. Nothing could stop her now.

A few more checks followed further on inside the main terminal but Harriet was confident that the worst was over and went through without a hitch. A quarter of an hour later she now stood outside the main entrance of London Heathrow Airport and there directly in front of her, was London.

Chapter 4

Harriet sat on a chair behind a small round table in the centre of Freda's kitchen. All the furniture and fittings in the room were quite small, but worked well in the space. To her this was possibly the smallest kitchen she had ever been in. It was not cluttered but did not seem big enough to fit any more things in it. It was also modern but Harriet had seen bigger, and in other cases better. Her mother's kitchen alone could swallow three of these easily. Some modern African homes were so impressive now that they easily rivalled those in advanced western countries. Amongst most Africans, bigger is most definitely better, and that is one way of showing how well you are doing.

Freda was upstairs changing out of her hospital tunic and as Harriet waited, she entertained a mug of coffee as she continued to study her friend's bachelor flat. It was a ground floor flat and not that big; plenty room for one person but would have never been enough to house a whole family. It was perfect for someone single or a couple with no children.

As she studied her friend's dwelling, Harriet's thoughts gravitated towards Freda. It had been such a long time since they had last spoken and she wondered whether her then-boyfriend, Sydney Chando, was still in the picture. Sydney and Freda had been together before Freda flew to England and he had eventually followed her sometime later. Harriet quickly looked around the kitchen hoping to pick up any photographic clues. She was conscious her friend would be down soon. She leaned back, tipping her chair and peered into the lounge hoping there might have been a picture or two of the couple on the wall, but there was none. Just a few of Freda's family in Zimbabwe and many other people whom she did not know. As Harriet continued on her nosy quest, Freda stepped back into the room.

"Oh my God Harriet, I can't believe you are here! Sitting in my house!"

Harriet sat back quickly, hoping not to have been caught snooping and produced a half-guilty smile.

"I can't believe it either sha. It's been so, so long."

"I know! Last time I saw you was just before I left Zim in 96." Freda reminded her.

"That long, really?" Harriet exclaimed in genuine surprise. She could not believe how much time had passed.

"Ye, I remember it very well because that's when I left Zim. I know we spoke a bit after that but the last time I actually saw you was back then."

"Wow, I can't believe how time flies. Look at us now, all grown!" Harriet remarked.

They both laughed briefly.

"You look good, Freda," Harriet continued," London seems to have embraced you."

"What are you on about, I'm ageing rapidly because of this so-called UK lifestyle. All work, work, work and no play. But I still try though, to go out and stuff. The life here demands it. It can be so stressful that if you don't make time to go out, you'll slowly go insane."

"The Freda I know didn't let anything stand between her and a good night out. You were the queen of Harare nightlife. The Mambo Club, do you remember? A party without Freda was no party at all."

"Oh my God, Mambo, don't remind me. I miss Harare sometimes. We did a lot of crazy stuff. London is good too you know. I have my spots; good music, good company. I'll have to take you, tell the London boys to look out, there is a new hottie in town."

Freda laughed as she went to give her friend a small high five. Harriet returned the high five but she knew she had to let her friend know about her current relationship status.

"The London boys will have to wait I'm afraid. Justin would kill me. You do know that we got engaged, don't you?"

"Serious?!" Freda exclaimed," That is brilliant Harriet! I didn't know, when? No one told me."

"Just before I left actually. He didn't want me to come all this way without us formalising things. We will wed as soon as I finish my studies and return home."

"Wow! Can't believe you guys finally did it. All those years together. You were definitely meant to be together."

"We have come a long way *sha*, and with what we've been through, I don't think anything can break us up now. He had a lot of issues with his family, with his dad, and I supported him through it all. He helped me go through some tough moments in my life too. Truth be told, our relationship grew much stronger from it."

"Oh my God, I'm so proud of you guys," Freda said, placing her hand on her friend's arm," Wedding, partying, I'm definitely there!"

They both smiled. Harriet thought it would be fair to find out how her friend was doing with her relationships, so she asked.

"What about you, what's happening to you in the love department?" Harriet asked, also gathering the guts to quiz Freda on her pondering earlier.

"Me? Well, been there, done it. I'm done trying to make relationships work. Doing very well on my own. I don't need anyone." Freda spoke with vehemence. It was not difficult to see that she had been through something that had left her wounded.

"What happened to Sydney. Thought you guys would be married by now?" enquired a puzzled Harriet.

"Almost," she said, regretfully. "Long story." Freda scoffed, displaying a false reluctance to go into the subject.

"Well, I am not flying anywhere tonight. What happened?"

Freda turned away with an expression of pure scorn.

"Men are dogs, Harriet," she snarled. It was evident Freda had a deeply cultivated bitterness towards Sydney. Harriet just sat on the edge of her seat and made sure Freda knew she had her full attention.

"Harriet, men are dogs," Freda repeated, as if Harriet had not heard it the first time.

"What happened?" Harriet asked sensing she had to come in to move the conversation forward.

"Um-m, sha, I can't even begin to tell you what he did to me. I gave him everything, Harriet, everything!"

"Sydney?" Harriet said, seeking confirmation.

Freda just looked at Harriet without uttering a word but the look on her face just confirmed it.

"What happened? Thought you guys had a good thing going?"

Freda slowly began to elaborate. "I can't believe it to this day how stupid I was, allowing him to use me like that. He literally took a large knife and pushed it into my heart. When I came up here we had planned it all. I was supposed to fly over, get myself sorted and once settled, get him up here. We had planned to get married once he had arrived and settled. Everything was arranged and the plan was solid. Well..., after a year, in line with our plans, I bought him a ticket to come up. I had started to hear a few rumours, things happening over there in Zim about him being seen with other women and all, but I trusted him and never made a big issue of it."

She paused briefly in contemplation then continued.

"When he came over I was over the moon. Finally, we could start our life together. Straight away though I sensed he was a little off but I just put it to us having been apart for a while. We had been talking regularly, all the time, but I felt being apart had changed us a bit."

"It would, a little I guess, obviously," Harriet agreed," But distance is nothing if two people truly love each other. So what happened anyway?"

Freda was now more sombre in her appearance as she relayed the next part of her story. Her words conveyed how much she had been hurt by it all.

"It was all true, the rumours." she continued," He did have other relationships in that whole year and coming up here did not stop him. It was the beginning of the end for us. Sha, can you believe that when he got up here he stayed in my house, ate my food, I bought him everything, only for him to carry on seeing this girl from Zim behind my back; she had moved to London as well months earlier. He would tell me he was going to visit his cousin in Slough for a week and all that time he would be shacked up with that whore, that slut! I hate him!"

"Oh, my gosh Freda. I can't believe Sydney would do that to you."

"That's just the half of it, *shamwari*. Just

before he left for good, he had maxed out my credit cards, stole my savings and left me with bad credit. He took out loans in my name, credit cards and spend them on HER! Left me in a really bad state."

"No way!" Harriet exclaimed in disbelief.

"For real, *shamwari**. It took me a long time to recover. I went into a deep depression for a long time and almost lost my job. He did me over good, real good."

Harriet was still sat forward in her seat, shaking her head in total disbelief. She could not believe what Freda had been put through. She knew Sydney and to think of him doing this was impossible to comprehend.

"That was evil," Harriet said softly," I can't believe he did that to you, I really can't."

Freda just shook her head too. She did not cry. She had cried enough already. This was the first time she had spoken about it in a long time and she was proud of herself for not having broken down again.

After what seemed a long moment of silence, Harriet asked Freda whether she had seen him since.

"He's lucky he hasn't seen me. I promise you that the day I meet him, that will be it, there will be only one place for me after that, prison. I am not joking, he'll live to regret it."

Although Harriet wanted to advise her friend against any violent acts of vengeance, now was not the right time. "What goes around comes around," Harriet managed to say.

"For sure," Freda agreed," His day will

* Sha or Shamwari – meaning: 'my friend' in Shona

come."

They had continued to speak more on the subject but they had not dwelt on it for much longer than it deserved. Harriet spent the following couple of days relaxing and sleeping quite a lot. She now understood what people referred to as "jet lag".

Never had she felt so tired, unable to find motivation or the energy to do anything. Before the end of that first day, the day she had flown in, Harriet had managed to ring home. She had spoken to her parents and her sister before finally spending quite some time on the phone with Justin. She was grateful to Freda for the use of her phone and after that, she had settled more and began to soak in the London atmosphere.

The one thing that Harriet quickly realised about being so far away from home was the fact that she now couldn't simply jump onto a bus or catch a cab whenever she missed her family and loved ones. Within a week she had begun to miss everything about home and occasionally she would question her decision to have moved so far. London kept her busy at times though. There were new places to be discovered, some places she had read about or seen in books, but now owed it to herself to actually visit and see.

In the first few weeks, Freda had taken Harriet around London just to get her used to navigating around the city, and finding her bearings. Later Harriet would venture out on her own, starting with nearer points of interest and soon she was venturing further. She was surprised and pleased with herself on how she had quickly got accustomed to moving around independently, learning bus routes and the London Underground train system.

She loved how accessible most places were and how easy it was to get things done. Gone were the ridiculous queues for ZUPCO buses and local minibus taxis, Combis, the two most popular but stressful ways of getting around in Harare.

Although Harare was nowhere near as developed as London, there were many buildings and features around the city that reminded Harriet of home. This was no surprise considering that the two cities had a shared history, the British colonial era. Some of the old buildings in Harare resembled the ones she was now seeing. Even many of the names of streets and towns were very familiar.

Besides getting to know the city, it also didn't take long for Harriet to get an insight into the lifestyles of the Zimbabwean expatriate community. She had been invited and gone to quite a few flamboyant Zimbabwean parties that were hosted pretty much on most weekends. Zimbabweans abroad seemed to have this need to constantly meet and drink themselves silly. Harriet could only conclude that there were many of these events because that was the only way Zimbabweans could relive their former lives back home, 'goch goch' as they called it.

The parties were typical Zimbabwean party's, despite being set in a foreign country. They started off with people arriving in their flashy automobiles, mostly hired as Harriet would eventually get to realise, each aiming to outdo everyone else. Couples would then emerge from these expensive vehicles dressed to the hilt, pretending not to take notice of the attention but drawing focus on themselves.

The event would begin peacefully until further into the evening when the alcohol would start to take effect; this is when the chaos would sometimes ensue. Most of the time it was a fight between two guys for a girl and vice versa, or sometimes just a fight for no other reason worthy of getting your face smashed in. Harriet did not particularly take to these events from the get go.

She had never truly been that sort of person although she did not mind going to a club or party once in a while. Freda, on the other hand, was a whole other entity entirely. She lived and worked for partying. Her whole life was a never-ending party. She worked hard but she also knew how to play hard.

From the moment they began living together, almost every other week Freda would tell Harriet of an upcoming event and rabbit on about how this was 'the' party to be at, the 'once in a lifetime and not to be missed'. Harriet would try and find a way to be excused, preferring to stay in with a book or watch a movie but as time went on she realised that this was a war she could never win. It was better to go and get it out of the way than to have to listen to Freda going on about it.

By the middle of May, a couple of months after her arrival, Harriet had finalised her University arrangements and would be ready to start at the beginning of September. They agreed that Harriet would live with Freda for the first half of her academic year and then move on to the University

Campus for her second semester. This would give them a chance to spend some quality time together and really get to catch up.

Although Harriet was grateful to her friend for helping her settle into her new environment, she found living with Freda also quite a challenge. She knew of her friend's active lifestyle from the time she was still in Zimbabwe but Harriet hoped London had mellowed out her flamboyant behaviour. This proved to be the exact opposite. London had given Freda more of a playground to thrive off.

Every opportunity Freda got meant going out to some club or party. Harriet struggled with this as she had not signed up to this lifestyle but would often go so as not to offend Freda. The other reason Harriet did not like going out was that she felt she would not be comfortable being out without Justin. Justin had always gone with her to most events she had been to; it felt strange being anywhere without him.

She had begun to miss him more every time they went out. Most people who came to these parties seemed to come with a partner and she wished if only it were possible for him to just quit his job and join her. That would have truly made her happy. As she contemplated on the two years she was going to be away, it began to dawn on her that two years was actually going to be quite a long time after all.

Harriet walked up from the street up to a glossy Black PVC door, which had two silver numbers nailed to it that read '29'. 29 Eccleston Close was the first address Harriet would always remember as her first London home. This was the address to Freda's flat.

She searched through the contents of a small handbag she held and pulled out a set of house keys. Inserting one of them through the keyhole, she gave it a twist and gently pushed the door open.

The door would not open straight away and felt jammed as she pushed. She then recalled that the postman had just been and probably some letters had wedged themselves on the underside of the door.

She lowered herself down and put her hand through the narrow gap in the door to remove the mail. Once cleared, the door freely swung open. Harriet picked up the letters as she entered the house and studied the names on the envelopes. None were hers but she already knew that. She had not been living there long enough to start getting any mail. She was, however, expecting the University to contact her with confirmation documents for her start date. She had given them Freda's address as her new home address but nothing had come through as of yet.

She dropped the bag and letters on the table in the lounge and went through the handbag again. She found what she was looking for; a small credit card size card and a coin. She then moved over to sit on the single settee near the house phone. She was excited; she had just bought an international phone card and was going to use it to call home.

She scratched the middle of the card to reveal a hidden code which she dialled into the phone and waited for further instructions. The automated voice instructed her to enter her chosen number and so she dialled her mother first, an obligation she felt she had, although deep down she desperately wanted to talk to Justin.

The phone rang and rang out as no one picked up from the other side. She surmised that both her parents might have been out.

She knew her father would definitely be at work, as it was only midday in London and the time difference being only an hour. Her mother, however, might have just stepped out, shopping or wherever.

She pressed the 'hash key' on the phone dial pad and that gave her the option to dial another number. She punched in Justin's work number and as it connected, she sat back into the settee and waited. She had not spoken to him in over two weeks and that was the longest she had gone without talking to him. She was excited thinking about how she was just about to hear his voice, that a little smile materialised across her face, even before he came on.

"Glenson & Glenson, good afternoon. Can I help you?"

Harriet knew this voice so well as she had heard it every time she called Justin at work. It was the distinct voice of the young girl who manned the reception desk, whom Harriet had also seen on her numerous visits to the Glenson & Glenson building.

"Hi," she replied," Can I speak to Justin Sangala please."

"Yes sure, I'll put you through," came the response. "Is that Harriet?"

Harriet was surprised that the receptionist knew who she was, as they had not really spoken that much.

"Yes it is," she replied, with that hint of surprise in her voice.

" I thought it was you. How's London?"

With even more amazement, Harriet replied, "It's quite nice actually. Different."

"Oh OK, good... I'll put you through to Justin."

"Thanks."

Harriet heard a few keyboard tapping sounds and then music began to play through her side of the receiver. It was a classical piece, probably Mozart or someone like that, she thought. Classical was not her favourite but she did not mind it. The music stopped suddenly as the call was picked up. The receiver did not answer immediately but was midway through another conversation with someone on the other side.

"No problem," the person spoke," Next week is perfect. I will call you."

"Sounds good," replied a female voice in the distance. "I'll be waiting."

Harriet had instantly recognised Justin's voice but she could not make out the female he was talking to. She was not the jealous type, ordinarily, but this was not an ordinary time in their relationship. They were countries apart and anything could happen.

As the female voice vanished, Justin brought his attention to the telephone receiver he was holding.

"Sorry to keep you waiting, this is Justin, can I help you?"

Harriet did not answer immediately. She toyed with him a little. She was not upset really but wanted to play him a bit.

"Hello. Hello!" He spoke again, raising his voice a little the second time.

"So who was that then?" Harriet asked, pretending to be annoyed at his interaction with the unknown female.

"Who?... Oh, hey babe!" Justin replied, having been initially confused by the question before he realised who was asking.

"OK, so as soon as I leave you are already making appointments to replace me." she accused him, jokingly.

Justin laughed and joked it off, "Oh, stop it you, crazy."

"Who was it anyway?" Harriet asked genuinely curious, as she began to move out of her ruse.

"Just one of our customers, a buyer. How are you anyway sweetie? Expected your call yesterday," Justin said, trying to move swiftly away from Harriet's inquisition.

"Sorry babe, I got a bit tied up yesterday and did not get a chance to get a phone card. I got one today."

"Oh, OK. What are you up to then? How are things going with University and all?"

"I am good to go really. I am just waiting for a start date. Should arrive anytime," she updated him.

" OK. That's good... Everyone misses you here."

"Who misses me?"

"Everyone. Me the most of course."

"Oh really? And by the way, who told your receptionist I was in London? Are you bosom buddies now?"

"There you go again. Stop it," Justin replied, with a half laugh," Everyone who knows me knows."

"Ye, I want you to tell those skanky girls to stay away. I got eyes and ears everywhere!"

Justin laughed again. He enjoyed how she always pretended not to be jealous. Even though he knew she was not really upset as they spoke, deep beneath it all he knew she was sending a message.

"You have nothing to worry about my dear. I know what you are capable of and I wouldn't want to be responsible for some poor girl's demise."

"You know me too well." This time it was Harriet who had a bit of a laugh of her own. She trusted Justin but she did not trust all other women. She believed that any man, once caught in a woman's web of seduction, was about as powerless as a fly caught on a spider's web. Justin being no exception.

"So what's London like?"

"Too busy for my liking but manageable."

"Have you met any other Zimbabweans yet?"

"What! Here? They are everywhere!" Harriet laughed. "Freda took me to a few parties. You should see how *MaZimba* show off here. They act as if none of this stuff exists back in Zim. I know people with better cars and houses back home. You know the ones I am talking about."

"Ye, I know," Justin agreed. "Parties, hey? Lucky for some."

"I go, but I'm not too keen on them. Freda lives for these parties."

They both sniggered.

"She hasn't changed much then?" Justin asked.

"Not in the slightest. She is worse now, I think."

"Well, be careful of those London boys and their flashy cars," Justin added sarcastically.

"You got nothing to worry about babe," she replied, giving him back a piece of what he had given her. "Anyway, how are things at work then?" Harriet asked, remembering how Justin had been the last night they had all been together.

Justin lowered his voice and discreetly replied to Harriet's question. "I am still furious. Worst is, if what I have heard is true, then there is more shit coming. But I am not going to let this one pass. I am going to cook up a huge storm over it."

"What? What's happening, what have you heard?"

"It's Sonders again. I swear one day I'm going to destroy that man. Apparently, he is appointing this kid, who just came out of UZ, for that post. And that's not even the worst of it; this boy happens to be his nephew. If this is true, I am telling you, it's going to be heavy around here for a while."

"Are you serious?" Harriet asked, horrified as to how brazen Sonderai was.

"That's what we have heard, this is from someone in his office. Harriet, this kid has not even worked anywhere, never in sales, and he's going to be my boss. Never! I am not going to let this happen."

"You have to take it up the chain babe, all the way to the top," Harriet encouraged him," That sorry excuse for a man has gone too far now. He thinks he can do anything he likes. It's not his company."

"You don't have to tell me. I am preparing a counter-offensive as we speak. I will call you when I have launched it. It's now or never."

"Do it! You deserve better than this." she encouraged him. Not long after, Harriet's phone card had run out. It was an abrupt end to the call but she was so pleased that she had spoken to him. As for her parents, well, she was going to have to catch them on another day.

Chapter 5

The morning rush hour madness in Harare was gradually diminishing as Justin arrived at the Glenson building. It was just a minute shy of 8 o'clock when he walked through the revolving glass doors; any minute later he would have been late. As he strolled past the main reception desk, the young receptionist looked up and called to him.

"Morning Justin." she smiled.

He turned and smiled back, "Morning Tina."

She got up from her desk and ran towards him, as he had already walked past the reception desk. He waited for her when he realised she was coming to him, somewhat curious as to what she so desperately wanted to say.

She got to him and relayed a message that all the senior marketing staff had been asked to meet up in the boardroom as soon as they arrived.

Justin was the last one in and they were probably waiting for him.

"What's going on?" he asked.

"Don't quote me on this but Flo, upstairs, told me that Sonderai was announcing the new Assistant Director of Marketing this morning."

"Oh OK, so it's happening today then?" he asked.

Tina nodded slowly in agreement, but her facial expression indicated that she knew more, and it was not good. Justin was not surprised; he knew what sort of a man Sonderai was and so did everyone else. The outcome of this post had already been decided and it was not going to be fair.

Without so much as another word, they had both turned and went about their business. Tina returned to her desk as Justin made for the staircase, to navigate his way up to the second floor boardroom.

He walked through the marketing department floor to where the boardroom meeting had been scheduled. He avoided eye contact with his other colleagues, who sat at their desks working. All he was focused on was getting to that boardroom and getting it over and done with.

He had made it to the back of the marketing department without interruption and turned to face the boardroom door. The door was shut and Justin could hear Sonderai talking from the other side; the meeting had already started without him.

"Shit," he said to himself. Justin did not like being late for anything, especially on a day like this. He did not like being the centre of attention either. He knew that this would happen the moment he opened that door, everyone turning to watch him as he walked in. He adjusted his tie, straightened his suit jacket sleeves and gave a big sigh before making his way into the room.

As he entered, everything happened as he had thought it would. He was reliving what he had just imagined a few seconds ago outside the door. Every face in the room turned to look at him. Justin averted his gaze to avoid eye contact with anyone at all cost, as he maneuvered past a few chairs, to an empty seat midway into the room.

Sonderai had stopped talking as Justin walked to his seat, in politeness, his aim only to further enhance focus on Justin.

"Thank you for joining us, Justin," he said in his usual slow and patronising manner.

Justin smiled back doing as little as possible to hide his annoyance. He scanned the faces in the room and noticed most of his usual senior marketing team colleagues were in attendance. He knew everyone, obviously, except for a slender young-looking man who sat on a chair adjacent to Sonderai, who sat at the head of the boardroom table.

The new fellow did not appear in any way rattled by the fact that he was the only stranger in the room; he presented himself like someone who had always been there. Justin knew instantly that this was the man who was about to be introduced as his boss. Sonderai went straight into it.

"OK, let's see," he began, as he studied the few typed papers he held in his hands. "First things first, I have the pleasure in introducing this young man sitting next to me. This is Lawrence Tafara and he will be taking up the position of Deputy Marketing Director with effect from today."

There was dead silence in the room. No one spoke. There was the odd shuffle, but the room remained as quiet as a moment of benediction during Mass. The air in the room felt so stale that you could cut it through with a knife. Everyone was thinking it, but no one dared speak. Everything about this announcement did not sound right and Sonderai was not doing a good job of hiding it. He knew, as much as everyone in that room, that there were capable people who had been passed from this opportunity without proper cause.

Sonderai continued. "Lawrence will commence his post immediately and I expect all of you to make him feel welcome and give him all the support he needs."

Justin sat staring at Sonderai, eyes ablaze with anger. Even though he had known it was coming, hearing it just drove the dagger even deeper into his torso. He had done so much for this company and if Sonderai did not see it, then he was going to have to go above him. He was not afraid of shaking this beehive.

For a further half an hour that followed, Justin's thoughts were no longer in the room. He had drifted off, working out how he was going to deal with this situation. He was going to expose Sonderai for the fraud that he was. He planned to go straight to the top of the company hierarchy and reckoned that they would be interested to hear all about the untoward practices within their company.

As the meeting drew to an end, everyone stood from the table and one after the other, they all lined up to meet and greet their new boss; everyone except Justin. He got up, picked up his Filofax and walked out of the room.

Back in his cubicle, Justin banged his Filofax on his desk and stood in silence for a few minutes, his hands perched on his hips. He felt like doing something drastic but that something was not coming to him quick enough. He stepped around his desk to his chair and collapsed into it. He sat there, for a further minute or two, leaned backwards, tapping the armrest of the chair with his fingers.

He was heavily engrossed in his thoughts when he caught the sounds of the others coming out of the boardroom and heading back to their desks. He sat up quickly from the back of his chair and opened his laptop. He did not want anyone to see how affected he had been by this. He knew they had all sensed how unimpressed he was with the announcement but he was not going to let anyone see him like that.

He heard them as they all passed by his cubicle but he pretended to be engrossed in his work and never looked up. They all noisily walked on and when the last one had gone past, it quietened down again. Justin kept his attention on his laptop but he could not focus. He tried to open a few files to start working on but he clicked them off again, unable to shake this situation from his mind.

He was stilled zoned out, trapped in his thoughts, when he noticed from his peripherals, a figure standing by his cubicle door. He looked up slowly and saw Lawrence, his new boss, watching him, leaning against the cubicle wall with his hands in his trouser pockets. Justin was surprised, not because Lawrence was by his cubicle but that he was just there, standing and eyeing him. He could not believe the nerve of the man and before he could ask if he could help, Lawrence walked in further into the cubicle.

"Hi, you must be Justin. I am Lawrence," he said, his arm now stretched out for a handshake.

"I know," Justin replied, reluctantly offering his hand in response. He was not sure how to react to the situation. He felt ambushed, forced into an awkward moment.

"You walked out before we had a chance to get acquainted," Lawrence continued.

"I did," Justin replied, still reluctant to give more to the conversation. He sat back in his chair.

Lawrence remained standing with his hands now back in his pockets, then said "Well, I hope we get a chance to get to know each other. I am informed that you are someone I can count on around here when it all heats up. I'm sure we will get along just fine."

"I'm sure we will," Justin answered with a hint of sarcasm. He was not sure what games this new man was playing but he could smell a seriously decomposing rodent.

Lawrence stood there for a further minute or so, still looking down at Justin, a big questionable smile on his face. It was as though he was challenging Justin to something; as though he had something niggling him and was not sure whether this was the right time to say it.

"Well, it has been lovely getting to know you Justin", he had said finally, preparing to move on.

"Likewise," Justin replied still wearing his

face of distrust.

With his hands still in his trouser pockets, Lawrence turned and walked away.

Chapter 6

"Hey, I thought we were just grabbing something quick to eat and then heading home," Justin grilled Ken when he realised they were about to enter Cloud 9 Bar, a popular local bar and club. They were just outside, by the steps leading to the entrance.

"Just a quick one. We will be out in no time. Besides, I've got a surprise for you."

Justin, who was still at the bottom of the steps, looked up at his friend doubtfully; Ken was already by the door. Justin knew that once he agreed to go in, one drink would lead to more. He had been out with Ken on numerous occasions and knew him all too well; things had a tendency of getting out of hand when it came to Ken.

"Surprise? What surprise?" Justin quizzed his friend, doubtfully.

"Let's just go in. You'll see."

Reluctantly Justin walked up the small flight of stairs and followed Ken through into the dimly lit bar. It was not crowded but there was a good number of people already sat drinking, far more people than Justin thought would have been out drinking on a Wednesday, being the middle of a working week and all.

They found an empty table at the back that had four chairs and sat down. Soon after, a smartly dressed waitress in a white blouse and a black pleated pencil skirt, walked to their table. She also wore a seductively alluring smile as she approached.

"Evening gentleman. What can I get for you tonight?"

"WOW!" Ken exclaimed, looking up at the waitress, with not even an ounce of shame in him. "You are gorgeous! How come I haven't seen you around here before"

The waitress retained her smile and replied. "Thank you, sir. I'm new. What can I get for you?" She was poised and in control, attempting to stir the conversation back to ordering drinks as quickly as possible. Although she was new to the job, she seemed to have the knack of how to deal with awkward customers.

Justin just shook his head, unbelieving of the nerve of his friend.

"Two Pilsners and a bottle of your finest red wine please," Ken ordered.

"Will that be all Sir?" she confirmed.

"For now," he answered, his face carved with a mischievous grin.

"Thank you," Justin stepped in, realising his friend was near enough making a fool of himself, if not already.

She nodded and walked back behind the bar.

"Bottle of wine?" Justin asked, confused. He knew neither of them was into red wine.

"Yes. That's the surprise."

"What? A bottle of wine?"

"No, no, no. I invited Flo from 3rd floor and Tina to join us."

"Flo? And Tina?" Justine retorted, still confused. He had never been anywhere with both women besides at work or some work-related function.

"Ye man. I thought I'd get us some good company tonight. We need to get you out of this work slump you're in at the minute," Ken said, feeling proud of his plan.

"By inviting people from work? How is that going to help me relax and forget about work? That's all we will be talking about." Justin replied sarcastically.

"Ye, but it's different. This is more of a social situation. There is something I haven't told you, just hear me out. You know Tina right?" Ken raised both his eyebrows at Justin twice, in a suspicious manner," She has it for you man. Flo said she talks about you all the time. Dude, that is a seriously easy slam and dunk."

Justin could only but stare at Ken in disbelief.

"Are you crazy man! Are you serious?" He questioned him." Harriet has barely left town and you are already trying to hook me up with someone."

"Hey, it's a harmless evening, work colleagues just out for a drink," Ken replied, attempting to water down the situation.

"Ye right," Justin responded, unconvinced.

"That's how it all starts, all innocent, and then before you know it, rumours spread and the whole world is talking."

"Oh come on, relax a little. No one is going to see you or say anything."

"You wanna bet?" Justin challenged him. He had a serious look on his face.

Ken just sat back in his chair smiling mischievously again, refusing to see the seriousness of the situation. Shortly after, the waitress returned with the order.

"Your order gentlemen," she said, as she carefully emptied her tray contents onto the table.

"Thank you very much, Miss? Sorry I didn't catch your name."

"I never gave it," She responded quietly but still smiling." It's Rachel anyway. I will be your waitress for the evening so please do not hesitate to call me if you need anything."

"Oh, OK, it's all strictly business, hey?" Ken said," OK, that's fine. We will definitely be looking for you later for another order."

"Thanks, Rachel," Justin stepped in, sensing he had to intervene yet again.

She nodded and walked off.

"You are unbelievable," Justin said, when the waitress was out of earshot. He reached over the table for his beer and took a big gulp.

"What!? Just having a bit of fun, that's all. Don't start getting all Holier than thou on me. Relax man."

Justin sat his beer back on the table after the swig and just shook his head smiling. Ken was never anyone to take too seriously.

"Instead of chasing skirts, we should be

talking about what to do with Sonderai." Justin began again, "We are not being serious enough and that is why he thinks he can just roll all over us and expect no retaliation."

"What are you going on about now?" Enquired a baffled Ken.

"I'm talking about us. Me, you and even all those people who work at Glenson & Glenson. We are the ones that run that company. We are the ones going out there, day in, day out, looking for new customers. When has Sonderai ever picked up the phone to talk to a customer? Those guys are living off our efforts and they get paid far more than we do."

"So true bro," Ken agreed, catching on to the conversation.

"My customer list alone is much more than most of the sales guys put together and I bet if I ever go anywhere else, I could take them all with me. Glenson & Glenson will be begging me to come back."

"Straight up bro. But why even take them to another company where you'll get the same shitty treatment. Setting up on our own is the best way to go man," Ken suggested.

Justin looked at him intensely, as he took another swig of his Pilsner.

"You have something there, son," He said pointing the mouth of his beer at his friend. " I like it. Start a whole new company with my customer base. Go after Glenson & Glenson's market share. Not a bad idea, not bad at all."

"If there is anyone who can pull off something like that bro, it's definitely you."

Justin did not reply as his mind had already

gone into overdrive, chewing up this new idea Ken had just brought up. He was already working out a plan in his head.

"This is it, it's now or never. This is the push I have been waiting for," he said finally.

As he spoke, two female figures walked up to the table.

"You have started without us boys?" Flo said as they got to the table.

"Just got here". Ken responded quickly.

"Hey ladies. " Justin greeted them straight after.

Tina was behind Flo and as they both sat they replied to the greeting.

"Wine ladies?" Ken offered. Picking up the bottle.

"Thanks, dear," Flo replied.

She was the older of the two women, not by much though. She was in her mid-thirties, very experienced receptionist and PA, having worked for Glenson & Glenson for over fifteen years. Tina was in her late twenties but very forward and mature in her manner. The two women were quite close friends as well.

Ken poured their drinks and one at a time they picked them up and took a sip. The sound system in the club was churning out some slow modern RnB music. The atmosphere in the bar was relaxing, the perfect setup for a bit of escapism. Justin and Ken had parked their discussion about the new venture and delved into more casual gossip with the two women. Ken was in his element, leading with the talking but Justin could not wait for all of it to be over. It was not that he did not like the company but he just had too much on his mind.

Besides, he had promised to call Harriet and she would be expecting his call.

"So how are you coping with your fiancé on the other side of the planet?" asked Flo.

Justin gave a little worried smile before answering,"I'm doing fine, thanks."

"Don't let him fool you," Ken jumped in." He won't last."

They all laughed except for Justin who just gave out another short smile.

"Men are weaker than women," Tina joined in. "She will be fine for two years but he won't go over three months before he starts missing things."

"You know us too well," Ken agreed with her.

"Speak for yourself man. I have no intention of doing anything," Justin resisted the idea of being typecast.

"That's what you say now, "Ken challenged him.

"How long has she been up there now?" Flo asked.

"Three months," Justin replied.

"0oh!" They all chorused and burst out laughing.

"It's starting now if it hasn't already," Ken remarked.

"No, it hasn't," Justin denied instantly.

"Well, I've got the perfect solution," Flo suggested. She smiled. "Your girlfriend, sorry 'fiancé, is away for a long time and Tina here has just broken up with her boyfriend. You both need someone for those cold nights. Talk about a perfect situation."

"Flo!" Tina exclaimed, and playfully

elbowed her friend.

"Sounds good to me," Ken said, reinforcing the idea.

"Don't you start," Justin warned him jokingly

"What! I'm only looking out for two of my dearest friends."

Tina picked up her wine glass and brought it up to her mouth to shield herself from the awkwardness.

"Stop pretending to be all shy now Tina. Aren't you the one who is always telling me how you find Justin attractive?" Flo continued to embarrass her friend.

"Oh my God Flo!" Tina exclaimed again." You are just so... so.." She could not find her words. If she were any lighter, she would have been as red as the wine she held. "I can't believe you guys."

Justin jumped in to rescue her, "Don't let them get to you, Tina. These two are troublemakers who thrive on creating chaos. Trust me, I have worked with them for years and I know what they're like."

There was more bunter and laughter until Justin glanced towards the entrance of the bar and his face changed. He leaned forward to take a closer look past Ken who sat partially obscuring his view.

"Oh shit!" he said, quietly.

"What?" Ken asked, as he also turned to look towards the door. He did not pick up straight away what Justin was reacting to. "What?" He said again turning back to face Justin.

"You don't wanna know who just walked in." Justin mumbled between his teeth.

"Who?" Ken asked.

"Beatrice, she just waked in. What's she doing here?"

"Beatrice? Harriet's sister, Beatrice?" Ken said, turning again towards the main entrance.

"Yep, and she's with some guy who looks way too old for her."

"Isn't she like 15 or something?"

"17 but that is still nowhere old enough."

Flo and Tina sat silently watching the drama starting to unfold. They were now all far from the joking mood of earlier moments. This situation now held more serious consequences for Justin, if Beatrice were to see them.

"What do you want to do? Do you want to just sneak out quietly? She hasn't seen you yet, has she?"

"No, I can't just walk out and leave her in here with a sugar daddy. If Harriet were to ever find out that I saw her and did nothing, that would be the worst. Even if she didn't know, it would still play on my conscience."

"If you go there, she will know you were here, with us."

"So what, there is nothing going on here." Justin said, defending his position.

"I think you are right Justin," Flo joined in. "You need to go over there and knock some sense into that girl."

Feeling empowered, Justin got up and walked to the table on the other side of the bar, where Beatrice now sat with her male companion. As he approached, Beatrice had picked up a menu and was looking through it.

"Beatrice," Justine said as he got to the table.

Beatrice pulled down the menu and could have died when she saw who stood before her. "Oh my God, Justin. Hi!" She said nervously. She was unsure what to do. Seeing Justin in front of her was the last thing she expected. She had been caught completely off guard and she did not know how to react.

"What are you doing in here, Beatrice? Who is this?" He asked pointing to the older man.

"It's not what you think. We are just having a drink."

"Excuse me friend," Beatrice's companion attempted to intervene, with a polite smile on his face.

Justine turned towards him with a stern look, as if to ask the man to stay out of it. He told him anyway," If I was you, 'friend', I wouldn't even open my mouth. Do you know how old this girl is, huh? Do you?"

The stranger stood up from his chair and squared up to Justin. They were nearly of similar height.

"I don't care how old she is. The young lady is with me, so why don't you crawl back where you came from."

Beatrice, realising that the situation could get totally out of hand, spoke, "OK. OK, I'll go home Justin. Please, don't tell mum and dad or Harriet. Please, Justin? Tindo, I have to go." She said, addressing her date.

Beatrice got up, picked up her purse and started for the door. Justin followed and caught up with her by the door.

"Wait here for me. I want to make sure you get home."

Justin went back to his colleagues and informed them that he was leaving with Beatrice. He had left the bar soon after and hailed a cab to take her home. Her only prayer, as the cab drove out the city, was that she hoped he would not tell her parents or her sister what had happened.

Justin's cell phone rang and he answered it immediately; it was Harriet. A day had gone by since the events at the Cloud 9 Bar and although he had not told Harriet's Parents about Beatrice's escapades, he could not keep it from Harriet.

"*Hi* babe," he began," Thanks for calling me back."

"*Hi*. Is everything OK? You sounded a bit off," she asked, deeply concerned.

"Not really, but nothing major to worry about. I needed to talk to you about something though."

"OK. What is it?" She asked, again still unsettled.

"Well, I don't want you to overreact on this but I thought you might want to know and have a word with your sister." He said, and signed briefly before continuing. "Yesterday, Ken and I went to Cloud 9 for a quick drink after work. You'll never believe this but moments later your sister walked in."

"Beatrice? In Cloud 9?" Harriet asked to

clarify.

"Yes, and she wasn't alone. She had this guy with her. Harriet, he was possibly three times her age!"

"What! Are you serious!?"

"Yep, I couldn't believe it; It's not like her to do this but she was there. That is what I don't get, she knows better than that."

Harriet's tone shifted to anger.

"Wait till I get hold of her. I can't believe she did that. You should have dragged her out of there by her hair."

"Well, I told her to go home and to be fair she came out straight away. I think she realised what she had done."

Justin was attempting to soften the situation, as he knew Harriet would make a much bigger deal of it. He was afraid that if this happened then his relationship with Beatrice would be irreparable.

"I am going to call her right now. I will call you back."

"Harriet, listen, just go easy on her. Talk to her rather than just shout at her. You don't want her to become even more rebellious just to spite you."

"Oh, you wait. I am definitely going to have a good talk with her," Harriet replied, sarcastically," She is so stupid! I have always told her not to do stupid things like that. I will call you in a bit Justin."

"OK, call me right back."

The call ended.

At Harriet's parents' house, Beatrice had just walked back into her bedroom from the kitchen, a sandwich on a plate in one hand and a glass of Mazoe orange crush in the other. There was no one else in the house and the only sound was that of The ZBC Radio 3 station blasting loudly from the stereo in the lounge. She could get away with having it that loud usually when her parents were not at home.

As she sat down on her bed and prepared to bite into her snack, the house phone rang in the corridor. She almost did not hear it due to the loud music from the stereo. She ran to answer when she heard it.

"Hello," she said as she picked up the call.

"Bee, it's me," Harriet said, her tone ready to attack.

"Oh, hi sis. You OK?" Beatrice asked.

"Turn the radio down," Harriet instructed, as she was struggling to hear past the loud music in the background.

"OK, give me a sec."

Beatrice had placed the phone receiver down on the small table, where the phone sat, and ran to turn the radio down. It was only then, as she came back to the phone that it hit her, why Harriet might have called and sounded flabbergasted.

"I'm back. What's up sis?" Beatrice said.

"Don't give me the innocent girl routine Bee. Justin told me everything. What the hell do you think you are doing?"

Beatrice was not quick with her answer but eventually said something.

"I haven't done anything! I was just in there with a friend for two minutes."

"A friend? You call someone who is that much older than you, your friend. Do you have a clue what you are getting yourself into?"

" I didn't do anything."

"You were in a bar with a man who is as old as dad. How is that not doing anything?" Harriet screamed into the phone.

"He's not that old."

"I don't care Bee. What are you trying to do to mum and dad? Did you stop to think about that, ha? What if you fall pregnant, what are you going to do then? Or catch some STD, AIDS even, then what will you say, 'I didn't do anything'," Harriet mocked her. "Think Bee, don't be stupid!"

Beatrice remained silent. There was nothing she could say now that could mitigate her situation.

"This is the first and last time. I never want to hear that you did something like this again. I should be telling mum and dad right now but I am choosing to spare them the stress of knowing. You better thank Justin for not telling them either."

Beatrice mumbled something quietly on the other side and Harriet heard it.

"What did you say, Bee? I heard you. If you have something to say you better come out and say it!"

"I didn't say anything."

"I heard you. Say what you said right now or else mum and dad will find out what you did!" Harriet screamed down the phone.

"I said if he's so perfect why was he there with two other women?" Beatrice shouted back.

Harriet was winded by this sudden revelation. "What are you talking about?" She asked, her tone easing off a little.

"He calls you and tells you about me but did he tell you he was there with two women, and that friend of his, in that bar?" Beatrice had sensed a window of opportunity to worm her way out and she exploited it.

"What women? Who were they?" Harriet asked calmly, sensing she had to ease off to get Beatrice to talk.

"I don't know who they were. Two slutty looking women. They might as well have been prostitutes."

"Bee, are you making things up now because I swear if you start making things just to get out of trouble I will tell dad everything!"

"I'm not making it up. Ask him yourself. If he is as honest as you say, he will tell you."

Harriet was silent for a moment as she worked it all out. She could not tell whether Beatrice was telling the truth or just being spiteful.

She trusted Justin and she knew he wouldn't do things like this behind her back. She had not been away that long even, not that this would have stopped him.

"OK," Harriet said eventually," I will speak to you again. This is not over."

"OK," Beatrice replied. Even though the heat was off her a little, she had started to feel guilty about it all, especially the can of worms she had just opened. But if Justin was indeed cheating on her sister, then she was happy with it all coming out into the open.

Justin's cell phone rang again. He moved away from the group of people he was sitting with in the staff canteen to answer it.

"Hey, babe. Did you manage to get hold of her," he asked, oblivious to his own drama that was about to unfold.

"I did," Harriet replied, but did not give anything more.

"Well, what did she say then?" Justin asked

"I haven't finished with her but there is something that I want to know first. Who were you with, in that same bar last night?"

Justin knew straight away that Beatrice had told Harriet about his drinks session with Ken and the two women. The best way, he thought to himself, was to come out with it and be honest with her.

"Look, babe, I was there last night but it was not my idea. Ken asked Flo from my work to come for a drink with us and her friend. It was all his plan and I only got to know about it once I was in the bar. You know Flo don't you, that older lady from 3rd floor."

"I don't believe this, Justin!" she said," Who was the other one? Who was the other woman?"

"Harriet, listen, I promise you, I really didn't have anything to do with this. You know how Ken can be. If I had known he had planned this I wouldn't have gone in."

"Who was she!" Harriet said, her voice slightly raised.

Justin sighed and then replied, "Tina. It was Tina."

"The receptionist girl?" Harriet asked recognising the name.

"Ye." Justin replied reluctantly.

"Oh my God!"

"Harriet, you need to stop. There is nothing going on!" Justin was starting to get enraged by where all this was going.

"Not from where I'm standing. I call your office the other day and this Tina knows everything about me and now I hear you are going for drinks with her."

Justin became even more enraged, "I have said it over and over again that I did not organise this. You are taking it out of context. Why is it so hard for you to believe me on this?"

"Why? Why Justin? I am all the way over here and you are over there. That is why!"

"Babe, it was nothing. I don't know how else to tell you. I didn't plan any of this. Stupid, I shouldn't have listened to him." He muttered to himself at the end of that statement.

"Ye OK, that's fine. You go ahead and let your friend organise your life for you, set you up with new people, now that Harriet's out of the picture."

"Oh my God, Harriet, you know what, here I am trying to tell you the truth about how things happened and all you want to believe is that something terrible happened. Well I am sick of trying to convince you. Call me when you're in a better mood!"

With that Justin forcefully pressed the call cut button on his cell phone and angrily walked back to his cubicle, not bothering to go back into the staff canteen.

"Justin! Justin!" Harriet shouted after him, unsure whether he had actually hung up. She lowered the receiver from her ear and looked at it in disbelief; he had actually gone. She could not understand it. If there was anyone who should have been more upset about this issue, it was surely her. She put the phone receiver back on its holder and sat back in the sofa, trying to piece together what had just happened.

Chapter 7

"What did I say," Freda said, rhetorically. "Men!"

Harriet did not respond. She was sitting on the bed, resting her back on its padded leather headboard, as she cuddled one of Freda's feather pillows. Freda was sitting in front of the mirror by her dressing table, vigorously applying foundation onto her face with a small make-up brush as she spoke.

"Men make me sick sometimes," She continued. "Us women give everything to a relationship, everything, and what do we get back, crap! That's right, crap. Men go out and do what they like and expect that when they get back, you'll still be there waiting for them with a big smile and arms wide open."

Again Harriet did not respond. Although she had brought up the subject of her fight with Justin, she had not counted on Freda going off on one of her 'I told you so' speeches. Harriet was upset about what had happened, but she still had this feeling deep inside that Justin may have been telling the truth. He had never given her reason to not trust him.

"Have you spoken to him yet?" Freda asked.

"No, not yet. He has been calling though. Called me a few times today alone," Harriet replied, passively.

"Guilt, that's what it is. That is why he keeps calling so much. He knows he messed up."

"He said he didn't organise it. His friend was behind it all." Harriet said, trying to give Justin the benefit of the doubt.

Freda stopped applying her make-up and turned to look at Harriet. Her face was so overdone with the foundation that she half looked like a clown.

"And you believe him?"

"You don't know him like I do, Freda. He has never done anything like this before. I can't see him planning to go drinking with some girls, even if he knows them well. He's not like that. That is definitely all Ken."

"Well, if that's what you want to believe honey, then it's up to you but be careful. Make sure you're not being taken for a ride."

Freda turned to face the mirror again and continued to even out the foundation on her face. Pleased she had done sufficient work, she placed the brush down and picked up a cotton swab which she began to use to remove and even out more of the foundation.

"He wouldn't do that to me, I know Justin. We have been together forever, and we have really solid plans for our future." Harriet said, looking down at the pillow, talking quietly as if she were trying to convince herself.

"That's well and good, dear, but I can tell you this from experience, there is something that happens to relationships when two people are hundreds of miles apart. Distance changes people."

"I won't allow it. We have invested a lot in our relationship and I won't let anything destroy it.... I think I should call him. This is all stupid and childish."

Harriet had started to feel that talking to Freda was making her feel worse. Freda had a lot of unresolved issues that she was bringing into this situation and it was not helping Harriet one bit.

"Hey, listen, call him tomorrow when you have your thoughts together. Right now, you need to get yourself ready. Hector said not to be late. This party is going to be crazy. Come on, get going."

Freda and Harriet had been invited to Hector's birthday party that evening; he was one of Freda's friends. They had ordered a cab to take them to the party later on that evening. Harriet threw the pillow she had been cuddling to the side and slowly dragged herself off the bed. She was still in her shorts and a cropped tank top, which she had been in all day. She walked lazily into the bathroom, turned on the shower before undressing and walking in.

London at night was hypnotic. As their taxi raced towards the central, Harriet peered through the window and observed the life outside. There were rows and rows of well-lit shops and hundreds of people walking in and out of them. It soon dawned on Harriet that London was seriously overcrowded and surprisingly multi-cultural. This was one thing that amazed her when she was out and about; the sheer amount of people who were not Caucasian or of 'white' background. She had always imagined London to be mostly white, a thought she may have picked up from the books she read, which depicted it as so.

"Did you say Piccadilly Circus, love?" the overweight taxi driver asked with a heavy cockney accent.

"Yes, Salisbury Hall please," Freda replied, with a miserable attempt at the cockney accent herself. Harriet had noticed this about Freda, and most Zimbabweans living abroad, how they seemed to change their accents when they spoke to the locals, which sounded so wrong sometimes.

After a few more turns, the cab pulled up in front of an old English period building that was now a blend of its historical past with modern glass fittings. It was probably listed, protected building, as were most buildings in London. A few people stood outside, smoking and chatting, as others arrived and walked in.

"That will be £15 love," the burly taxi man said.

"Thank you," Freda replied, as she passed him the money through a small opening on the transparent shield that separated the driver from the passengers. This was a feature that London black cabs had as a protective measure for the drivers, to keep them safe.

When the fare had been paid, the pair got out and began walking up the steps towards the entrance into the building. They had both made an effort to look good and they were enjoying the glances from some who stood outside .

"Oh my God, so many people," Harriet shouted into Freda's ear as they walked in. The music was very loud that you could hardly hear yourself think.

Freda just nodded in agreement. This was no surprise to her. They walked further into the hall and as they did, Freda stopped several times to hug and greet many people she recognised. This was near enough everyone in the hall. It happened so many times that Harriet began to feel as though she didn't exist.

They got to the other side of the room, where all the food and drinks had been laid out and began to help themselves. There were a few empty tables and chairs on the same side, so they sat down to eat. Although the music was still overwhelmingly loud, it seemed less noisy that other side; they were able to converse a little better.

"Wow! I can't believe it. Everyone is here," Freda said, visibly excited.

"Quite a lot of people," Harriet repeated. She was feeling overwhelmed and a bit out of place.

"I know. Hector is very popular. He knows many people, Zim celebrities too."

"Really? Who?" Harriet asked enthused. She was still sceptical though, as Freda sometimes enjoyed adding her own details to flavour a story.

"Peter Chuma. He knows him, and he introduced us a few months back."

"Peter Chuma, the footballer?"

"Yes, the very same. Hector said he might actually turn up tonight. I seriously hope he does." Freda said, a mischievous smirk etched on her face.

"Serious?" Harriet asked pleasantly surprised.

"Ye, for real," Freda confirmed.

"That's interesting. Who else?" Harriet was intrigued.

"Tich Mutasa, CJ, most DJ's you know of."

"Really? Wow! I didn't know he was that well connected when I spoke to him last time. He seems such a quiet and humble guy."

"That's Hector for you, well connected but doesn't like to let it show."

"How was he when you met him then, Peter?" Harriet quizzed her friend.

"Oh my God he is so adorable," Freda answered excitedly." He is so well built, my knees almost buckled when I first met him, and he held my hand as he talked to me. I swore that very day that I was definitely going to make him my future husband." She spoke with so much excitement that it sounded as though she were already in a relationship with him.

"You are in love my dear," Harriet remarked but deep down wondering whether Freda was shooting far above her level. This was Peter Chuma, a celebrity. Could Freda truly nab him or was he into more of the sophisticated type of woman.

They finished their food and sat drinking for a little while. The party had now picked up pace and a few people had already invaded the dance floor.

Freda got up and grabbed Harriet's hand, "Come on, let's go dance. I like this tune."

Harriet refused, embarrassed to get up and remained glued to her seat, shaking her head.

"Don't be shy. No one cares here. Come on."

Reluctantly Harriet got up and followed her friend to the dance floor. The large hall was now very dim with the only source of light being the coloured disco lights flickering in sync with the music. Soon they were immersed in their own little world, totally submerged under the spell of the music. Once in a while, the DJ would disrupt their bubble by saying a few words and then the music would come up again.

A few moments later, after a couple more songs, the music came to a complete stop and they heard people whispering from everywhere around them. Harriet looked up to see what all the commotion was about when the voice of the DJ came booming over the speakers.

"Ladies and gentlemen, we have royalty in the house tonight! Make some noise for PETER... CHUMA!"

The whole room roared with excitement. PETER! PETER! PETER! They chanted. Harriet turned in the direction of the entrance and coming into the room, surrounded by quite an entourage, was the Zimbabwe International Striker Peter Chuma.

He was a little shorter than she had imagined but more handsome than she had thought. He wore an expensive looking suit and fit the part of someone with a seriously healthy bank balance. Everyone wanted to shake his hand and talk to him.

Others tried to force themselves on him but they were gently ushered away by his entourage. Harriet now understood why he had to have people around him. Some women in the crowd were going out of their way to disgrace themselves, all in an attempt to get near him. It was embarrassing to see what they were willing to do just to get his attention.

Harriet moved away from the dance floor and went to stand at the back of the room. She didn't want to be associated with this shameful behaviour. Some moments later Freda came looking for her.

"There you are. I was beginning to wonder what had happened to you."

"I thought I'd come back here, away from the madness."

"Yes, it got a bit crazy, didn't it? Have you seen him, Peter? Freda asked, quite enlivened.

"No, I wasn't going to get trampled on, just to say 'hi' to a guy, celebrity or not." Harriet replied and smirked.

Freda just laughed. "You should come and meet him. Come, we'll go find him."

"No Freda," Harriet protested, overwhelmed by the prospect. "What would I say to him,"

"He's nice. I will introduce you." Freda reassured her.

Again, Harriet reluctantly followed her friend through the crowds to the other side of the room, where now only a few people stood and in their midst was Peter Chuma. Harriet grew even more nervous as they approached. She grabbed Freda's wrist and pulled her back.

"Freda let's just go back over there."

"Oh, come on, he is harmless. Don't stress, I'll do all the talking."

"Those guys won't let us near him." Harriet said, pointing out to the huge burly men that stood guard near him.

"Don't be silly, they all know me now. Besides, look, Hector is there talking to him too."

They advanced further and as they got to where Hector and Peter stood, the bodyguards recognised Freda and let them through. Harriet was impressed with her friend.

"Hi Peter, how are you?" Freda asked, as they approached.

Peter turned to them and replied. "Oh, hi. How are you? Hasn't Hector thrown quite some party here?" Hector smiled sheepishly, like a child receiving praise for chores done well.

"He has. It's been quite a lovely evening." Freda responded. "This is my little sis." She said gesturing towards Harriet. "Her name is Harriet. Just flew in a few weeks back."

Peter turned to Harriet, cheeky smile on his face, "Harriet, that is a lovely name. Nice to meet you." He stretched out his hand to take hers.

"Likewise," Harriet replied, trying to be extremely reticent about her real feelings. She was ecstatic being in the presence of a real celebrity, but she was not going to let anyone know that. He had a deep confident masculine voice that she couldn't help notice and would never admit that it made her a little excited.

"So, what do you think of the UK? Are you homesick yet?" Peter asked.

"It's OK, I'm used to things now. I do miss home though, sometimes, but not that much yet.

Maybe later I'll miss it a lot."

"Hope these guys are taking good care of you," he continued, gesturing to Freda and Hector.

"They are," she replied with a smile.

"Great! I guess we will be seeing a lot of you around then. Hector, are you bringing her to my party next month?" he said turning to address him.

"I haven't asked them yet but you are coming, aren't you ladies." Hector forwarded the question.

"Of course we are," Freda replied," We will definitely be there."

Harriet just smiled.

"Good," said Peter. "I look forward to it."

Harriet woke up the next morning exhausted. She could not remember the last time she had been to a party and stayed out so late. She had tried, several times during the party, to persuade Freda to end the night and go home, but Freda was having far too much of a good time. By the time they had got in, sometime in the early hours of the morning, all Harriet wanted to do was sleep. She had managed to get upstairs, disrobe and straight under the covers.

Harriet pulled the bed covers off and crawled out of bed. She was still naked, only in her underwear, having not bothered to get into her night dress when they got in. She staggered out of the spare bedroom, which she had now made her own since moving in with Freda and walked into the small bathroom at the end of Freda's upstairs corridor. She got in and closed the door behind her.

Harriet stood by the sink and looked into the square mirror on the wall just above it. She looked rough and she felt it to. Her face felt heavy and plumb, and her hair was spiked up in all directions. She grabbed a handful of her hair extensions and after examining them for a bit, she concluded that she would have to change them soon.

She opened one of the taps and let the water run for a bit until it was warm. Using both hands she got some of the water that had collected in the sink and brought it to her face, as she also leaned down to meet it. She washed her face for a few minutes and then reached out for a small towel that was on the radiator next to her to dry.

As Harriet walked out of the bathroom and back into her room to get dressed, she heard Freda downstairs, in the kitchen cooking. She wondered what time it was. She had not checked since getting up but it felt late, and she could not tell if it was breakfast or lunch that Freda was preparing. Some moments later, dressed, she walked downstairs to the kitchen to join Freda.

"Morning princess," Freda said, closing the oven door where she had just been checking the bacon and sausages.

"Morning," Harriet replied lazily.

"Tired?" Freda asked.

"A little. Got a bit of a headache too."

"It's probably the loud music. That place was banging." Freda said with a big smile and she also did a little dance.

"Ye, absolutely," Harriet agreed, as she plonked herself on a seat by the kitchen table. "Do you need any help?" She offered, with all hopes that Freda would decline. She did not have the energy for anything.

"No, it's OK dear. I have it covered."

"Oh good; I wasn't getting up anyway," she said with a weak laugh behind it. Freda smirked too.

"How fab was that party though? What do you think?" Freda asked.

"It was good, really good." Harriet said. She had eventually loosened up and genuinely enjoyed it.

"Peter Chuma showing up though, that just made it a different class, didn't it?"

"It did! He is SO not how I imagined," Harriet confessed.

"How so?" Freda enquired.

"Well, firstly he wasn't as tall as I thought he was, and secondly I was amazed at how humble he is. Very nice guy."

"First time I met him I thought the same. I near enough wet myself," Freda said, laughing.

"You know you are truly into someone when you find yourself unable to control your bladder," Harriet responded, laughing too.

"He seemed quite kin on you though," Freda remarked, changing to a slightly serious tone." What was that all about?"

"Was he?" Harriet replied, pretending that she had not noticed.

"Of course he was. He was giving you the eye and all. When he said, 'Harriet, what a lovely name', and when he asked Hector to make sure he brings you to his party, that was him making moves on you. I know how men work."

There was hint of despondence in the

manner Freda spoke.

"I think that was an invite to both of us," Harriet said, trying to shift focus from herself.

"No, he specifically asked if Hector was bringing you to his party."

"Ye, he was probably being polite since I'm new here. I think he meant for you and Hector to take me to his party, since he already knows both of you. You are invited by default anyway."

"Stop trying to deflect, Harriet. Be honest, did he or didn't he show a little more interest in you?"

Harriet sensed a tiny hint of hostility starting to emanate from Freda, but she could not quite figure out why this was. She hadn't made any efforts to try and make Peter notice her.

"I think he was just being nice, not just to me but to everyone. Why are you trying to make this into something?" Harriet challenged her.

"I'm not making it into anything. I'm just saying it as I saw it."

"Oh, stop it, Freda," Harriet said jokingly, still attempting to defuse the worsening situation.

"Ye, like you didn't like the attention," Freda joked back, beginning to ease off." What girl doesn't want to be a celebrity footballer's wife."

"Not me," Harriet refused, a statement that she truly did not believe but seemed the best thing to do, in light of the situation." I don't care for money or riches."

"I do," Freda said, laughing.

"Well, then you should do something about it. Last night you should have stuck to him like glue, who knows, you could have woken up in his palace this morning," Harriet teased her, relieved that Freda was now calming down about it.

"Nah, I am not sure he is ready for someone like me."

"Why not? You are an attractive, young, single woman. What's not to like," Harriet said, exploiting the opportunity to shift focus to Freda. She was being overly generous though. Freda was a decent looking woman, but attractive was a subjective word. Besides, her reputation as a party girl was well known in the Zimbabwean expatriate community and Peter would have heard about it, being friends with Hector.

Harriet on the other hand, had a raw, natural, untainted beauty. She did not need any make-up to enhance her features and she hardly used any. She took pride in being all natural and detested vanity. Harriet never put too much time thinking about her looks and was not one to put anyone down. She believed that everyone had an individual look, that everyone was beautiful in their own way.

"Now you are just trying to make an old girl feel good, "Freda replied.

"No, I'm not. If you really like him you should do something about it, regardless of whether he is Peter Chuma or not."

Harriet was attempting to sound genuine in her efforts to urge Freda on, to go after her man, but deep-down Harriet was trying to suppress her own feelings. She had noticed how Peter had been looking at her all night, and as flattering as it may have been, she was not going to entertain any of those thoughts, especially with the way things had gone with Justin the last time they spoke. What sort of person would that make her?

"Hey, listen," Harriet spoke again, sensing

Freda's depressive state," Next month we're going to that party and you, my dear, are going to knock his socks off. We will make you up so good that he will be singing your name by the end of that night, trust me?"

Freda smiled, but her eyes were filling up.

"Ye," she said, her voice quivering, about to burst into tears," We will do that.... Check the bacon for me please, I'll be right back?"

Freda left the room quickly and went upstairs. Although she tried to hide it, Harriet had noticed that she was upset and crying. Harriet could not understand what had made Freda so upset. It was strange, for someone to be that emotional over someone she was not in a relationship with. Harriet got up from her chair and moved to the oven. She checked the bacon and switched the oven off as it was done. She decided it best not to follow Freda. Whatever she was going through, this was one thing she had to deal with on her own.

Chapter 8

A month later, Harriet and Freda had done what had now become a frequent ritual; getting dressed up to go to some social function or other. It was not just them, but it seemed to be the most popular pastime for many expatriates. This one was going to be special though; it was gearing up to be a much bigger affair than the last one they had been to. Hector's party, in central London the other day, had been a pleasurable experience for both of them, but Peter Chuma throwing a party was most certainly a function of another level. Every Zimbabwean in London, in the UK even, wanted to be there.

It had gone around all Zimbo circles, that this party was definitely happening, and many had tried everything to get an invite. It became evident, closer to the time, that this party would be so exclusive that only Peter's closest and a chosen few would be attending. Even if you made it to Peter's private mansion in Richmond, Surrey, there would be a battalion of his security guards to get through first.

Richmond was quite an upmarket, affluent area of London, mostly home to the rich and famous. Property there was priced in the millions and this was one of the only few areas in London that you could buy real estate with descent yard space. London homes were characteristically small, crammed with little to no outside space; and these were what most people could afford. Only those with deep pockets could afford to buy as much of the UK's most expensive commodity as they wished, land.

Being a footballer in Britain, playing for major teams, was a very rewarding profession. Peter had been scouted by Chelsea Football Club, a premiership team, when he was back home playing for his local team, The Rufaro Rovers. He had also worn the Zimbabwean National Team captain's armband, playing for his country for many years, and when Chelsea came knocking, he did not hesitate.

He was ready for the big time and he did not disappoint. For over two years, his name would be encapsulated in song by the Chelsea fans, as he guided them to the top of the premier league. Fans, young and old, clad in their blue and white team shirts, would often call out his name, wrongly pronouncing it as Cha-you-ma, but he did not care. He knew how to handle a soccer ball around the field and that was good enough for them.

The more famous he became, the more the sponsors came seeking, and soon his wealth accumulated. Peter became internationally known and also became one of the wealthiest footballers of his time, more than what a boy who grew up in the dusty suburbs of Harare could have dreamt of. He quickly built a healthy investment portfolio of property and assets, both back home and abroad. His house in Glen Lorne, a low-density suburb of Harare, was one of the best-built homes known to locals; it was famous in its own right. The only unfortunate thing, however, was that it lay dormant for most of the year and only saw use when the cleaners went in, or when Peter himself was in town.

Sat in the back seat of Hector's Ford Mondeo, Harriet could not help thinking to herself how pleasant the weather was, as they sped towards Richmond. It was a gorgeous, warm summers afternoon and so perfect was the weather that it made the trip past London's finest homes even more captivating. It was the first time since arriving in the UK that Harriet had experienced warm weather in England. This part of the world appeared to have had a curse of bad weather bestowed upon it. Not only were the winters icy cold but the summers were also wet and humid on most days. This day, however, was a welcome exception and Peter could not have picked a better day to throw a party.

Harriet was grateful Hector had offered to pick them up. First of all, he knew how to get there and most of all, Harriet had not been looking forward to a train or bus journey, or forking out on an extortionate cab fare. She was glad to have had the stress of getting there taken away from her. This meant, however, that they would be at his mercy all day.

They would only be able to leave when he was ready; taking away their choice of an early escape if the party got sour.

Three quarters of an hour later, the Mondeo took one last turn into a private road and pulled up in front of a set of very tall, well veneered, wooden gates; all framed within a shiny black metal skeleton.

The large gates were attached to two boundary walls running either side. The walls were quite high, which meant nothing on the other side was visible from the road outside. Peter had gone to great lengths to protect his privacy.

Just outside the gates, erected next to the cobalt driveway, was an intercom system. There was a car parked next to it and as they pulled up behind it, the driver had stretched out his arm from his car window and pressed one of the buttons. After a few seconds, a voice was heard over the intercom, which asked for the name of the driver and his passengers. After a few exchanges, the driver angrily stuck his head out his window and barked at the intercom.

"Of course, I was *bloody* invited. What person just turns up somewhere where they are not invited. Check again!"

The voice on the intercom went silent and then a few moments later returned with the final verdict; the driver and his passengers could drive in. Almost immediately the large wooden and metal gates began to open slowly, like theatre curtains, and for the first time, everyone saw what lay beyond the high walls.

Some distance from the gate was a large, white residential building that looked so grand that

Harriet did not believe the house belonged to one man. Surrounding it was an impressive display of well-manicured lawns, shrubbery and trees. This was a house you only saw on television or in movies and Harriet could not believe she was about to drive into this dream space.

As the car in front drove in, Hector roared his into life and drove next to the intercom. His window had been lowered already in preparation and he too stretched out his arm to press the intercom button.

As they waited, the car in front had begun to disappear further up the drive, at the same time as the gates began to shut slowly. There was a bit of a delay as they waited for a response to their call on the intercom, but then the gates began to open up again without the questioning voice from the intercom. Both girls looked at Hector with bewildered gazes. They had expected some sort of interrogation before being allowed through. It seemed they had underestimated Hector's relationship with Peter.

"Wow, check you out Hector," Freda said, turning to face him from the front passenger seat. Hector smiled sheepishly.

"He is Mr Connected this one," Freda added, this time turning to the back seat of the car where Harriet sat, behind the driver's seat.

Harriet just smiled. She was still trying to take in the beauty and extravagance of this new world she had just entered. She had been in the United Kingdom for a few months now and visited many Zimbabwean expat homes, but she had not been to anything this extravagant.

"How did we get through that easy though?"

Harriet asked, snapping out of her trance for a second. "How come they just let us through?"

"Security cameras. Didn't you spot them above the gate pillars," Hector answered, attempting to further showcase his knowledge and closeness to everything of Peter Chuma.

"Is that what those were. Wow, I would've never guessed," Harriet said, even more intrigued.

At this point, Hector had driven into the compound and was headed for an overcrowded car park on the far side of the mansion. As they neared the car park, two men in suits with high visibility vests strapped over them, were beckoning and waving to usher them to where they could park. Hector manoeuvred his vehicle in the direction indicated and found a reasonable spot where he parked.

Hector opened his door and got out of the vehicle. He stood outside and stretched a little before proceeding to open the rear passenger door on his side to let Harriet out.

As the door came ajar, he noticed that Harriet was still sat back in her seat, a tiny make-up mirror in one hand held up to her face, and a stick of lipstick in the other perched onto her lips ready to apply.

She expertly covered the upper lip, then the bottom and then brought her lips together to gently massage each other to even out the application. She put the mirror down onto her lap next to her handbag, and using both hands she rolled back the lipstick and re-sheathed it. She then threw it into her handbag. She picked up the mirror again and did one more quick check before finally using the tips of her fingers to run through her hair, like a comb, raised and flattened any uneven areas.

Hector was getting visibly impatient and Freda, who was in the front, was not helping. She too was doing her last minute making up in the car vanity mirror on the front passenger side.

"Come on ladies," Hector whimpered.

"A-ah Iwe!" Freda snarled at him, making sure he understood that he knew better than to rush them. It is a woman's prerogative to be afforded the time to look good.

Freda snapped her makeup mirror shut, placed it back into her handbag and turned to exit the vehicle. She stood next to the car and made a last minute adjustment of her outfit. She wore an extremely tiny, body-hugging black dress that was so short that it kept riding upwards every time she moved; she did not care. She could have worn tights, but she wanted to show her legs. She was on a mission to try and catch someone's attention, and her legs were her best asset. On her feet, she wore a pair of high-heeled Jimmy Choos, her dearest and most prized pair of stilettos, that she had worked so hard to purchase. They complimented her outfit and further helped to extenuate her long legs and the rigidity of her calves.

Harriet, on the other hand, had decided on something a little more conservative. She had settled on a long sleeveless purple chiffon dress and a cream coloured silk scarf resting over her shoulders. Hanging from her arm was a matching cream ladies handbag that went well with the flat evening shoes she wore. She still felt new to the expatriate social groups and did not want to be seen as trying too hard to fit. All she had to do was dress decent and avoid any unwanted attention towards her. If she was going to survive without Justin, this was what she was going to have to do.

"Let's go in," Hector said, and began to lead them towards the mansion doors. The house was even more grand now that they had moved closer, at least two stories high.

They walked towards the entrance, past the two ushers, who greeted them as they went in. There was a small flight of steps to negotiate before they could enter through a set of heavy doors into the foyer, a large room with a very high ceiling and a grand staircase that lead to the upper rooms. Just as you entered, your attention was stolen by a large crystal chandelier that was the focal feature in this space. From the foyer they could see all the way through to the back of the mansion where a large gathering was assembled. The house was well illuminated by light slicing through the glass panels that formed part of the roof and back walls.

"Oh my God! Wow!" Freda said quietly but visibly excited at how beautiful the house was. Harriet shook her head too in awe, overcome by an intense sense of admiration. "This is the life! I am moving in guys," Freda continued.

They all laughed but Harriet knew that Freda actually meant it. Freda had been quite clear in conversation, after Hector's party, that she had her sights set on Peter. Harriet knew, though, that this would not be an easy task. Peter had not shown any interest in Freda at Hector's party and besides, Peter was the most eligible bachelor in Zimbabwean circles anywhere and could have any woman he so desired. Why would he want to tie himself down?

However, that wouldn't have been the only obstacle for Freda. It was also common knowledge that most foreign black football players usually went for local blonde white girls. This was a stereotype that had often been proved true. Harriet concluded that this might turn out to be a fruitless endeavour for Freda but she was not about to drop the bombshell on her friend.

They got to the end of the long foyer and exited the building through the open French doors, onto the backyard decking that overlooked the rest of the garden. This had now been transformed into an organisation of tables littered with all manner of food types. The backyard was a large rectangular space that had a pool house to the left stretching down the yard, next to a 12 by 48 foot in-ground swimming pool, and the rest was green lawn, block paved pathways and a lot of plants and shrubbery. In the centre of the garden was a large water fountain, which was attached to a walkway leading all the way back to the main house.

The size of the crowd attending the party, was testimonial to Peters popularity. There were groups of people gathered around the tables, picking food and placing it onto their plates, whilst others stood around in smaller numbers, engrossed in conversation and downing the various drinks and beverages that were on offer.

Most were Peter's friends and the rest were invited people from his social and professional circles. There was also the odd one or two gate crashers, who had wormed their way in somehow, determined in their resolve to be there. To be known to have been at Peter Chuma's party was a measure off an unimaginable scale on the social ladder. Women, in particular, had no problem getting in. Peter's parties could sometimes be easily mistaken for a Miss World pageant or a professional modelling shoot.

As the three stood on the balcony overlooking the party below, Harriet could not help but feel slightly inadequate at being at this event. There were a lot of smartly dressed and significant looking people dotted about. There were people of all sorts, a concoction of colours and cultures, all mingling and interacting. This was further evidenced by some in attendance who opted to be draped in their national dress. It was easy to spot those who were from the north African regions with their bubas, kabas and abeti-ajas. Those of Asian and Indian culture were distinct too in their saris and Lehenga Cholis and a few Sikh turbans were unmissable in their bright vibrant colours.

"OK guys, go down there and enjoy yourself. I'll be back." Hector said, his hands on their lower backs, ushering them forward like two reluctant young school girls nervous about walking into their first day of school.

"Where are you going? You can't just leave us," Freda sneered at him.

"I'm just going to hunt down a few people. I'll be right back."

"Don't disappear on us," Harriet joined in.

"You'll be fine. I'll find Peter and bring him to say 'hi'. I'm hundred percent sure that he wants to meet you, well, one of you more," he said with a naughty grin spread across his face.

"What? Who? What do you know? Did he say something?" Freda quizzed him, the questions coming fast like a machine gun spitting bullets.

Hector just smiled and began to walk away, evidently indicating that he was holding some knowledge but was not about to reveal it just yet. He turned and grinned at them again before disappearing.

"Come back here! Hector!' Freda shouted quietly after him, but he was long gone. "Err, that boy drives me crazy sometimes! What do you think he is up to? What do you think he knows?"

This time the tirade of questions was now targeted towards Harriet.

"I have no idea but if I were to guess, I'd say that he meant that Peter has interests in someone. It's you obviously. I saw the way he looked at you at Hectors party." Harriet lied.

"Oh stop it. He has more interest in you. You think I didn't notice. Besides…....," Freda did not finish.

"Besides what?" Harriet asked.

Freda did not reply instantly. She was debating with herself whether to say or not. "I like him but it's complicated. It's nothing serious though. Don't worry about it." she continued to be elusive.

Harriet was confused. She sensed that there was more to Freda and Peter's story that she had not been privy to.

"No seriously. I saw him checking you out and the way you look today, girl, I have no doubt that by the end of the night it will be a different story."

They both giggled like two pubescent teenagers and then proceeded to descend into the party below.

The sun was slowly setting, and night was creeping in. The party was in full swing, and with the backyard now wondrously illuminated by a cascade of colourful lights, the drinking and dancing continued. Harriet and Freda had found their feet eventually and had managed to get acquainted with some of the party attendees. Hector had not made much of an appearance but could be seen dashing around the place attempting to look busy and important.

Freda and Harriet had been dancing, in between the eating and drinking, but they now sat on two pool loungers, watching the bustling crowd. Besides the deafening waves of the music blurring through gigantic speakers strategically positioned around the yard, you could still make out the humming sounds of people conversing, and a few laughs here and there.

"I could get used to this," Freda said, as she stretched and straightened her legs on the lounger.

"This is how the other half live," Harriet agreed. "Not bad I guess."

"What!" Freda said, challenging her trivialisation of what they were experiencing. "What more would you ask for?"

"I'm not saying it's not nice, I'm just saying there is more behind all this. Not all that glitters is gold."

Freda laughed," I don't care what else comes with it, as long as I have the money, I'll buy someone to sort it out."

Harriet laughed too.

"I swear I'm going to kill that boy when he finally decides to show up", Freda huffed as she turned to look around for Hector.

Harriet, whose head was resting on the lounger headrest, turned to look at Freda. She knew her friend was only upset with Hector because he had not taken her to meet the host. Harriet knew that something had to happen, and happen fast, because going home with a disappointed Freda was not something she was prepared for.

"OK, I'm going to have a wonder around," Freda said, as she dragged herself up off the lounger and sat on its edge for a few minutes, wrestling to put her Jimmy Choo's back on.

"Don't you go and disappear on me too, Missy," Harriet warned her friend.

"I won't be long sweetie. I just need to talk to Hector."

"OK, don't be long. I don't want to spend the rest of the night fighting off drunk idiots by myself."

"I won't abandon you, I promise." Freda said, now stood up and adjusted her dress. She pulling it down a little then bent down to pick up her purse, before disappearing into the crowd.

Harriet sat back in the lounger and closed her eyes to absorb the music and the party ambience. For a moment her mind drifted to Justin and she wondered what he might have been up to. She had not spoken to him all day and she created a mental note in her head that calling him would be the first thing she did the very next day. Harriet wished if only he were there with her. She could not shake the feeling that having a great time without him was like cheating on him in some way.

Justin trusted her though and would have encouraged her to have fun, but she was happy feeling this way; this was the only way she was going to stay on the straight and narrow path back to him. She was pleased with herself so far, how she had managed to stay away from trouble. She was trying, incessantly, to not get herself carried away, especially with some of the attention she had been receiving from guys at these parties. Truth be told it was quite flattering at times to have guys swarming around her, but she had to be good.

"Is this lounger taken?" A voice sounded frighteningly close to her face that she jumped.

"Oh gosh!" she exclaimed as she sat up on the lounger, realising who was asking.

Peter sat himself on the empty lounger next to her, not waiting for an answer to his question, and leant back to make himself comfortable. He was holding a half drank bottle of Corona beer in one hand which he took a swig of and then placed it on the ground. She had not seen him throughout the day and all evening and at one point had wondered to herself what sort of host would arrange a party and not be present to meet the guests.

He was dressed in all white, a light cotton summer shirt, unbuttoned around the chest, and very thin cotton trousers. On his feet were navy suede deck shoes but no socks. He was very casual but it was fitting with the occasion.

Harriet had not responded quickly enough as she had been trying to process the fact that not only was the party host sat next to her, in plain view of everyone, but this was the very person Freda was prepared to give up everything for. Unfortunately Freda was not there to take her chance.

"How have you found the party tonight, its Harriet isn't it?" Peter said, rescuing her from shock and loss of words.

Harriet was never one to be lost for words, but she froze for a few more seconds just trying to come up with an answer that would not leave her sounding like a rambling mess.

"Oh yes. Ye, its has been such a lovely evening," she responded nervously.

She was uneasy, not sure whether to stay seated or get up and look for Freda.

"That's good. Glad you are enjoying yourself," Peter responded, still sat back on the lounger.

"Have you had a tour of the place?" He said, turning to her.

"No," Harriet answered smiling, trying not to making eye contact and still slightly perplexed by the awkward situation. She could not work out whether he was just being gracious or whether he was making moves on her.

She prayed for Freda to return as this was making her seriously uncomfortable. On the other hand, though, Harriet could not work out why this situation was making her so uneasy. All she needed to do was to be civil, answer the man's questions and be mature about it.

"No, I haven't. It's a very lovely place. Is it all yours?" Harriet said, attempting to enhance the quality of the conversation but she failed dismally. As the words came out she knew instantly that the moment of stupidity she was dreading had just happened. She closed her eyes and wished for the ground to open and swallow her whole.

Peter just laughed. He had found the question rather amusing but knew it had emerged from nervousness. He had been around many people who often babbled talking to a celebrity. He was used to it. Again, to help her, he did not answer the question but got up from the lounger and made her an offer that all single ladies, even those taken, would have loved to have.

"I'd love to give you a personal tour of the place. May I?" His arm was stretched out to offer her a hand up.

She looked up at him with a reluctant, shy gaze, her body wanting to reach out to him but her mind saying otherwise. He kept his hand stretched out towards her and Harriet realised she was going to have to go along with it as people were beginning to stare. She gave him her hand and he helped her sit up on the lounger.

She put her shoes on and then he took both her hands and helped her stand. As he got her up to her feet, Peter pulled with a little more strength than needed that she fell forward into him. This forced them into a position where they stood so close to each other that they seemed like they were about to kiss. If it had not been awkward enough for Harriet before, then now it most certainly was.

Time seemed to stand still for a moment, and Harriet was surprised and overwhelmed by the warm feeling she was experiencing at what was happening. She zoned out briefly into some bubble with with him and forgot where she was or who ever might have been watching. Perfect situations are seldom planned, and Harriet felt her whole self sucked into what was a near perfect cinematic moment; she felt her knees buckle and her throat dry up. She swallowed visibly and stepped back away from him, in a moment of realisation that she may have just crossed so many lines.

As she gathered herself and prepared to

move this on, she turned and to her right, standing watching the episode unfold, was Freda. She too appeared frozen in time, as she witnessed, in disbelief, what was transpiring before her.

"Freda!" Harriet exclaimed, shock and relief both engulfing her simultaneously. "We were just coming to look for you."

Freda did not respond but kept her gaze on Harriet, with a look that registered both confusion and disappointment.

"Peter wanted to show us around, so we were going to come looking for you," Harriet continued, still attempting to convince her friend that nothing suspect had occurred.

"I can see that," Freda replied softly, with a hint of sarcasm noticeable in her tone. "It's ok, you can carry on. Wouldn't want to intrude."

"Don't be silly. What do mean intruding? We were coming for you," Harriet insisted defiantly but also untruthful. She did not know how best to get out of it.

"I'd be most happy to show you both around," Peter joined in. This did not help.

"Hi Peter," Freda said turning in his direction with an over produced fake smile," It's nice to see you. Thanks for the offer but please go ahead and take her around. I was just going to look for Hector to take me home."

"Why the rush, the party is just beginning?" Peter asked.

"I don't feel well all of a sudden and I need to go." Freda said, as she walked past them and went towards the balcony, which was also the way out to the car park.

They watched her walk away and both were unsure how to carry on. Harriet was now visibly upset. She had not asked for this.

She had not set out to cause any problems or hurt anyone. How is it that she suddenly found herself in the middle of this situation?

"Wow," Peter began, with half a smile on his face. "I'm not sure what started all that but I hope she's OK."

"I'm sorry, Peter. Thank you for the offer and the invite but I have to go too," Harriet interrupted him quickly.

"Why? Do you have to? I'm sure Hector will make sure she gets home safe. I can get a car for you later. Stay, please?" There was an almost boyish charm to his pleading that could have melted any heart, had the situation been different.

"Thanks for the offer, but I'm sorry I can't".

With that, she too walked away towards the balcony in search of her friend.

Chapter 9

Freda's flat was quiet and all that could be heard were cars passing by on the street, beaming their headlights into the lounge as they zoomed past. The car tyres made a whooshing sound as they drove over rain water that had collected in the gutters a few moments earlier. What had started as a bright and sunny day, had turned dark and wet without much warning as the evening played out.

The room was quiet and lifeless, and the only other sounds that could be heard was the occupant shuffling in their seat for comfort and the occasional sigh. The lights had been deliberately dimmed and the clock on the wall could be heard ticking away the seconds. The occupier seemed on edge and sat waiting.

A few moments later, keys began rattling on the door as another occupant was making attempts to enter from outside the property. After a few fiddles with the key and lock, the door slowly opened and a silhouette appeared, aided by the street lights outside. The silhouette paused by the open door and turned the lights on to full beam, revealing Freda by the door, still in the same clothes she had worn to Peter's party, her purse in one hand and her Jimmy Choos in the other. She appeared to have walked home barefoot. Also revealed by the lights coming on was Harriet, who sat on the other side of the room facing the door. She got up and walked towards Freda.

"Freda, where have you been? Are you OK? It's so late and I was getting very worried." Harriet began, having been genuinely concerned for the welfare of her friend.

Freda ignored her and slowly turned to close the door. She turned back into the room and made for the stairs.

Harriet tried again to engage her, "Hector and I looked everywhere for you at the party. He brought me straight home, hoping you were here, that maybe someone dropped you off. I was quite concerned when I got here and you weren't."

"There was no need to worry about me. You should have stayed. Things seemed to have been happening for you there," Freda replied, in a slow and very low sounding voice. She sounded much more intoxicated than she had been at the party.

"Freda please. What happened today was just one big misunderstanding. I want you to know that nothing happened. What you saw was nothing."

Freda, who had already got to the foot of the staircase, stopped and turned to face Harriet. She stared at her intensely with a piercing sharp gaze.

"Nothing. You call that nothing." Freda

replied." I know what I saw and that did not look like nothing to me."

"What do you think you saw, Freda? We had just got up to come and look for you." Harriet said moving closer towards Freda by the staircase.

"You were literary in his arms Harriet." Freda fired back. "Anybody who saw that knew what was happening. Do you think I'm stupid?"

Harriet exhaled heavily and shook her head. She folded her arms and turned her face to the floor. Although she accepted that the situation looked compromising, she truly had not intended for that to be the case; convincing her friend of that was going to be a struggle.

"Look, I know how it might have appeared to you but please believe me when I tell you that I had no intention whatsoever, of that happening."

"Oh, so now you accept that something happened."

"No!" Harriet replied, almost pleading," It just looked like something happened but please, please listen to me, nothing happened."

Freda paused and looked up the stairs, as if contemplating the climb. She was visibly upset. She tilted her head backwards and closed her eyes for few seconds, then slowly turned to face Harriet again. Her eyes had welled up and disappointment written all over her face.

"It may have been nothing to you, Harriet, but he clearly wanted you. Don't you see, it's you he wants and that was so blatantly obvious tonight. How can I compete with that."

Freda spoke with such softness that her voice echoed the hurt that her heart was screaming. She felt so defeated. Her only chance of real happiness had just been snatched from underneath her feet, and the worst thing about it was that it was by someone so close to her.

A few days later, following the incident that had caused such a rift between Harriet and Freda, things had begun to settle and the feud seemed to be fading away. By the morning of the fourth day, the two had started to exchange pleasantries and it looked as though they were getting back to normal again. Harriet was most happy about this happening because not only was she still Freda's guest, but there was also Justin on her mind. If this were to ever come out, this could create unwanted problems and wreck everything they had worked towards; their engagement and future plans.

Harriet had called Justin the day after the party and told him about it. However, she deliberately left out the details of what transpired between her and Freda, as she thought this would generate negative thoughts in Justin's head. Her logic dictated that talking about it would have turned this into a problem, a problem that did not exist. She was not prepared to go down that road.

Justin had finished work and was at his flat when she called. He was in the kitchen laying out a juicy piece of steak onto an oven tray, which he had just oiled and salted. He was just closing the oven door when his cell phone screamed and vibrated from the other side of the kitchen counter. He took his time to wash his hands and as he dried them with a cotton dish towel, he peered over to see who was calling. He threw the cloth onto the counter and with a grin on his face, he picked up the phone and answered it.

"Hey, Miss London, what's up?"

"Hey, sha, ndeipi?" Harriet's voice sounded from the other end. She was calm and collected.

"I am good. How was your day?" Justin enquired.

"Chilled really. Still not much to do, just waiting. I'll be starting uni soon, then I'll have something worth talking about. It's going to be good though, getting myself behind some books. How about you, how has your day been?"

"Solid, really good," he responded, confidently. "I have a few things I have been working on. Ken and I have been talking and for the first time in a long time, I feel good about something."

Justin walked into his lounge, phone perched on his ear, and planted himself on a one seater leather sofa that was directly facing his 23 inch colour TV. The TV was turned to the local ZBC TV and broadcasting a wildlife documentary.

The flat was not heavily furnished and in addition to the single leather sofa and a 2 seater version, there was also a small dining table with four metal chairs around it. The room had a wooden floor, and no carpeting, which made it bare and not very homely. Justin liked it that way. It was a fully functioning, small bachelor pad with only the essentials he needed. It was a space devoid of any form of female touch.

"Really? You and Ken had a grown up and uplifting talk? Can't even imagine how that went,"

Harriet said sarcastically, openly expressing her doubts.

"We actually did," Justin said, coming to Ken's defence,"he said something that really made sense to me and I am really inspired. Think about it Harriet, who has brought in the most clients and holds the biggest client list at G&G? If I leave, I bet I can take them all with me."

Harriet agreed but was not convinced.

"And then what? Go join another company and make another group of ungrateful buggers millions?" Harriet pointed out.

"No, not this time," Justin replied, with even more enthusiasm in his voice. "I need to think about setting up something of my own. I have to do it, it's now or never."

"Serious?" Harriet asked, half of her excited and the other half unsure whether she should be supporting such a big move. She had not heard all the details yet.

"Yes, why not? I have been working for these guys for far too long and I am sick and tired of being used. I know every aspect of this business because I set up most of the structures. I can easily replicate it somewhere else and also even improve it, without having Sonderai looking over my shoulder all the time."

"Wow, you have given this a really good thought, hey?"

"Definitely! It's now or never. He can keep that new boy of his and let's see where it gets them."

"You know I will always support you babe, no matter what. That sounds like a really sure thing. I know you can do it."

"It's definitely happening," Justin confirmed. "....So what have you been up to?"

Harriet took a small but uncomfortable pause, as she felt that the question required her to answer with tact.

"Nothing much. All quiet really. Hey, guess who we met this last weekend, well, who's party we went to I should say?"

There was a reluctance from Harriet to give out much more than that, out of fear of revealing too much.

"Who? Do I know him?"

"Ye, very famous," Harriet said, throwing in a clue.

"Oh wow, really? A celebrity? From Zim?"

"Yes." Harriet confirmed.

Justin paused briefly to think then said, "I don't know sha, can't put my finger on anyone. Who was it?" He was now quite eager to know.

"Peter. Peter Chuma!" she said, trying to keep her tone as normal as possible. She could not work out why, but the mere mention of his name had sent a shiver down her spine. It did not make sense to her that someone she had only met twice, and she did not know much about, could influence her body to behave like that; it was unlike her.

"Peter Chuma? The footballer?" He replied astonished. Justin was a football fan and Peter was the one player he admired the most.

"Ye!" Harriet answered, with a hint of excitement. "Freda was invited and she asked me if I wanted to come." she lied, emphasising the point that she had only been a tag along.

"Wow, that is so cool. Where was it? What is he like in person?" Justin asked, now hungry for details and Harriet had to oblige.

"It was at his house, oh my God Jussy, he has the biggest house you could ever think of, the biggest mansion you have ever seen! I couldn't believe how huge it was. And the grounds, oh my God, just immaculate. The party was outside, in his backyard, and it was laid out so beautifully. It was just spectacular!"

"Wow! Lucky you," Justin responded, quite envious, "Harriet Sande mingling with Zim Royalty now, huh? You won't be talking to us mere mortals soon." He mocked her and laughed.

Harriet laughed too and continued to tell him how Freda had introduced them, how down to earth Peter was and all the gossip she had acquired on the night. She made attempts to paint the picture as an innocent, controversy free affair and even went as far as telling Justin of all the women present, including stories of Peter's infidelity she had overheard.

"You should've seen the amount of skanks there. He's a typical 'good boy gets rich and goes bad' example, surrounding himself with tons of women. It was quite embarrassing really, so I asked Freda if we could leave early."

"And why shouldn't he surround himself with beautiful people?" Justin laughed, "Let him enjoy his money. He worked hard for it."

"Ye, he has earned his money, but surely one woman at a time is enough. He could do so much better". Harriet was doing her best to come out as though she had been repulsed by Peter's lifestyle, all in an attempt to try and distance herself from him. Justin was too busy being a fan to notice.

"You should have been there sha," she continued,

"I'd have been much happier."

"Now I wish I was. I'll have to fly up sometime when you are settled. You had a good time though?" He asked, half of him hoping she would say no. It was not that he didn't want her to have a great time but he did not want her to enjoy herself too much without him, and start to forget him.

"It was OK, just too many people though. A few drunk and crazy ones too."

"Crazy? How? Did anyone do anything to you?"

"No, no, nothing to me. Just people being drunk and stupid," she tried to dismiss the issue.

"Hope no one tried to make moves on you?" Justin quizzed her.

Harriet gave out a small nervous laughter.

"Oh my God no! I wouldn't entertain anything like that. I had my serious face on, you know the one I use on you when I am upset?" She was now trying desperately to infuse humour to diffuse the intensifying conversation.

Justin laughed. "Ye, I know that face. The death stare."

"Hey!" she warned him, jokingly. "You'll get the stare through this phone if you keep going. I have the power you know, it's possible."

They both laughed, and naturally their call came to an end. It was never easy to say goodbye and sometimes it was the phone card timing out that helped. Speaking to each other often was the key to keeping things going between them, but it was also a strong reminder of how they were worlds apart and how much they missed each other. They would often comfort each other with the hope that it was not going to be long before they spoke again. They had even planned for Justin to visit once Harriet was settled. This was definitely something that was keeping them going.

Chapter 10

The London underground train glided to a halt at Liverpool tube station. Harriet was already up from her seat as the train came to a controlled stop underneath Oxford Circus Station. The sliding doors rolled open and trails of people scurried from the train onto the platform. It was like a human stampede as they all migrated in the same direction towards the escalators leading to street level. Harriet had decided to go on a window-shopping trip, on one of the most affluent and renowned shopping streets in the world, Oxford street. She was not sure whether she would be able to afford much, if anything, as she had to keep her finances in check for university, but she was more than happy to just have the pleasure of being there and seeing shiny beautiful things.

She jumped onto the escalator, behind the

other commuters, and waited patiently as it ferried them all the way to the top. Just in front of her was a Caucasian woman, dressed in a smart business suit and holding an expensive looking Louis Vuitton bag, dropped down by her side. The bag had caught Harriet's eye and she was impressed by how elegant the woman looked. She surmised that the woman was probably some top boss in a big company, but she wondered why she would be on the tube; surely she could afford a car and chauffeur. Affluent people back home never took public transport. Harriet did not realise that the London underground was the fastest way to get around and many business people prefered it to driving.

As she neared the top, Harriet gently tapped the woman on the back. Making conversation with strangers was not a typical London thing but Harriet had not long arrived, and didn't know any different. The woman turned slowly, with a look that spoke volumes, clearly unimpressed at being disturbed. Harriet ignored her expression and continued in her quest.

"Your bag is very nice." she complimented the woman, smiling.

The woman smiled back and murmured an awkward and confused 'thank you'. She appeared unnerved that this strange woman was talking to her and commenting on her personal belongings. She gingerly turned to face forward again and clutched her bag up to her chest, clasping it tightly. As they arrived at the top of the escalator, the woman quickly got off and sped away as hurriedly as she could, turning a few times to check if Harriet was following her.

Harriet was puzzled by the bizarre behaviour and a little bewildered by the lack of appreciation of the compliment, but she did not dwell on it too much. Her thoughts had quickly shifted, as she walked from the darkness of the subway onto the refreshing brightness of the street level.

She had arrived on Oxford Street and it did not take her long to get stuck in, browsing. As she had predicted, most of the merchandise was priced out of her reach. She could not understand how they could justify some of the prices she was seeing, but she had to remember where she was; she was right at the heart of the world's richest business centre where the wealthy came to spend.

Besides it being midweek, Oxford Street was packed. Most were shoppers, hoping from store to store, some struggling to carry their large branded shopping bags. Harriet would later find out that Oxford Street was always that busy, regardless of whatever day it was. This was one of London's busiest shopping boroughs and was very popular with those in the middle to high class on the social ladder.

She crossed the busy twin road that cut through the shopping district and had to run a little, the last few feet to the curb, all in an effort to avoid being run over by the Number 10 London City bus that was passing by. She had spotted 'New Look', a popular fashion outlet she had been advised by Freda to visit. She knew instantly that she would love this store as the fashion and prices displayed outside were more to her taste.

Harriet walked in and began to move from rack to rack, scanning the items on sale. She felt like a child in a sweet shop, unable to contain herself, with all the pretty dresses on offer. She pulled out a few items from the rack and placed each one against her body to see whether they would suit her. There was a mirror next to the rack, which she would walk over to and use to confirm whether they would look good on her.

Harriet was in the New Look store for what seemed like nearly an hour and was enjoying the experience. If she could take every single one of the items she had picked, she would have easily filled the whole of her room at Freda's flat. She could only pick one or two outfits, she told herself. She took her final two from the rest and went to the long mirror again, just to make sure she had made the right choice.

Deeply engrossed in the mirror, as she interchangeably placed the dresses against her body, she almost jumped as she realised through the reflection that there was someone behind her, watching her. The watcher had been partially obscured by one of the clothing racks but then walked into view.

"I think I'd go for the red one," he said, as he came towards her. "Yes that would definitely look good on you."

Harriet froze on the spot. She couldn't believe he had done it again, sneaking up on her like that and almost shocking her out of her skin.

"Oh my God, Peter! You scared me half to death." She exclaimed, still trying to get over the shock of not only discovering a stalker but also that the stalker was the one man she wasn't prepared to meet at that moment in time. A lot of thoughts raced through Harriet's mind. How was he here? What some coincidence bumping into him in a city so big.

How had he even spotted her in this big crowded store, with tall clothing racks that could conceal anyone.

Peter smiled and generated a small chuckle as he was gaining pleasure from seeing how confused and uncomfortable this was for her. She was unsure how to react. He had completely taken her by surprise and she had not been ready for him.

"What?.....What are you doing here?" She stammered.

He smiled again. "Well, I was out shopping, trying to get a few things and I thought I recognised a familiar face."

She knew he was lying. There was a hint of deviousness in the manner in which he spoke. Harriet did not buy it.

"Um-mm, OK?"she replied, her face showing how unconvinced she was.

"Ye, this is my territory. I come here all the time."

Harriet did not respond but contorted her face to indicate that she was still not convinced. She did not believe this was just coincidence but had no reason to doubt him either. It was truly an awkward situation for her to meet Peter like this. What would have been better for her is to have never laid eyes on him again.

Their last encounter took a lot to put it right and now that she and Freda were talking again, this 'chance' meeting might fail to be viewed as just that. This, however, was one part of the battle she was fighting. Since the night of the party and the incident by the pool, Harriet had been trying everything she could to get that scene out of her head. She could still smell his cologne every time she closed her eyes, and she could still visualise them both, standing so close to each other, and the explosive concoction of feelings that erupted in that moment. This was a dangerous encounter and she needed to make distance before she was drawn in deeper into something she could not come out of.

"Well.., it was nice seeing you again Peter, I should go now, don't want to miss my train," she said, hurriedly gathering her things to head to the paying counter and out.

"Hey, why the hurry?" He said, placing his hand on her arm. "You not trying to escape from me again, are you?"

Harriet shuddered slightly when his hand made contact with her arm; she had not expected him to touch her. She remained still, not wanting to offend him by seeming jumpy and over exaggerated, yet deep down, another part of her felt intrigued; there was something about him that seemed to disorientate her. She felt like a deer caught in the beam of the headlights of an oncoming vehicle. She wanted to move, leave, but somehow she felt glued to the spot, trapped by the moment, unsure whether walking away would be a decision she would always regret.

Seeing how conflicted she was, Peter decided to put her at ease. "Hey, listen, it's OK. You can leave if you want to but I thought you could help me out with a little problem that I have. I promise to treat you to a coffee afterwards or a meal even, that's if you have time to spare." He was still wearing that cheeky, alluring smile that she was now starting to find irresistible.

"Help? With what?" She enquired, feeling a bit unsure as to the extent of the request.

"Nothing major. Nothing you wouldn't be able to handle I'm sure," he reassured her.

"How do you know I can do whatever it is you are asking?" She came back with a slightly fiery response.

He chuckled again.

"You seem to me like the girl who can handle pretty much anything. But please, I promise you, you will be doing me a huge favour."

She took her time with her response but she was already hooked. He wanted something from her, but what was he after and how much could she trust him. She did not know him that well and from what she had already heard about him, she was not sure if she should actually be agreeing to anything. Peter's reputation with women was known world over, he lived the true bachelor footballer lifestyle. He could have any woman he wanted, whether he wooed her or bought her.

"Hang on," she said, snapping out of the bubble she had now found herself in and dropping back into reality, "How can you want my help, we just bumped into each other. What if you had not met me?"

She had now folded her arms across her chest, with the two dresses she had chosen clasped in between. Her handbag was hanging from her shoulder.

"I am very lucky I guess," he replied, still trying to push his cheeky charm upon her.

"No one is that lucky," she argued.

He laughed. "OK, OK, whatever it is, luck, coincidence, I am just glad I bumped into you, because firstly I really wanted to see you after that day at my house but secondly I really do need your help today."

A big lump formed on Harriet's throat which made her swallow hard. He had just confessed that he had been thinking about her but now she was also curious about what he could possibly want from her that he couldn't either ask for or just pay someone to do for him.

The store was still buzzing with shoppers and a few staff dotted around, tidying up racks and picking up clothes dropped on the shop floor by some unforgiving customers. Harriet was oblivious to everything that was happening around her as she had been whisked into her own little universe, where the only two things that existed were her and Peter. She was not supposed to feel like this but she did.

"What is it that I am supposed to help you with?" she asked coyly.

He smiled. "OK,..so there is an event at the club house this afternoon, where all our sponsors will be coming. Its a wine, dine and entertain situation, that sort of thing. That is why I am out here. Just need to look for something smart, not too formal, to wear to the event and that is where you come in. I just can't seem to make up my mind."

Harriet remained silent, still considering what he was asking her to do. She wondered why he thought she could do this with him? She did not know him that well to even know what his taste in clothes was. Besides, did he not have people employed to do this for him? If she had his wealth she would have people like that, so she asked him.

"Don't you have someone on your payroll, an assistant or something, someone who does this for you?"

"No," he sniggered. "Well, I have an assistant but she helps with my schedule and stuff at my house. That's as far as her services go."

Harriet considered it for a moment, then asked another question.

"What about your wife? Girlfriend? Surely that's her job?'

This time he laughed out loud.

"Have you not read the news, I divorced a year ago and I am as single as they come."

He had just finished that line when a young female store assistant appeared next to them. She was attractive, blonde, and very presentable, with a name tag that read 'Holly' right above her left breast.

"You guys alright?" she enquired, with a warm smile that was typical of a sales person.

"We are ok here thanks," Peter replied, with a smile of his own to match.

"OK, great! Please call me if you need anything."

"Thank you.. Holly," he answered again, his eyes scanning her name tag. He was trying desperately to show little interest in this new arrival. He wanted to reassure Harriet that his focus and attention was on her.

As they were about to resume their conversation, the store assistant, who had turned to move on, turned back and stared at Peter.

"Do I know you from somewhere? Not sure, but you seem awfully familiar," she said, as she walked back towards them and getting closer to Peter.

Harriet turned to look at her, with a stare that could have been interpreted as a succession of profanities had this been spoken word. This did nothing to deter the store assistant, she got even closer. Peter knew this all too well, it was an everyday occurrence for him where people knew him from football but for some reason could not put that together.

"I'm Peter and I am sure we haven't met before, Holly, but you might have seen me play football, maybe?"

The penny dropped straight away for the store assistant.

"Oh my God! Yes! That's where. My dad and brother adore you!"

"Thank you," Peter replied humbly. He always tried to be amicable when it came to his fans. He had seen situations where celebrities ended up on the front page of tabloids for small and insignificant incidents.

"Wow!"She continued, reaching out to stroke his arm, her smile now even broader. The situation became a little awkward for all of them. "Can I please have a picture with you? My brother will be so jealous."

She did not even wait for a response but reached into the front pocket of the black skirt and pulled out her mobile phone. She turned towards Harriet.

"Can you take a picture of us?" She demanded, as she turned on the phone and passed it to her.

Harriet slowly unfolded her arms and reluctantly took the phone. Her face was a picture. If this had been any other time, she would have responded differently to this situation but she did not want to be rude in front of Peter. Holly pulled closer to Peter, clasped her arms around his and tilted her head to lay it on his shoulder. Harriet could do nothing but raise the phone to her eyes and snap them into frame. Holly had suddenly changed from helpful and smiling sales assistant to a clingy and annoying groupie.

It took a while to get rid of Holly after that but as soon as she was gone, they thought it best to leave the store and continue their conversation elsewhere. They walked up the road from New Look and went into a coffee lounge where they bought two coffees and continued their discussion.

"Wow, what was that?" Harriet said, laughing. She was now sat opposite Peter in a nearby coffee lounge, in front of them a small round table made of dark veneered oak, with a solid steel base at the bottom.

"That's nothing," Peter laughed back, his elbows on the table as he stirred his coffee playfully.

"What? Are you saying this happens to you all the time?" She asked.

"All the time,"he replied, casually.

"Wow," she responded, riveted by the thought of such a lifestyle. She was now more relaxed and secretly enjoying his company. "Doesn't it annoy you though?"

"It used to, but you get used to it. People over here are obsessed with the celebrity culture. Sometimes you just have to bite your lip and go with the flow."

"I have noticed that, but I'm guessing that you don't complain much with these women falling at your feet and trying to touch you." She said, sitting back in her chair, her coffee mug gently cuddled between both her hands.

"It's not how you think. I guess when you are starting out you can't get enough of the attention but you soon get tired of it. There are times when I really hate being recognised. Sometimes you can't even go out for a quiet meal without someone wanting a picture of your dinner." They both laughed.

There was a chemistry forming between them that made conversation quite natural and fluid; they were bouncing off each other's statements. Harriet was worried at how easy being around Peter was getting. She was so comfortable around him that she almost felt as if she was starting to forget how it felt being with Justin.

She had not seen Justin for a few months and her biggest fear now was that she would start to feel even more distant from him.

"So..., tell me truthfully, did you really bump into me by chance or was it just a rouse to try to talk to me. Besides, I thought you had people with you all the time?" She asked, looking around the lounge area and also outside through the large window into the street.

He gave out his signature short laugh, complimented by the now all familiar cheeky smile." Well, I guess I have to make a little confession, just a little one," he smiled. "I kinda knew you were here."

Harriet's eyes and mouth opened wide in

disbelief. She could not believe that he had actually planned it all. Weirdly, she was also flattered that he had gone through all the trouble of tracking her whereabouts.

"How?" She asked in total astonishment.

"Well," he said, still smiling," I seriously hope you don't think me to be a stalker but I wanted to see you so badly, so I asked Hector to do a bit of digging for me. He found out from Freda that you would be coming to this part of the city and then I asked one of my boys to let me know when you got to the station."

"Freda knows about this?" She asked, her face changing instantaneously. Harriet was unsure whether to be upset or pleased that he had done all this to see her. On the one hand it was so romantic that he had gone to such lengths to find her but the other side of it felt a tad sinister.

Sensing how alarmed Harriet was about Freda being involved, Peter became more serious and responded quickly to reassure her.

"No, no I don't think Freda knows it was me who wanted the information. I think Hector asked her casually, in conversation, where you were and if anything I think she thought Hector was the one interested in you."

Harriet sat back in her seat in both relief and disbelief. She was ruminating at how he had had her followed, only so he could spend time with her. Who does that, she thought to herself? She concluded that this was probably something only rich people were likely to do.

For Harriet, this was an extremely perplexing situation now. On the one hand she was pleased to have seen Peter again, but she was also fighting another huge battle within. She could not understand why she was developing feelings for him, yet she was still very much in love with Justin. The future did not offer much solace, appearing even darker and unclear. She did not know Peter that well yet and was definitely unfamiliar with the world he lived in. Her biggest mistake, if she allowed her feelings to flourish, would be allowing her visceral impulses to drive her down the wrong path.

"Wow, this is...so unbelievable," she said eventually.

Peter gave a half smile and also sat back in his seat. He did not say anything to allow her chance to assimilate what she had just discovered.

"So you're not alone right now then?" She asked, still trying to put the pieces together.

"I do have a few helpers around," he said, a hint of gloating in his voice.

"Seriously? Where are they?" She asked, turning to scan the room again.

Peter turned to look over his shoulder and then waved. Two men sitting at a table near the door waved back. One was black and the other white, but they looked so inconspicuous, just two guys having coffee. Harriet had seen them but had not even clocked them as being Peter's aides.

"That is Tau and the other guy is Jeff. Two of my finest." Peter informed her.

Harriet gave a short wave back, her expression still exhibiting a mixture of disbelief, confusion and titillation. How was she here? Coming to London had been all about progressing academically but never had she thought she would find herself sitting in a coffee lounge, with a

Zimbabwean celebrity, and going through all these emotions. All this made her even more anxious, just thinking about it. What if Justin saw her now? What would he think of her?

Still sitting back in her chair, her arms folded and her legs crossed, Harriet took a deep sigh and shook her head. She was also smiling a little, as she deliberated on all her thoughts of the current and previous events. She had always been a conflicted character. She knew always to do the right thing, but she was also driven by a rebellious nature, an adventurous side that liked to take chance encounters, even if they were filled with uncertainty.

She still had people to think about though. This was going to hurt the two people who mattered to her right at that moment in her life. Freda was in love with Peter, even though she had not told him nor had she even admitted it out loud.

The other elephant in the room was that Harriet was engaged. People had attended and witnessed as she got engaged to marry Justin. Why was she doing this now? How could she allow herself to forget something so reverent.

She finally managed to get a few words out, after a little while," I can't believe this. This is something I tell you. I'll give you top marks for determination but *eish*…" She paused again and shook her head, "I don't really know what you want from me. Truth is I am not even sure I can do what you want. I am engaged to someone else and I have university coming up soon. I don't think I can be who you want me to be. Besides…" She didn't finish, he cut her short.

"Hey, don't stress." he said, calmly and reassuring,"I only want to get to know you. I like you and I think we can really get on well. I liked you the very first time I met you."

She was surprised that he still thought about the first time they had met in that way. Of all the people that could have captivated his attention that night, he had elected to narrow his focus on her. Why though, she thought? She wondered whether he truly found her attractive or was it all just a game to him; preying on innocent newcomers from home.

"Look, I can't. I can only help you today with choosing your outfit but I really can't see you in any other way after that, besides just being friends. There is a lot that you don't understand."

"And that's all I want," he lied."For us to get to know each other."

She gave him a pained smile and pretended she was happy with what she had just said. She was drawn to him, his cool, calm and collected demeanour, and it made her feel safe and secure. If it had been under different circumstances, her being single to start with, she wouldn't have hesitated to be with him. There were others involved and she had a responsibility towards them, despite what every fibre in her body was saying.

She could not figure out what it was about Peter that made her feel this way. She loved Justin but she had never felt her insides move the way they were, sitting there with Peter. It was as if her whole cellular structure was reacting to every word and every touch he made. These were new feelings and she felt guilty that she was feeling them for another man other than the one she was supposed to.

Some time later, they left the coffee lounge

and visited a few men's fashion outlets, where Harriet helped Peter pick his outfit for the day. She had a lot of pleasure doing it as well.

"That was fun, I could do this for a living," she had said at the end, just before they parted.

"You were very helpful. You have quite an exquisite sense of style," he complimented her.

"Thank you," she replied shyly.

"You have to let me return the favour somehow," he offered.

"You don't have to," she refused, politely.

"It's only fair I do. Leave it with me," he smiled. "Hey, are you sure you don't want us to take you home?"

Harriet did not think this would be a great idea, in case Freda happened to see her coming out of Peter's car.

"No, its fine. I will take the tube back."

"OK, till next time then."

"Ye, till next time."

And then they parted.

Chapter 11

The days that followed, after Harriet and Peter bumped into each other on Oxford Street, fell on a weekend and both Harriet and Freda were home that morning. Freda, however, was on shift at the hospital later that night and was trying to make the most of the time she had to rest.

You couldn't say that Freda truly loved being a nurse but she didn't mind it; it paid the bills. She had grown disillusioned with her profession over the years, the stress of the job and the never ending ward politics.

Looking after patients was the easy part. The real work was having to deal with some not so pleasant colleagues and bad management at the top of the organisation. What frustrated her the most was that there were people with top positions who had not stepped onto the wards for years, and these people had forgotten the hardships of slaving away on the units, yet they were the ones in charge of making policies for everyone else. You did not want to get Freda started on this debate.

It was a Saturday, around ten in the morning, and both women were still fast asleep, when the doorbell sent a shrieking sound across the flat. The first ring did not wake them up, so the visitor zapped on it again. The second one got Harriet's attention and she opened her eyes slowly, trying to orient herself with what was happening. She did not move off the pillow but stayed and listened to make sure it was definitely the doorbell that had gone off.

Almost immediately the shrieking sound went again and this time Harriet slowly pushed the covers away from her body and got up out of bed. She walked out of the spare bedroom and went past Freda's room, noticing that the bedroom door was open and Freda was still fast asleep, she thought.

"Who's that, at this time of the morning?" She heard Freda groan from her bedroom. She had heard the doorbell ring too but had not bothered to get up.

"I don't know. I'll check," Harriet replied, in a sleepy voice still.

Harriet gently made her way down the stairs and halfway down, the door bell shrieked again.

"OK! OK!" She mumbled to herself, making her way towards the door. She was not particularly impressed by the impatience from the unexpected visitor.

She got to the door and began fumbling with the key. She managed to get it unlocked and slowly cracked it open, just enough to see who it was first. As she did, the sun rays from outside shown in her eyes and for a moment she could not make out who it was. She raised her hand towards her forehead to provide a visor for her eyes and had immediately realised who was outside. It was Hector.

Harriet kissed her teeth in annoyance as she opened the door the whole way and moved to the side to let him in.

"Why are you so impatient Hector?" She rebuked him, her back to him as she walked back into the lounge. She wrapped the silk house coat she had on tightly and tied the coat belt to secure it; all to cover up the sheer nightie she had on. Both the nightie and the coat were quite short, only reaching as far as the middle of her thighs, but she did not mind Hector that much. She had grown to regard him as she would a brother.

"You guys sleep a lot," Hector said as he came in and shut the door behind him.

"It's the weekend. Why would we want to get up at all, unless it's because of inpatient unexpected visitors?" She replied teasing him, but still quite annoyed about having been disturbed.

Hector had a habit of turning up without warning and would go about the place as if he lived there. The girls did not mind him much, as long as he came at appropriate times and if he rang to let them know he was coming. He also seemed quite good at timing his visits around meal times. He lived alone and the girls surmised that he probably did not know how to cook or did not enjoy dining alone. Either way, they did not mind feeding him.

Harriet went into the kitchen and picked up the kettle to fill it up. Hector was taking his coat off near the front door and when he had finished hanging it up, he followed her into the kitchen.

"Miss Freda still asleep?" He asked, as they crossed paths in the kitchen, Harriet walking towards the gas cooker to put the kettle on, and him towards the fridge.

"No, not yet, well, she spoke to me before I came downstairs to open the door but I guess she went back to sleep."

Harriet's voice still sounded sleepy, she had not fully woken up still. They had not been out the night before, like they usually did, but they had stayed up to watch 'Bridget Jones's Diary', a film adaption of the book by Helen Fielding. It chronicled the life of Bridget, a single British woman in her thirties, battling issues and decisions surrounding her life, career and relationships. Little did Harriet realise when she was watching it that she too would soon be faced with such dilemmas.

As the water was heating up on the hob, Harriet reached up into one of the top cupboards and brought down 3 coffee mugs, which she placed on the counter. She leaned over the other side and grabbed the jar with tea bags and popped it open. She pulled out 3 tea bags and distributed them into each mug.

Hector shut the fridge door and took a bite of the piece of sliced ham he had pulled out of its packed. He turned to face Harriet and spoke. "I am actually glad Freda is still asleep because it's you I wanted to talk to." He said with his voice lowered so as to avoid it travelling upstairs.

"What about?" Harriet asked, turning from making the tea to face him; her face unable to cover her derision. She knew where the conversation was headed.

Hector, who was leaning on the counter, took another bite of his ham, preparing himself to answer. He had somewhat of a silly grin on his face. He could sense that Harriet knew what he was going to say but he did not know whether she was going to be pleasant about it.

"OK, so...the thing is, I have a message for you. Peter wants to see you. Tonight!"

"What?! No, iwe, you know I can't do that!" She said, as quietly as she could. She moved to the kitchen door and stuck her head out to find out if Freda was up.

"Hector, you need to tell him to stop. Freda will freak out!" She said, as she turned back into the kitchen.

"I know Freda has a thing for him but he wants you. He has been calling me, almost everyday. What am I supposed to tell him?" Hector replied.

"Why is he calling you... and why haven't you told him this can't happen?"

"He won't take no for an answer," Hector said.

"No I can't. I'm actually mad at you for what you did the other day. Telling him I would be out in the city" She said, pointing at him and still whispering.

Harriet turned to listen outside the room again. There was no sound from upstairs. The kettle behind her began to whistle. She turned quickly and moved to the hob to turn it off; this brought the whistle to a whimpering stop. There was a quiet pause between them for a moment. Harriet was trying to work out what to say next and as she did, she picked up the kettle and poured the boiling water into each cup. She placed the kettle back on the hob and went to the fridge. Hector had to step out of the way to allow her to open it and get the milk out.

"You have to convince him that I can't do it," she said, as she took the milk to the mugs of tea and poured a bit into each.

"What do you mean you can't?"

"I just can't. I'm with someone else. I can't just simply start liking another guy."

"Come on Harriet. The guy likes you and it's Peter Chuma we are talking about here. What's not to like?"

Harriet turned abruptly to him and gave him a stare that spoke volumes. What sort of girl did he take her for? She was not the type to get caught up in all the glitter and fame. She wasn't going to deny that she had been tantalised by Peter's relentless efforts but she was still unsure what it was about her that had enchanted him so much.

She stirred the tea in one of the mugs and handed it to Hector. She had made him a few cups of tea before and knew how he took it, white with two sugars. He accepted the mug and took a sip.

"I don't think it's a good idea for me to see him," Harriet said as she picked up one of the remaining mugs and left the kitchen.

She disappeared upstairs for a little while whilst Hector remained in the kitchen nursing his beverage. She did not take too long and was soon back in the kitchen. She leaned against the counter, and looked at him, her mug of tea next to her.

"Is Freda up now?" Hector asked.

Harriet nodded. "She's jumped into the shower," she confirmed.

"So let's sort this out before she comes down. What shall I tell him?" Hector asked.

"I don't think it's a good idea. Why tonight? Where even?"

Harriet felt the pressure starting to mount, not only from outside but from within herself. Although she was a sensible girl, she was susceptible to feelings most women would have. The idea of dating a celebrity and the lifestyle that came with it was a fascinating prospect for anyone. Any woman would desire a man who is capable of providing beyond the means of most men.

But Harriet was also sensible enough to know that roses can prick. She had seen her friends enter into relationships they had later regretted, yet again, that was the nature of relationships. You always go in blind and hope it all comes together in the end. This was a different situation though, she thought. She was not single, but neither was she married. She felt compelled to honour her word to the man she had promised to marry. Justin was innocent in all this and he would definitely end up bruised.

"I can't," she muttered to herself. She didn't want Hector to hear, in case he would judge her for her stupidly, for not realising what was on offer.

"Listen," Hector said, realising the dilemma she was in. "You don't have to commit to anything tonight. Just meet up with him, go on a date and see how you feel after. It's that simple."

"Easy for you to say," she came in, staring at the kitchen floor tiles." I don't even know him that well, well, you know what I mean. I mean like know him, know him.

"Of course you don't know him, but that's how you get to, by meeting up, getting together and having a great time. I know him, he is a good guy and he will treat you well."

"My God! How much is he paying you," she laughed.

He laughed back, relieved that she was finally warming up.

"Nothing. He's my friend and I can vouch for him."

"Hm-mm, I don't trust you guys. You probably have some kind of boys club where you get innocent girls and mess them about."

"Nah, we don't," he laughed. "Clean, through and through, thats us." He had a smug grin spread all over his face.

"Clean? I don't know about that. Especially you Hector, you look seriously dodgy."

Hector laughed. He was not bothered about the comment as long as she was engaging with him. He had cornered his pray and could smell the blood. He didn't speak, waiting for her to say what her final word was. She made him wait.

As they stood there quiet, they heard Freda's footsteps upstairs. She had just finished her shower and was heading to the bedroom. Harriet decided to quickly put an end to the discussion.

"OK, I will meet him tonight but only this once," she whispered. "And it better be the last time."

Hector smiled excitedly, as if it were his date he had secured. He moved towards her to embrace her.

"Get off, get off," she said pushing him

away playfully, and then went on to give him one final warning.

"You better make sure Freda doesn't find out or else I will kill YOU!" she emphasised, jokingly, whilst pointing at him. She too was excited but was not going to show it. Deep down, her adventurous nature was intrigued by all the secrecy and deception. The fish line had been cast and she was slowly being pulled into the game.

At 7:10pm Freda walked downstairs, fully clad in her navy London City Hospital nurses tunic, a matching cardigan and light brown sheer tights. She had no shoes on as yet, as they usually lived near the front door. On the right side of her chest was her name badge and nurse's watch, pinned to her tunic and both visible through the gap of her open front cardigan.

Harriet lay on the sofa in the lounge watching television, covered all the way up by a cosy faux fur throw that was part of Freda's lounge decor. She was portraying very well the image of someone who had no plans of going anywhere and was not going to be moving for anyone for the rest of the night.

As Freda walked into the lounge, focused on locating her bag and car keys, Harriet turned to look in her direction. "All done?" She asked, in a tired sounding voice.

"Ye," Freda answered, sounding uninspired by the prospect of work and also still engrossed in her search for her bag.

"Your bag and keys are on the kitchen table," Harriet came to the rescue, noticing how frantic Freda was starting to get with her fruitless search.

"Oh my God, I'm getting old," she remarked, as she headed towards the kitchen, remembering that she had put them there earlier.

Freda grabbed her bag and forced open the long zip, dropped her car keys into it and zipped it up again. She made her way back into the lounge.

"Well, I'm off now," she said, towering over Harriet, "I will see you in the morning."

"OK sha, have a good shift and I'll see you tomorrow."

Freda made her way to the front door and spent another two minutes putting her shoes on before walking out and locking the door behind her. The house fell silent, with the only sound remaining coming from the television set.

Harriet gave it a good fifteen minutes after Freda had left before springing up from the sofa and dashing upstairs. She had to get ready in record time before Peter's arrival at 7:30pm. She had planned it meticulously, leaving only a small window from the time Freda left to the time Peter was to arrive. She had been praying on that sofa for everything to go smoothly, like clockwork, and as things stood, all the pieces were falling into place.

She went into her bedroom and straight to the wardrobe. She had bathed earlier, before Freda had. Freda would not have thought of it as being suspicious as Harriet always had a second bath around the same time every evening. Harriet pulled out a black casual evening dress she had bought from New Look the day she had met Peter on Oxford Street. Now she had a reason to wear it. An unexpected sense of exuberance enveloped her and she was not thinking of anything else at that point except meeting him.

By the time the clock got to 7:30 pm, Harriet had transformed herself from a sofa slacker to a gorgeous lass ready for a magical night out with her handsome suitor. She now waited on every second to hear that doorbell ring. Unlike earlier in the morning when she had resented the bell ringing, this time she wanted it and it was not coming soon enough.

Several minutes after 7:30 pm, the familiar shrieking sound filled the flat and Harriet felt her heart skip a beat. She could hardly control her breathing from both anxiety and excitement. Yet again, she could not fathom why this man was so capable of rendering her unable of controlling her own body. As she walked towards the door, her legs felt like jelly, like they were just about to give way. It was definitely nothing to do with Freda's black stiletto Jimmy Choos Harriet had 'borrowed'. Thank God they wore the same size, she thought to herself, because the shoes really complimented her dress.

She managed to get to the door and slowly cracked it open. As both the street lights and the lights from the house caught him, she smiled as his ruggedly handsome figure came into view. He smiled back, revealing a clean set of healthy gnashes. He was quite composed and seemed pleased with what he was seeing. She looked perfect in her black dress, every curve pronounced and short enough to exhibit her smooth light toned legs and well moulded calves. Her makeup was decent too, even though she had had very little time to put it on.

"You are late," she said, joking with him straight away in an attempt to break the ice and initiate conversation.

"I am, my apologies," he replied. "Got caught up trying to get this side of town."

"Oh, don't worry," she reassured him."You are not that late really. Come on in."

She stepped to the side to let him in and as he made his way in, Peter turned towards her and gave her a quick hug. This threw Harriet off her game a bit as she had not expected it, however, she succumbed and reciprocated.

As they embraced, she caught the pleasant scent of his cologne, a rustic masculine fragrance that added more to the spellbinding effect he always had on her. He had a well toned body, very athletic and she felt every inch of his ripples through the thin shirt he wore. He felt hard and muscular, but still gentle when pressed against her body. Somehow this also gave her the feeling that she was safe with him.

As he pulled away she felt this intense desire to stay connected with him. She wanted him to turn back right there and hold her again, this time for much longer. She had not counted on feeling such pleasure and a deep sense of satisfaction, just from being held by him. If Justin had crossed her mind in that moment, she would have been awash with emotions of endless guilt but he did not. She had not actually done anything regrettable yet, but it still felt as though she had just given away something sacred, her promise to someone else. She snapped herself back into reality, adjusted her dress that had hiked up when she hugged him and offered him a drink.

"Erm, would you.. erm.. like a drink or something," she stammered, clearly rattled by all the emotions she had just experienced.

"Ye sure, cold please. Just a quick one I guess. Got us a booking for 8:30pm, and can I just say you look really amazing tonight." he said, scanning her from top to bottom.

"Aw-ww, thank you," she responded, impressed by how charming he was trying to be.

Harriet walked into the kitchen and left him to wonder in the lounge. She put together 2 glasses of tropical juice and walked back in moments later to find him looking at a few of Freda's pictures on a small corner bookshelf.

"Is Freda OK with you seeing me tonight then?" Peter asked, as he accepted the drink she held towards him.

Harriet was a bit surprised by the question. She did not see a reason why he would ask her that, unless he knew that Freda fancied him.

"Well, to be honest, she doesn't know we are together tonight. Why?" she asked.

"Just wondered." he responded, not wishing to give away more.

Harriet thought to use this chance to suss him out.

"She likes you, you know," she told him

"Does she? Really?" He asked, trying to sound surprised but failing dismally. What he also failed to realise in that moment was that this was all a test to see how he would respond to hearing of another woman wanting him.

"Oh, yes she does," Harriet added." She's the one you should be with tonight, not me."

He smiled before responding. "Well, I have no doubt whatsoever that I am with the right lady tonight."

She smiled too and took a sip of her juice, using the glass cup to cover more of her excitement. Her efforts had been useless, he had already noticed how relieved and pleased she was to hear this.

"So, shall we?" He said, casting a glance at his wrist watch.

"Yes, sure," she replied, placing her glass on the coffee table and picking up her scarf and purse that were on the single seater sofa nearest to the door.

Peter was first towards the door and out of the flat. Harriet followed, locking the front door behind her. By the time she joined him, he was now standing by the passenger door of his Bentley Continental GT with the door open for her. She got into the car as elegantly as she could, and as she sunk into the two tone leather seats, Harriet could not help but feel special. There was something about that moment that made her realise that there was much more to life than she knew and whatever else was out there, she wanted it.

That first dinner date lived up to more than what Harriet could have ever imagined. Never in her life had she been exposed to such opulence. It was a teaser into a whole new lifestyle she was not familiar with and not only did she like it, she wanted more of it.

They had driven into central London and parked outside the prestigious Ritz Carlton, right by the entrance. A man in a tall black hat and a long sea captain coat came down the steps of the hotel entrance and walked around the car to open Harriet's door. She was not accustomed to being pampered this much that she felt a little shy about it. He opened the passenger side door and stood aside. Harriet turned to exit the vehicle and as she did the door man offered his hand and helped her out.

"Good evening Ma'am and welcome to the Ritz Carlton," the man spoke, with the most distinguished English accent.

"Thank you," Harriet replied, in a low timorous voice.

They both walked around to the other side and joined Peter, who was now stood below the steps to the hotel entrance.

The door man addressed him too, "And a warm welcome to you too Sir. May I?" He put his hand out and Peter passed him the keys to the Bentley.

"Thank you Sir. This way please," he said, and gestured them up towards the main doors. They both started up the steps and as they did, Peter put his hand in the small of Harriet's back, to support her up. This pleased her very much. His hand on her back made her feel wanted and protected. She loved his chivalrous nature.

They reached the top of the steps and another man, also dressed similar to the first, opened the door and repeated the welcome greeting. They obliged and proceeded into the main hotel lobby.

The sumptuous surroundings of the Ritz Carlton were breathtaking. The lobby was sparsely but beautifully decorated with furniture that gave it a presidential feel. The lighting was well thought out, with soft darkened areas and also well lit in areas that needed to be. The ambience was so relaxing that all you wanted to do was sit on one of the presidential looking settees and never move.

As if two people were not enough to meet and greet them, they were intercepted by the concierge as they entered the lobby. He was a shorter man, also in uniform but with less layers, more of an indoor version of the same uniform.

He approached them with a large beaming smile, "Good evening sir, madam. This way please."

Harriet was astounded by how elaborate it all was, how the staff were so fluid in their roles and made the experience easy. She could not help wondering whether Peter was a regular visitor there. Maybe he had dined many other women here, she thought. But she was not going to let these thoughts ruin what was already promising to be a perfect evening.

By the time they got to the dining hall, Harriet was having this nagging feeling, an anxious feeling of being out of place. This feeling had been further exacerbated as she scanned the dining hall and realised, for the first time since they walked in, that they were the only people of colour. She was hardly nervous around anyone, regardless of race, but strangely being there she was. She latched onto Peter's arm and clung to him. He sensed how uneasy she was.

"Are you OK?" He asked in a gentle voice

She just smiled up at him.

"We can go somewhere else if you don't feel comfortable."

She was surprised he had asked her this, that he would be willing to forego this lavishness to please her. She was not prejudiced in any way whatsoever, but she had just been overwhelmed at being in a closed environment and realising they were the only ones different from the rest. What did not help were the stares from some in the room, who appeared as though they had never seen black people before, or maybe they hadn't, not this close anyway.

"No, it's fine", she said quietly, trying not to let anyone hear.

They were lead to a table for two that had been dressed to perfection with all manner of shiny silver cutlery and fancy folded napkins. A lit scented candle flickered in the middle of it to infuse an element of romance to the arrangement and a couple of small flower arrangements to compliment it. It was aesthetically pleasing to the eye.

As soon as they sat down, the hotel staff put on yet another show. They were first approached by the bar waiter who took their drinks order, then the supervising waiter who kept milling around and asking if they were OK, and then eventually the

food waiter who took their meal order. It all appeared over the top, an over indulgence, but Harriet would soon realise how addictive being fussed on could become.

They had not spoken much since the car journey, but a moment became available between food ordering and waiting for it to be served. As they sipped on their £150 bottle of Dom Perignon, Harriet made a comment about her new experience.

"Oh wow, mind blowing," she said, with a hint of mockery. It was not too much to upset her host.

He smiled forgivingly, as he empathised with how disconcerting it might be for anyone if they had never been exposed to this kind of lifestyle.

"I know," he agreed with her,"But like anything else, you get used to these kinds of things. You will get used to it."

Harriet looked up at him, realising he had just made a remark that eluded to a future for the two of them.

"Will I? How do you even know there is going to be a second date?" She said, with a cheeky smile of her own.

He laughed and decided on playing the game.

"Well, it's because I always get what I want. You are here right now ain't you?"

Harriet gaped her mouth in disbelieve at how brazen he was. She made a pretend angry face and even picked up her purse as if to leave.

"OK, OK, I'm joking," he laughed.

She sat back down and smiled to assure him that she too had been toying with him.

Some time later their meal had been served, both having ordered an Aberdeen Angus sirloin steak, well done, accompanied by mashed potatoes with Cajun spice, a vegetable goulash and mushroom sauce. There was no doubt in the quality and taste of the food. It had been prepared by the finest and most experienced hands, in portions that were not too much but kept you hungry for more. As they ate they got to know each other a bit more. Harriet was the first to ask questions. She wanted to know as much as she could about him.

"Seriously though, if anybody told me that on this date, at this time, I would be sitting in a posh restaurant eating dinner with Peter Chuma, I wouldn't have believed them. But here we are." They both smiled. "So do you come here a lot then?" she continued.

"Sometimes,"he replied..

"Bet I'm just the next one in line of women you have brought here?" she said, avoiding his gaze but preferring to look down at her steak instead. She cut off a small piece and forked it into her mouth.

He laughed. "Why do you always think my life is filled with loads of random women?"

"Just asking," she answered, still trying to avoid looking at him. "It's just stories I hear."

"About me?" He asked, but not bothered by it really. He had heard and read so many stories written about him in newspapers and tabloid magazines that were not all entirely true.

"Not all of them about you. I'm just saying that you hear many stories about footballers and their playboy lifestyles, that's all."

"That's just the papers cooking up stories. The reality is very different. I have worked very hard to be where I am and I won't apologise to anyone for my success, choices and mistakes. I am just like anyone else, money or not, and I make mistakes like anyone too."

She felt for him and understood him in that moment. There was genuineness to what he was saying and she sensed that he had probably been through a lot of hurtful situations in his life.

"I can imagine it must be hard sometimes to be in the spotlight all the time. Everyone thinking you got it all just because you are rich and famous."

"Having money isn't always as glamorous as people think. There're many things I hate about being in this position. I have lost a lot of family and friends, just because they thought I would be handing out cash as and when they asked. It doesn't work like that."

"That doesn't surprise me at all." Harriet agreed."So what happened with your wife then? How come you guys divorced?"

Peter hesitated to answer for a few seconds trying to find a way to answer the question.

"Well, to be honest, the marriage just got to a point where we were living in two separate worlds. My career grew and she couldn't handle what came with it."

"What things would drive a woman away like that?"

Peter placed a forkful of his food into his mouth and paused to chew before he answered.

"Not much happened but it was enough to drive both of us crazy. I was going away a lot and she was listening to a lot of bullshit from a lot of people. People she shouldn't have been listening to."

Although he was still quite calm, there was a lot of trapped anger in the way Peter spoke about it.

Harriet did not want to probe further down this route. They ate for a few more minutes in silence before Harriet asked again.

"So why me then? Why have you been so persistent to go out with me. There are plenty of other women, far better than me, you could have chosen."

The smile came back to his face. "To be honest, I just had this feeling about you when I saw you. Can't explain it but I liked it. I just knew I had to speak to you."

"Really?" Harriet asked shyly.

"You don't know how it feels being with you right now. It just feels right."

Harriet was enthralled by every word that was coming out of his mouth. She was glad he was saying it because she felt it too. It seemed like something just destined to be.

She was so engrossed in that moment when suddenly the thought of Justin flashed in her mind. Her demeanour changed. She knew she had to tell Peter the truth if this new development had any chance of taking off. But another thought told her that this might put Peter off her straight away. She decided to tell him anyway.

"Well, there is something I haven't told you yet about myself. I was engaged to someone before I left Zim. I haven't broken up with him and that is not an easy thing to do." she began.

"I know," he said. She looked at him surprised that he knew. "Ye, Hector told me," he said, noticing her surprised expression.

"And you still pursued me?" Harriet asked, with a little smile peering from the side of her mouth.

"Why not?" He said smiling. "I want you and I didn't care what other man is in your life. I have to have you."

"Have to have me? Like your next purchase or something?"

"No, not like that," he laughed, "I just mean I want you so much that I don't care what man stands in my way."

She was enjoying torturing him a bit but also liked hearing him talk about how much he wanted her and how he had to have her. She was exhilarated.

"So what now?" She asked, as if she did not know what had to happen next.

"Well," he answered," You need to ring him up and tell him that things have changed."

This was the only obstacle Harriet feared the most but before she could even think of all that, she needed some assurances.

"How do I know that after shutting down all these doors, you won't just use me and dump me for the next pretty face?"

He leaned forward across the table and reached out to put his hand on her arm. "I swear that's never going to happen. I want you and I want us to be together. My feelings for you are growing deeper every time I see you. I think I am falling in love with you and I will do anything to be with you."

Harriet stopped eating and looked at him as he spoke. The warmth of his voice melted every inch of her heart with every word he uttered. Harriet knew she was now at that point of no return. Peter sounded like he truly meant what he was saying and she could actually see them being together. In that very moment she knew that her life had taken a whole new trajectory.

Chapter 12

Three weeks on from the day Peter picked up Harriet and took her on their first dinner date at the Ritz Carlton, they were now seeing each other more often. They were still officially not in a relationship as yet and they had to make sure it did not become public knowledge before they were ready. There was a lot that needed to happen first, a lot of issues that Harriet had to work on before she could fully commit. Peter made her know that he would be patient, as long as he could see or talk to her, he was happy. He understood that she needed to do what she had to, to find closure.

They did not see each other every day as Peter's schedule with the club could be hectic, but he would call her when he could. He had brought her a mobile phone so they could keep in touch but Harriet could not always pick up his calls when Freda was around. She always kept it off, especially when Freda was home, and onlyswitched it on to check if he had sent her a message.

The first thing that needed to be dealt with before Harriet could freely be with Peter was to tell Justin that she was moving on. She had avoided him for many weeks now, ignoring his calls and emails, not having the courage to face him. If he had been a bad boyfriend then her conscience would have been clear; she would have found it easy to start up something and end it, but he had always been more than caring, the first person who had truly got to know the real her. They had been together for years and no one had any doubt that they would eventually settle down together and build a family. Harriet had convinced herself that Justin was the only man she would ever be with, but now she could not believe what she was about to do to him.

She had weighed up the situation in her head many times, playing it over and over again, just trying to convince herself that she was not making the worst mistake of her life. She would always come back to the same conclusion though. With Peter there was definitely something different and in many ways strangely pleasurable. Ordinarily, he was not the type of guy she would have gone for but she felt that there was a fire that he had managed to ignite in her, a strong desire that seemed to always pull her towards him. She had never felt this way for any other man before, ever!

Justin, on the other hand, was true boyfriend material, loving, caring and always there; dependable. But he was not as outgoing, preferring quieter nights in. He was prim and proper in all areas that mattered but unless he was pushed, he was rather boring at times. This made Harriet's decision ever more difficult because both of them had qualities she really considered to be good; Justin being the sensible, predictable choice and Peter, the intriguing wild card.

The other reason, however, which was making Harriet lean towards Peter was a selfish one on her part, but she was not going to lie that it had not been a factor she considered. Justin was ambitious, but Peter was rich. He was already made and all she had to do was step into his world and she was done. People spend years to get to that place but here it was, an opportunity of a lifetime, an immediate transformation from obscurity into a whole new life of celebrity. This was not selfish at all actually, she would think to herself, this was common sense.

The other obstacle standing in their way was Harriet having to tell her parents. If anything, this was the part she dreaded the most. She was not bothered about the wider family, her aunts and uncles who had taken part in the engagement, they would catch on.

Her parents, however, would be a much steeper upward climb she would have to take on. She could visualise her father ranting at her non-stop about the shame she was bringing to the family, and her mother's disappointment as she was quite fond of Justin.

Harriet hoped that they would all eventually learn to respect her decision. Besides, if they got wind of who she was with now, they would all be clamoring to get back into her good graces. Most of her family were football fans and fans of Peter nonetheless.

There were also other things to be

considered before their relationship could become public knowledge. Peter was not an ordinary guy and every aspect of his life was deliberated first by his management team. Harriet had not considered this until she got a hint of it when they met for their third date.

They had gone into central London again, but this time to Peter's favourite club, Cirque Le Soir. Harriet made sure that the night out would coincide with Freda working nights. She did not want to risk Freda becoming suspicious about where she was going and so she waited until Freda had left for work, as she had done previously. Harriet aimed to return before Freda got back in the morning.

The first thing that puzzled Harriet on that third meet was that when she opened the door expecting Peter, she found Tau instead, one of his aids. Her initial thoughts had been that something terrible had happened but she thought Peter would have called her instead of sending someone.

"Oh, hi!" she exclaimed, puzzled." Thought Peter was picking me up?"

The burly man did not smile but simply said, "Change of plans. You coming with me."

"Where is he though?" she asked. Somehow another man picking her up was making her a bit uneasy, even though she knew he had been sent by Peter.

"Don't worry, you will see him soon enough." Tau replied, with no empathy in his voice whatsoever.

Harriet was not enthused by his character. He seemed too stern, rushed and abrupt. She was not happy about the change of plans either. Why had Peter not come for her as he had done previously. Even if the plans had changed, she would have wanted him to let her know rather than just being sent for.

As she sat in the back of the Continental, having refused to sit next to this brute of a man, a man with no ounce of chivalry in his bones, she nagged him for answers.

"So how is it that things changed tonight. Why didn't Peter come for me." She asked, half expecting a snotty response.

"He was busy." the reply came. He didn't disappoint, the response was cold.

"Busy, really? Wow! But he never mentioned he was going to be busy."

"Something came up. Told me to take you to the Club. He will meet you there."

Harriet realised that whatever the reason was, she was not going to get it from this man. She wasn't too upset as Peter had still made an effort to see her. She would have probably been more disappointed if he had cancelled. The fact that he got busy and still wanted to see her meant that he cared.

The Bentley cornered through the tight London streets heading yet again into the city centre. The driver was quite confident with his abilities to navigate through this urban jungle and he did it swiftly, like he had done so many times.

Later Harriet would learn that it was one of the main criteria that Peter had considered for his drivers, someone with extensive knowledge of London who could navigate alternative routes and occasionally have to escape the paparazzi.

They arrived at the club just before nine o'clock and Harriet had to have yet another wait before being reunited with Peter. Tau managed to get her through the crowd to the VIP area at the back of the club, where she sat alone for a little while observing the club goers. There were many elegantly dressed people, mostly in smart casual. Harriet was intrigued by most of the young females who all seemed to have been in some competition to see who had the shortest dress. Some dresses were so ridiculously short that she wondered how they managed to keep their modesty when they sat down.

Peter emerged a while later, flanked by a couple of his entourage. He navigated through the crowd, his head down to avoid being recognised, and as he got to the VIP booth, the two accompanying him just seemed to fade into the background.

"Sorry to change plans on you like that, sweetie," he said as he slid in and sat next to her. "There was a bit of a situation, nothing major." He moved in straight away to put his arm around her and gave her a peck on the cheek.

Harriet did not respond but just looked at him. She was trying to communicate that he was not going to get out of this one that easy. The music in the club had got a bit louder and many were now on the dance floor.

"Are you OK babe, hope you not too upset. Something came up which we had to sort out," he tried to convince her after noticing that she appeared a little off.

"I'm good," she replied, her expression still indicating that she was not going to be satisfied with half an explanation.

He sensed it and explained further.

"OK, I'll tell you the full story. The truth is that someone found out about us and wanted to write about it, a reporter. Well, they were not hundred percent sure but was looking for proof and so my team thought it would be best to be cautious and just travel separately."

Harriet was surprised to hear how involved Peter's team was in his private life. She had never taken time to think of it. This bothered her a little and especially the covert operations that had taken place to even make their date possible. She obviously did not want the whole world to know about them as yet, with everything the way it was, but she did not want to feel like she was in some secret affair either. Maybe the story coming out might have not been a bad thing, she thought to herself. This would have solved all their problems in one go, everyone knowing at the same time.

"Reporter? How did they find out?" Harriet asked, also trying to work out why Peter and his team had gone to such considerable lengths to stop it from coming out. Were there people that Peter did not want knowing about her, she thought.

"Not sure how they got wind of us really. It could have been the hotel staff at the Ritz trying to sell a story. Who knows. But listen," he said,
turning to face her,"We are just starting and the last thing we need is the media breathing down our necks. We will let everyone know when we are ready."

Peter was doing his best to convince her that this was the right thing for both of them. She agreed with him in parts but she wanted this period to be over as quickly as possible so that they could just focus on being together. She was becoming impatient, not only with him but with herself as well. She was still to call Justin and needed to make that call soon if she wanted things to move fast.

"Would it be such a bad thing if it all came out?" She tested him.

"No, not at all," he replied. "Everyone will know soon enough anyway. We just need to pace ourselves and do it right."

She gave him a half smile.

They had stayed in the club for quite a while after, drinking, dancing and mingling with some of Peter's friends. Most were other footballers and their partners and some were part of his management team. Harriet did her best to blend in and even began to have a good time, putting behind her the disappointment of how their evening had started.

They left the club just after midnight and had taken the south western express-way back to Peter's Surrey Mansion. Harriet had been there before, the day of the party, but had not returned since. Peter had not managed to get the chance to give her the tour that night of the party, as he had hoped to. Harriet had been hesitant to go back to his at first but he had managed to convince her that he would get her home in time, before Freda got in. It was not Freda that was primarily on Harriet's mind at that point but it was more the fact that this seemed to be an even bigger step, being alone with him at his house.

The drive through the mansion gates and up to the house was a different experience for Harriet this time around. Unlike in the day, the gardens at night were a different spectacle, illuminated by a range of light fixtures that trailed the path to the house. Harriet was awed into silence at how magical the experience felt and envied Peter for owning this wonder; he had the pleasure of experiencing it every day. On that night Harriet finally got to see more of Peter's home and it was much more than she had originally thought.

Once inside, he had taken her first through his two lounges, the first being bigger with a humongous central fireplace feature on one of its walls, a mounted eighty-inch flat screen television above it and a series of other electronic gadgetry on either side of it. This was Peter's main TV room and the sofas in that room allowed for serious lounging and relaxation, with heavy fat cushions and thick backs. They were off white in colour and Harriet thought that it was lucky that there were no children living at the house as these would not last.

The second lounge was smaller, with more of a grown up feel to it and Harriet was informed that this was where people could sit and converse over drinks. This room had more rigid settees in a different shade of cream with black vertical stripes which strongly resembled the type she had seen at the Ritz Carlton. She made a comment about her observations.

"These look similar to the ones at that first hotel we went to." she said, as she ran her hand on the soft silk material.

"They are indeed. I liked those at the Ritz and went out looking for the same ones. I didn't find the exact kind but these seemed near enough."

Harriet nodded as she further scanned the room, pleased with herself for having made the connection. She also noticed a black piano in the corner of this room and wondered whether Peter played.

"Do you play?" She asked, pointing to the piano.

"Oh no," he laughed." That's just for show. I thought it completed the room quite well."

They had moved on and he had taken her through some interior glass doors and down a corridor towards the kitchen. They entered the kitchen which was an open plan design, a combination of the cooking area that housed a six plate hob and all manner of cupboards, all in bright white. This colour seemed to be the theme of the rooms in the downstairs area.

In the middle of the kitchen was an island, with a glossy beige granite top infused with high grade polyester resin, quartz and recycled glass, and a chrome sink at its centre. There were more cupboards underneath the island and several high stools surrounding it. On the other end of the kitchen was a dining area with six chairs, all wrapped in white leather, around a rectangular glass top table.

Before showing her the upper levels of the mansion, Peter had taken Harriet to his basement level, where she was even more shocked to find another complete and self functioning living area. This was his man cave, which had pretty much almost everything she had seen upstairs, including a bedroom and an office suite. Instead of just a TV room, this space had a small cinema area with a roof mounted projector and a large screening area on the wall opposite. And to further compliment the room, a bar sat on the far side, fully stocked with almost any alcoholic beverages you could think of. A large pool table also sat near by.

"This is where I do most of my indoor entertaining, especially when the boys come over after practice or something," he had informed her.

She was still exploring this new area, still quite amazed at how thought through it all was.

"Wow, never thought there was more down here," she had replied, genuinely surprised and impressed.

"I usually hold parties in here too, mainly because it is isolated from the main house. People just drive up and they can come straight in here. Come I will show you."

He had led her to a door at the far side of this sub level living space and through it they had emerged in his garage. This room was also large, housing 4 shiny supercars, a Ferrari 458, an Aston Martin DBS, Lamborghini Spyder and modified Range Rover Sport Overfinch. Harriet was astonished at how clean the garage was with a series of shiny black and white glossy tiles on the floor, the walls painted in a hazy light grey colour and a collection of motor racing memorabilia hung all over the walls.

The main garage doors opened up to the driveway, with a slight incline to get to the ground level and Peter had explained that his guests usually parked their cars just outside and walked down a stairway into the basement through the garage entrance. He liked this and this is the reason why he had made the garage into some kind of a 'museum' to showcase his love for cars, something his guests could enjoy as they walked through.

They had gone back through the internal

door into the basement apartment and right next to the door was a small elevator that Harriet had noticed before they had stepped into the garage. She had wondered where the elevator led to when they had walked past the first time. As they got back into the basement living space, Peter mentioned the elevator, answering Harriet's curiosity.

"This,"he said pointing at the silver elevator door,"is a shortcut to my bedroom, especially if I have had a long day and want to avoid people. I just park up, come through this door and straight up to my room'.

Harriet nodded to acknowledge that she was taking it all in. She could not hide how much she was in awe of his property and lifestyle. He gestured for her to step into the tiny elevator, which could only reasonably take two people, and they were ferried up to the mansion's top floors. As the elevator doors opened, they found themselves in a large thick carpeted corridor that lead to various bedrooms. Peter's bedroom was at the end of that corridor. As they walked towards it, he also showcased the rest of the upper level comprising of different themed bedrooms, all stylish and elegantly put together. Harriet was taken by his house and she could not believe the level of detail and thought he had put into the place.

They got to the end of the corridor and through two large brown mahogany doors, they stepped into his bedroom. Immediately, Harriet had been struck by the overwhelming feeling of grandeur that the room exuded. It was the largest bedroom she had ever been in and everything about it screamed comfort, softness and cosiness. All you felt like doing in this room was kicking your shoes off, diving on the enormous king size Tempur-Pedic bed and get comfortable under the silk sheets, thick duvets and fluffy throws. Even the floor was inviting, covered by thick under heated carpet and a few shag piles scattered around.

Harriet had gone and done exactly that. She took off her heels and walked towards the bed, enjoying the soft feel of the carpet and heat underneath her feet. She sat on the edge of the bed for a moment before lying back and looking up at the patterned ceiling above.

"Wow! So comfortable. I love this bed," she had managed to utter, as she soaked up the experience.

"You like it?" Peter asked, walking from the door towards her, his hands in his pockets.

"I do," Harriet replied as she sat up, having sensed him walk towards her. She had not realised how suggestive she might have just been, but she did not think he would do anything.

She battled with her thoughts for a few seconds wondering what she would actually do if he did start something. Surely it was too soon for anything of a physical nature as yet, she thought, or was it, kissing maybe. The thought of what could happen had made her a little nervous that she got up off the bed completely but it was a little too late. Before she could move away he had got to her and they now stood quite close to each other, just as they had been by the pool at his party. He had done it purposefully, moving in on her, his intentions clear. He went further and put his arms around her waist and pulled her towards him, something he had been itching to do all night.

Harriet was unsure of what to do. She was now like prey caught in his trap and she felt overwhelmed by his presence, sending her heart into a frenzy. She wanted him too but she was not sure she was ready for how far it could all go. As he held her tightly against his body, feeling her frontal curves against his, she was gently trying to resist, attempting to pry herself from his embrace.

It was not that she did not want him but she was not sure she would have the will to stop herself from going further. As she looked up at him with a combination of a longing desire to stay in his embrace and confusion, he moved in and kissed her, feeling the warm air of her breath as their mouths touched.

As they kissed, her mouth trembled from both excitement and worry. This was the first time she had kissed another man. He was gentle with her, as he explored her lips and tongue, still clutching her tightly as if he was trying to stop her from escaping. She stopped her tiny efforts of resistance and sank into him. For a while they managed to stay on their feet, mouths locked in a passionate kiss, but it did not take long for them to urge backwards towards the bed.

Gently, he lowered her down onto it and still towering over her, he stared into her eyes longingly, before slowly moving down towards her and planting his lips against hers yet again. Harriet made a quiet moan of exhilaration, which almost sounded like a cry. It could have been a sign of how connected she felt to him in that moment but it could have also been a cry for what she had just given up. Only she knew.

Chapter 13

"Hello. Hello." The person on the other end answered. The line had not connected well. "Hello!"

"Hi! Sandra, it's Harriet. Can you hear me?" Harriet spoke louder as if this would have improved the connection.

The line crackled a little more and then the receiver came on again.

"Oh my God, Harriet, hi!' came the ecstatic response from Sandra. "I can hear you now. Can you hear me?"

"I can now," Harriet confirmed,"How are you?"

"I am good *sha*. How about you? What is this, you disappearing on me like this?"

Harriet had not kept in touch with her friend as she had promised.

"I know, sha, I am so sorry," Harriet apologised," I can't even begin to tell you how it has been for me, crazy busy. How's things over there?"

"Things are going really well, you know, just the usual, same old me. How's things up there for you? I was beginning to worry that you had forgotten all about me?"

"Forget you, nah, not in a million years," Harriet replied, sincerely feeling she owed her friend an explanation for the silence." I just got wrapped up in a few things this end and it took me a while to get organised. I was going to call soon as things settled." There was a tinge of mis-truth in what she was saying but that is all Harriet had for now.

Yes, things had moved on at an exponential rate since Harriet's arrival in London, some four months ago, but she could have made contact with Sandra on numerous occasions. She could not quite work out what had stopped her from calling her friend but she soon worked out that life in Britain was so fast paced and there was always something that needed doing. Harriet was even more ashamed of herself when she recalled that she had not spoken to her family for nearly two months.

"Don't be like that, sha,"Sandra pleaded with her friend," Even you mum was asking me when we last spoke. You need to call them."

"I will. I am, today, after I finish talking to you," Harriet replied in a sombre tone, as the feelings of guilt enveloped her." How are they? When did you last see my mum or dad?"

"I spoke to your mum just the other day. Everyone is alright except your dad who had another turn. I would call your mum if I were you but don't worry too much. Your mum said he was better now and didn't need to stay in hospital."

"Did he? Was it his heart again?" Harriet asked, now even more alarmed. This was one thing she had feared the most, especially being so far away from home.

"I think so but it wasn't too bad. They managed to get him to the doctor's and he was home in no time. I think she may have mentioned that he is now on some new tablets and he seems to be doing well on them."

"Thanks for letting me know, sha. I will definitely call my mum straight after." Harriet said.

"Ye sure, no problem. So tell me, Justin, what's going on with you guys. He called me yesterday and said he too has not heard from you in weeks. What's going on?"

Harriet was bursting to tell Sandra about the latest developments in her life but she was not sure how Sandra would react to the news. Sandra had been there from the start of Harriet's relationship with Justin and this situation with Peter was most likely to break her too, as it would him. Harriet needed her though at this point. Things were moving much faster and further than she had anticipated and she needed to talk to someone, fast!

"It's a long story my dear, but it's one I really need to share with you."

"What is it? What's happened?" Sandra asked, her tone elevated with concern.

She had never known there being a major issue between Harriet and Justin that would have had Harriet speak in the manner she was. Something intense had to be happening.

"You won't believe what has happened to me this side. I never imagined it or thought it would happen like this but it did. It's a huge deal." Harriet started. She exhaled deeply, sending Sandra deeper into worry.

"Harriet, what's happened?" Sandra asked, still deeply concerned.

Harriet hesitated again for a few seconds, then answered," I met someone, over here. We have been seeing each other for weeks now."

"What?!" Sandra exclaimed,"Are you serious?" Her voice now registered a mixture of both worry and confusion.

Harriet did not respond. This immediately gave Sandra the confirmation that this was true.

"Oh my God, Harriet! When? I mean, what about Justin? What are you thinking?" Sandra interrogated her friend, going straight for the hurtful truth. They had always had that type of relationship.

"I don't know how it happened sha. I don't even know how I am going to tell him." Harriet replied, her voice riddled with guilt and defeat.

"How far has this gone with this other person? Anyway, who is he? Where did you meet him?" Sandra had a lot of questions and thoughts racing through her mind, quite astounded by how Harriet had moved on in such a short space of time.

"You know him, but you have never met him before."

Sandra did not get what this meant. How could she know someone she had never met.

"What do you mean I know him but I have never met him. Is it someone you have mentioned to me before?'

"No', Harriet replied." It's someone you

would know about anyway."

The confusion did not leave Sandra.

"Who is it then? Just say." Sandra insisted.

"Peter Chuma."

"Who?"

"Peter Chuma, the footballer," Harriet added.

"Peter Chuma, the Zim national captain?" Sandra replied, not quite believing that this was one and the same person.

"Yes, him", Harriet confirmed quietly

"Oh my God! Where did you meet him?" Sandra asked, shocked and intrigued simultaneously.

Harriet had gone on to share the events of the past few weeks with her friend, details of how they had met at Hector's party and further dates after that. Sandra was mouth agape as she listened to Harriet narrate. Part of her remained intrigued but another part was irate with Harriet for not having shared this sooner. So she confronted her.

"I can't believe you, Harriet. You didn't even think to share any of this with me when it was happening. You should have called me the very day you met him."

"I didn't plan for anything to happen and to be honest I didn't want anything to happen. You know how much I love Justin and I knew if I let this happen, I might as well have just stuck a knife into his heart. But things happened and I don't know how I got here."

Sandra felt some empathy towards her friend. She had sensed that Harriet was in genuine turmoil over the matter and what she needed at that moment was her best friend.

"This is definitely something big," Sandra began, now a bit more relaxed and caught up." So how far has it gone? You haven't done anything stupid like sleep with him, have you?" Sandra was hoping the situation might still be salvageable.

Harriet did not reply.

"Oh my God Harriet!"Sandra exclaimed again down the phone. She could not quite believe how far the affair had gone. "You slept with him?"

"I like him, so much. I wouldn't have if I didn't like him," Harriet attempted to justify her actions.

"But you just met him? You don't even know him that well, do you? Is he worth destroying everything you have built with Justin for?" Sandra asked her.

"He's a lovely guy and I like how he makes me feel, how we are together. It's different."

"More than what you had?"

"Far more, I think," Harriet replied, hesitantly.

There was a silence as they both reflected on their thoughts and prepared their next words.

"So what are you going to do about it? When are you going to tell Justin, how even?" Sandra asked.

"I don't know, sha. That's why I have been ignoring his calls. He calls everyday and I can't get myself to talk to him. What do you think I should do? Can you talk to him for me, maybe? It might be better for him coming from you."

"E-ee sha, I don't even know how I would start that conversation with him. Don't you think it's better if you spoke to him directly?"

Harriet did not respond. She knew that it

would be the right thing for her to talk to him but she was too fearful of hearing his response, the agony of having to hear the news tear him apart.

"Please Sandra? You have to help me, please? At least start it off for me and I can deal with it once he knows."

Sandra thought for a minute. This was not going to be easy for her either but she had somewhat of a good relationship with Justin, having talked to him in the past when issues had arisen in his and Harriet's relationship. Sandra told Harriet that she would try talking to Justin but could not guarantee the outcome. Harriet thanked her friend immensely for her understanding and taking on this heavy burden off her shoulders, well, at least for now. They would speak again a few days later.

Harriet caught up with her mum that same day, after talking to Sandra, and had also managed to speak to her father and sister. She was happy she had called them, although details of her father's illness earlier in the month had worried her. Her mother reassured her, as Sandra had done, that they were hopeful the new medication would help him.

They all missed her immensely and she missed home too. It had only been a few months since her arrival in the UK but she felt as though her life had been moving at breakneck speed, and if home were close, she would have gone back just to reconnect and gather herself. She felt like a boulder that had been pushed down a steep hill and now rolling out of control.

As Harriet spoke to her mother on the phone, her thoughts were on her earlier conversation with Sandra. Now that the cat was out the bag, she wondered how all this was going to end. She knew that Sandra was going to see Justin in a few days and tell him what was happening. She was not certain how things would then progress from there but she surmised that Justin would obviously inform her parents, something she was not prepared to do herself. This action would then escalate the issue to a whole new level, extended family summoned and gathered, as Africans tended to do. She respected her culture but viewed some of the practices as over performed, making mountains out of mole hills.

This was no small matter though. Harriet had decided to end a betrothal, a sacred vow to unite with someone, a vow now broken. Africans did not take this kind of thing lightly. She would be mocked, ridiculed and her family looked down upon. People had been invited, gathered and witnessed the event happen. Breaking it would be a mockery to their time and the effort they spent.

All these thoughts bothered Harriet but she knew that what was done was done. All she had to do now was wait and see where it all went next. There was one thing, however, that she could not ask anyone else to do for her, a fight she would have to take on herself. She had one more onerous task of having to face Freda. Sooner or later she was going to have to tell her and so she decided to wait, at least until Justin was aware of it.

That wait did not take long to come, because a couple of days later Sandra met up with Justin. She had called him the day before and asked if he would be home on the Saturday morning, perfect day as they both would be off work. Justin had agreed to see her but wondered what it was that would warrant Sandra to insist on seeing him in person.

He had woken up an hour earlier and was now sat by his dining table, entertaining a bowl of cereal and reading Saturday's Herald newspaper. He had managed to nip out to the local shop to pick up both a cereal box and newspaper, something he did most weekends. It was around ten o'clock when a knock sounded from outside his flat door. Justin got up, newspaper still in hand and peered through the peep-hole. He unlocked it realising it was his anticipated guest on the other side.

"Miss Sandra!" he said as he opened the door and allowed her in.

"Hey Jussy, how are you?" Sandra greeted him as she walked in.

"I'm alright thanks. How about you?" He reciprocated, politely.

"OK, thanks. Just glad to be off work today. Soaking up the weekend."

"Totally, same here." He agreed, closing the door and walking back to his seat by the table. "So what brings you this end of town. Just decided on a social, did you?"

She laughed a little but it was not her usual care free laugh. This one was marred with anxiety at the prospect of the real reason for her visit.

"Thought I'd check up on you, see how you getting on," she lied, as she sat down on one of his settees, not bothering to wait to be asked.

"Ye right," he said, catching her bluff." What's really going on? You never visit me, and when we spoke last I sensed something was wrong. What's up? You can talk to me."

Justin was preparing himself to help and advise Sandra on whatever problem she had brought to him. He had been there for her before, on several occasions when she had been stuck with her personal issues, and now he wondered whether this was another one of those.

"I was having some cereal before you came. Would you like some, maybe breakfast or tea?" He offered.

"No, I am OK for now thanks. Maybe later," she declined.

"Oh OK, no problem." He said, as he lowered himself into his seat." So… what's on your mind? How can I help?"

Sandra did not realise how hard this subject was going to be to start, but she was here and he was expecting her to say something. She froze for a moment, but then gathered the courage to begin.

"I spoke to Harriet two days ago," she started, her tone subdued.

"You did?" Justin asked, perplexed as to how she had managed to get hold of her and yet he had been struggling for a while now.

"Yes," Sandra confirmed.

"And?" Justin asked, a frown across his forehead. He wasn't upset with Sandra but with Harriet for avoiding him.

"She is fine but there have been a few developments that she wanted me to talk to you about."

"Developments? What developments? And why isn't she talking to me about it herself?"

Justin instantaneously had this feeling at the pit of his stomach that he was not going to be enthused with what was coming. But whatever it was, he was more upset that it was not Harriet telling him herself.

"Justin, you know Harriet wouldn't do anything to hurt you on purpose," Sandra continued tactfully," She was more concerned about your feelings to what I am about to tell you."

"Sandra, just tell me!" Justin demanded impatiently.

Sandra paused again, composing herself one last time. She could no longer delay it any further.

"She is breaking off the engagement," Sandra said, her tone still quietened and laboured.

"What?!" Justin roared from across the room."When did she decide this?"

"I don't know exactly but she told me this when I spoke to her," Sandra replied.

"Why?!" Justin barked at her again, his gaze sharp.

"I am not sure of the exact details but all she told me is that she has been seeing someone else over there."

"You've got to be kidding me?!" He yelled, getting up from his seat and forcefully swiping the cereal bowl off the table in anger. "What is this bullshit? I want to speak to her, NOW!"

Sandra just sat there, eyes to the floor, and allowed him time and space to vent. She had expected him to react this way.

Justin went into his bedroom and returned with his cell phone which he shoved across the table towards Sandra. "Call her now! I want her to tell me herself what this nonsense is all about."

Sandra picked up the phone and before dialling, she rummaged through her handbag to find her note book with Harriet's number. As she did so, Justin was pacing the living room, muttering to himself and vocalising obscenities at how selfish Harriet was being for doing this. Sandra found it and slowly punched in the long number.

She pressed the green telephone icon before slowly raising the phone to her ear. She waited as it rang, praying that someone would pick up on the other side.

Unfortunately, her prayers were not heard on this day. The call went to an answering system. Sandra slowly lowered the phone and placed it down on the table.

"There is no answer," she informed him, expecting another bout of screaming and howling.

Justin snatched up the phone from the table and pressed the redial button. He too waited for an answer but to no avail. He walked into his bedroom yet again and this time came out with a jacket in one hand and his car keys in the other.

"I will drive you home," he said to Sandra, now much calmer but still visibly upset.

She picked up her bag and notebook and followed him to the door. They both exited the flat.

Chapter 14

Justin raced his Nissan Sunny Boxster sedan towards Cranbourne, a middle-class suburb east of Harare, heading towards Harriet's family home. Sandra sat next to him on the passenger seat, not only fearful about what lay ahead when they reached their destination, but also whether they would even get there, judging from the speed at which Justin was driving. Neither spoke to the other for a while.

Mid morning in Harare produced the best weather you could get, in this southern African country. The sun was usually closer to the earth's horizon which meant that it was not too bright and neither was it too hot. The temperature at this time of the day was optimum for basking and as they drove past many of the suburban homes, they saw many people, young and old, doing exactly that. Most did not work on weekends and neither were schools open, so many would have been at home, making the most to recharge after a long week.

Some businesses were open too, as they normally did at this time of the morning, grocery shops especially. Many people could be seen going in, and others pouring out of them, clasping plastic shopping bags. Most bags contained breakfast essentials such as bread and milk, but others included eggs, for the fortunate ones. Eggs, butter and milk were a luxury for some families but there were other easily attainable alternatives that could be sourced to enhanced the family breakfast. These included items such as avocado to spread on the bread, tomato and onion soup to dip the bread in, or even shredded green leaf vegetables, usually left over from a previous evening meal.

That morning, the Sande's, Harriet's family, were going through the same Saturday morning ritual like everyone else. As Mr Sande took his bath, the female members of the house were getting on with the house chores and cooking breakfast. Even after so many years of advancement socially and technologically to match the rest of the world, there were still some practices accepted within African culture that other societies might have viewed as prejudicial.

Men were typically viewed as the bread winners and women there to serve their husbands. This was still very much alive in modern day Africa. But ironically, some of these practices were also quite prevalent in other countries that claimed to have advanced social systems; Africa just happens to be upfront about it.

The Sunny Boxster left the main road and turned to face the metal gates of the Sande family home, which was surrounded by a high *Durawall*. You could not see the whole house behind it but just its red roof tiles gleaming in the African sun. The *Durawall* was supposed to be light grey in colour but was now a combination of that, and a red tint caused by the red soil near the property that had wafted up and stuck onto it. A good run on it with a water hose usually solved the problem, and cleaned it right off, but it would only be a temporary fix, as cars passing by would just raise more dust and the wall would be covered up again.

Justin got out of the car and went to open the gate. He put his hand through a square gap, right in the middle of the two gates and pulled the locking system sideways, which released the two gates and they flung open. He had been there several times and knew that the gates would not be locked at this time of the day. As the gates flew open, Ginger the family dog came up from the house, barking at the intruders. She quickly recognised Justin and moved coyly towards him, head down and tail wagging vigorously.

"Hey Ginger," Justin said, stroking the dogs head. She liked it and moved her head around his hand, exposing her canine gnashers and trying to snap at it playfully.

From the house, someone popped their head out the kitchen door and looked towards the gate. Justin 'shooed' the dog back to the house whilst he stepped back into the car and drove it in. He parked it just outside the kitchen door and they both alighted. As they did so, Beatrice walked out the house to greet them.

"Hey, guys! Welcome!" She said once they were out of the vehicle.

They both gave a stone faced response, indicating that not all was well. Beatrice picked it up and did not think it her place to probe further.

"Come on in, mum and dad are in the lounge." Beatrice invited them.

"Thanks," Justin said. "I will close the gate."

"No, it's OK. Mkoma Shingi will do it," she stopped him. She then proceeded to call out for Shingi, their resident gardener, to go up and close the gates. With labour so cheap in Zimbabwe it was common for most working class families to employ either a maid or gardner, or sometimes both. A scrawny looking man in dusty green overalls came running from the back of the house and ran towards the gates. As he did, they all walked into the main house through the kitchen door.

Harriet's parents sat in the lounge having their breakfast in front of the TV. The coffee table had been pulled towards the two seater sofa they were sitting on, and it housed a large pot of tea, a plate with bread mounted on it, two individual plates with eggs, tomato soup and 'Polony' sausage, plus two mugs both with half drunk tea.

As the three walked in, Beatrice introduced them, "Mum, dad, Justin and Sandra are here."

Both parents turned towards the visitors," Oh, welcome my children," Harriet's mother spoke first."Come on in. Take a sit. " She was gesturing to the empty three setter on the other side.

They murmured a few 'thank yous' as they casually walked and sat down.

"What a pleasant surprise. We weren't expecting anyone to visit at all today. You have blessed us." Mrs Sande continued. Her husband just hummed a supportive response but did not say anything. He was a very quiet man who enjoyed silence and his own space. This intrusion of his weekend rest was not usually welcome but he was not one to make a scene.

Beatrice walked out of the room as they sat down and returned with two extra mugs. She placed them in front of Justin and Sandra, who both immediately and politely declined the offer of tea.

"Oh don't be like that my children. No-one has ever been harmed by a cup of tea. Please, please, have some," Mrs Sande insisted.

They had relented, again out of politeness and Beatrice went ahead and poured tea into both their mugs. As they sugared and picked up their tea, Justin knew he had to go straight into why they had invaded the families weekend bliss.

"Mum and Dad," he began. "You know I would never come to you with anything unless it is really important. Well, today I got some news from Sandra here, news that did not please me at all."

"What has happened my son?" Mrs Sande asked, with obvious concern.

"Mum I don't know what has got into Harriet. I have been trying to get hold of her for weeks and weeks now, but she has been avoiding me. Today I found out why." He paused for a second

"E-eh?" his future mother in law said, urging him to keep going.

"Sandra told me this morning that Harriet, from her own mouth, has said she is breaking up our engagement."

"What?!" This time both parents echoed each other. Harriet's father, who had been seated in a slouching position, sat up and straightened himself.

"Harriet herself, said this?" Her father

asked, the question directed at Sandra.

"Yes, baba," Sandra replied.

"Oh my God this child!" Mr Sande cried out.

"Why has she done this? Did she say?" Harriet's mother asked.

Both Justin and Sandra were not sure whether they should tell Harriet's parents the real reason for this situation. Justin, though, thought it was best if they knew the whole truth.

"The truth, mum and dad, is that Harriet seems to have met another man over there, whom she has apparently been seeing for a while now."

"Another man?" Her mum gasped in shock. Her father sighed.

"Yes mum," Justin replied.

"It's Peter Chuma, the football player. That's who she has been seeing," Sandra added.

Justin turned to look at her, he too shocked at learning this new piece of information. He had not thought about asking who it was. He had just assumed that it was probably some random guy she had met out there.

"Peter Chuma?" Justin asked her.

"Yes." Sandra confirmed.

Justin's world shut down for a moment. He had not anticipated that his competition would be someone of the likes of Peter Chuma. He felt small in that moment, inadequate and doubtful as to whether he could even compete with that.

Harriet's parents were lost for words too. They had sensed something was afoot when she did not ring them for a while but her mum had spoken to her a few days before, same day Harriet had called Sandra, but nothing had been mentioned.

"We are going to have to call her, Dad. You need to speak to her and find out what this nonsense is all about," Mrs Sande said, addressing her husband.

"Yes, we need to do that," he replied softly, both feeling let down and embarrassed by their daughter.

This was unlike the Harriet they knew. They could not believe that she could have moved on to someone that quick, mere months since moving out. It would be even more disgraceful if she had only been enticed by his fame and wealth, they thought.

"We are going to have to get to the bottom of this, son," Mr Sande continued, addressing his future son in law." If this is true, then Harriet has let us down and brought shame upon this family. For now, please, do not be hasty with your decisions but wait on us and we will try and get a resolution."

He had spoken to everyone as reassuring and as comforting as he could, trying to stay level headed and project his role as head of the family. Everyone in the room knew there was nothing any of them could do. They had to wait now to hear what Harriet's next move would be.

Later that morning Justin walked back into his flat, closed the door behind him and threw his cell phone and car keys on the coffee table. He sat down on his single seater sofa and rubbed his head several times with both his palms. It was as if he was trying to rub his brain into action to try and pop out his next move. He threw himself backwards in his seat and stared at the black glossy glass screen of the television, which was switched off. It responded by throwing a hazy transparent image of his sorry-self back at him.

The flat was dead quiet except for noises filtering through from outside, cars with bad exhausts, kids shouting playfully on the streets below and a few vendors bellowing at the top of their voices as they desperately taunted for a sale. This was supposed to be a normal weekend break for Justin, but now he sat alone, feeling even more alone that he had ever been since Harriet left, and now ever more uncertain whether he would be able to get her back.

He got up from sitting back in the sofa and picked up his cell phone from the table. He pressed it to life and flicked through to the last dialled numbers. He clicked the number Sandra had used earlier which was Freda's home telephone number in London and waited. Harriet had also given him this number when she moved in with Freda. He did not hesitate or even think about the cost to his mobile phone contract, but just went ahead and dialled it.

The phone rang several times and Justin wondered if Harriet would pick up this time. A few rings later the phone made another clicking sound as it was picked up on the other side.

"Hello," came the response.

"Harriet?" Justin asked, not recognising the voice straight away.

"No, its not. Harriet's out. May I know who's calling?" The response came, cold and unwelcoming.

"Freda, it's Justin. How are you?"

"Oh, hi Justin," Freda replied, her voice now more pleasant after realising who was at the other end.

"I'm ok thanks, well, not really to be honest. Where is Harriet? I've been trying to get in touch with her for the last two weeks but she hasn't returned any of my calls."

"Really?" Freda replied, quite surprised by this herself. Harriet had not mentioned any problems between them. "She has gone into town to sort out her Uni fees and stuff, but she will be back shortly I'm guessing. She never said anything about you guys not talking though. When did this start?"

"She stopped calling me and responding to my messages about two to three weeks ago. I have called this number a few times now but no-one ever picks up, and this one time I think someone put the phone down on me. It might have been her, I don't know. Why is she avoiding me? What's going on over there? Do you know anything?"

Freda felt herself being pulled into something she did not want to be part of. She had not picked up anything from Harriet's movements or talking with her.

"I don't know anything about what you are talking about Justin. Harriet hasn't told me anything, and neither have I noticed anything. Wait, did you say she stopped talking to you about three weeks ago?" Freda asked, beginning to piece a few things together, based on events that had happened around that same period. She did not have to wreck her brain too long.

"Yes, that's about right," Justin confirmed. "Listen, do you know whether she is seeing anyone, or have you heard her talk to anyone since she arrived?"

"No, not to my knowledge," Freda replied, her mind now racing as she spoke. This came through her voice and Justin picked it up.

"Do you know anything Freda? Please tell me if there's something going on?" He pleaded. He could sense that she seemed to know more than she was letting on.

"I don't," she replied. "I was just trying to work out what could be causing her to shut down on you like that, maybe something I might have missed."

Justin made a deep loud sigh on the other side and decided to ask the question he was dreading the most. The answer to this would seal the fate of his relationship and the end of his engagement.

"Last conversation I had with her, she told me that you had both been to a party and met Pater Chuma the footballer. Is that true?"

Freda's heart skipped a beat and she felt it, as it struggled to gain its natural rhythm. She was shocked and aghast, not only because Justin know about this, but that Harriet might have gone further with Peter, to the extent that it had reached the ears of people back home. A few things began to come together in her mind, times when she had wondered where Harriet was, and days when she came off nights and Harriet would also sleep in the day. It was all beginning to make sense now.

'U-um," she huffed."Yes we did. We were invited to his house for a party. What do you know?"

"Sandra told me that Harriet confessed to her that she is seeing him. You know Sandra, don't you? Do you know anything about that?"

Freda was stunned and felt so betrayed.

"No, I don't know anything about it. It doesn't surprise me though, and I know why she wouldn't tell me. Oh my goodness, this is not good, not good at all." Freda sounded irate and her tone revealed someone plotting.

Justin too, was destroyed hearing that something could have definitely happened between Harriet and Peter Chuma. He closed his eyes, still holding the phone to Freda, and shook his head. When Freda had finished, Justin implored her to tell Harriet that he now knew and wanted to hear her side of the story. Freda promised to pass on the message and told him that she too would be straightening out a few things with Harriet on her return.

Chapter 15

"What the hell, Harriet!" Freda confronted her, quite aggressively, as Harriet walked into the flat.

Harriet was stunned and taken aback by Freda's vicious tirade towards her, and the vehemence in her tone. Never had she spoken this sharp to her in the several months they had lived together. Harriet had been in the city all morning finalising the payment for her university fees, and making last minute purchases of what she needed. The money her father had borrowed from the Standard Chartered Bank back home, to fund her studies, had come through and she was quite thankful for that. Little did she know that she would be walking back into a fight, after such a productive day.

"What's the matter? Why are you angry with me?" Harriet asked, her tone defensive.

"Don't pretend like you don't know, you

sneaky sly bitch!"

"What the hell Freda!" Harriet shouted back, not in any way impressed by the name calling. "What have I done to you that's so bad?"

Harriet sensed that this might have something to do with her and Peter. There was only one issue that could evoke such aggressive emotions from Freda.

"For all I have done for you, letting you live in my house, you go behind my back, lying to me everyday, knowing full well the shit you were pulling?"

Harriet knew the game was up, but she was not sure how Freda had found out. She decided to play ignorant.

"What are you talking about?" She pretended not to know.

"Stop treating me like a two year old Harriet!" Freda screamed back. "You know exactly what I'm talking about. In actual fact, call your fiancé, he's looking for you. That should definitely be an interesting conversation. You're such a disgrace!"

Harriet knew the net had closed in but she was not going to just stand there and be abused.

"Seriously Freda, I don't appreciate the tone or the insults. If you have something to say to me, then just say it!" Harriet was now wearing her own aggressive stance and was prepared for anything else that was coming.

"For weeks and weeks, you have been lying to me, sneaking out to see him, all this behind my back, yet you knew how, ...you knew how I felt about him. Oh my God, it all makes sense now. I used to see things out of place and wondered what had happened, but somehow it never crossed my mind, that this is what you were up to."

Harriet did not respond. She was still stood near the door, arms folded, and with an intense fixed stare towards Freda, as she watched her rant.

"You knew how I felt," Freda continued. "You know I have feelings for him and still, you went for him, betraying me, your fiancé and your family in the process. Who does that? Are you not ashamed of yourself?"

"Listen, I never wanted any of this," Harriet hissed back. "I am sorry if you feel I stole something from you but I did not set out to get involved with anyone. I came here for my studies and yes, I know I am engaged, but I never planned to fall for him."

"What? You expect me to have sympathy for you. You came into my house, my life and you think you can take what you like?"

"Oh my God, Freda!" Harriet screamed, both hands raised gesturing her to stop," You are not even seeing him. It's not like you are in a relationship with him!"

"That's not the point! You knew I liked him and as my friend, someone who knew exactly how I felt, you should have stopped yourself!" Freda screamed back.

"He came after me. Don't forget that!" Harriet reminded her.

"And you should have stayed away from him! Besides, you are engaged. When did you forget that? Your family must be feeling the shame right about now."

The mention of her family shame did not help the situation. Harriet decided to fire back.

"Leave my family out of it! You just can't hack the fact that he wanted me. I never asked for this and I tried everything to keep away from him. He clearly chose who he wanted, so come to terms with it!"

Freda stared at Harriet, eyes blazing. She felt betrayed and humiliated, and was hurting terribly inside. She had always wanted Peter from the moment she met him. She had been around him on several occassions, and even though they had talked, he had never said the things she wanted to hear. She had never stopped trying, and hoped that one day he would realise how she truly felt for him. Things changed later, however, and something happened between her and Peter, things she had never shared with Harriet. Freda decided to use this now, to gain her advantage over their fight.

"Really!" Freda snarled at her."Really? He chose you, huh? Well, let me tell you something you don't know, Missy. Peter and I have been much closer than you could possibly imagine. Take a guess?"

"What? What are you talking about?" Harriet glared at her questioningly.

Freda sneered at her, an unnerving look spread across her face. "Peter and I have been sleeping together, long before you showed up. How about that for your big pompous back side!"

Harriet was shocked into silence and left feeling run-over by the sudden turn of events. She had not seen this coming. She had never picked up that things had gone that far between them. She was not sure whether Freda was telling the truth or just intending to wound her in that moment; in some conniving revenge move.

"You are lying!" Harriet challenged her.

"Am I?" Freda sneered again."Well, go and ask your precious new boyfriend. I am sure he'll tell you, if he really likes you, and please call your fiancé whilst you are at it. I am sure you two have much more to talk about. Oh wow, the drama!"

Freda concluded her rant with an acidulous laugh, which sent Harriet out of the room in a huff. Roles had reversed, Harriet, now the one feeling betrayed. In all the weeks she had known Peter, Harriet could not understand why he had not thought it best to tell her far he had gone with Freda. She was angry, and blamed him for where she was now.

A black cab pulled outside Freda's London apartment and the driver sounded the horn. It was mid-afternoon of the same day that Harriet and Freda had wrangled over Peter. They had not spoken, and the tension in the apartment was so heavy that one could slice right through the middle with a knife.

Harriet had been fumbling upstairs for a good half an hour, before storming downstairs holding a small overnight bag, stuffed with some of her personal belongings. She had concluded that it was best if she left, not wishing to aggravate the situation any further.

"I will be back for the rest of my things," Harriet informed Freda. She was much calmer by that point, slowed down by guilt, of how Freda had been gracious enough to host her and now they had to part, abruptly, under such sketchy circumstances. She hoped to end this chapter as quickly as possible.

"Wow, ok," Freda gasped. "So now you are just going to take off. For all that I have done for you, this is the way you are going to go? That's the "thank you" I get?"

"Freda, I don't want to argue with you. A lot has happened and we can't be in the same house right now." Harriet responded, defending her decision to leave.

Freda shook her head. "No, it's fine, go! I am sure your rich boyfriend is waiting to take care of you there."

"I am not going to him. What do you take me for?"

"I don't need to remind you what you are. You know exactly what you are!" Freda barked at her.

"You know what, I am done!" Harriet said, as she moved towards the door, swung it open and slammed it shut behind her.

She marched down the few steps onto the pavement and walked to the waiting taxi. She got in the back and as she sat down, the driver asked for her destination.

"Where can I take you, ma dear?" The driver asked. He had a very cheerful and brazen character about him, oblivious to how agitated his passenger was.

"Can you take me to any hotel please, anything reasonable, not too up market?"

"There is the Premier Inn on Bell street?" The driver said.

"That will do, thank you," She agreed,

without taking much consideration about the suggestion.

With that, the taxi had pulled off the side of the kerb and joined other vehicles on the main road, heading south towards Bell Street. In less than twenty minutes the driver had parked his cab outside the front of the hotel and relayed the fare to Harriet. She pulled out a £20 note, handed it to him and after messing with his bag of loose change for a bit, he turned and handed her change from the £20 note. Thanking him, Harriet exited the vehicle and walked into the hotel reception.

She was grateful yet again for her father's generosity, as this day would have been much worse if she could not afford somewhere to stay. Her plan now was to base herself at the hotel for a day or two, whilst she contemplated her next move. She would have to get something reasonable soon though, as the cost of staying in a hotel would be unsustainable for her long term.

There were rooms available at the hotel and so Harriet booked herself in for the next 2 days. She thought this would be ample time for her to plan where to go next. She had made payment for the room in cash, money she had withdrawn earlier to buy some essentials for her studies. She would have to replace it later.

After getting her room key, Harriet slowly walked away from the reception desk towards an elevator on the other side, leading to the upper level rooms. She stepped into the brightly lit silver metallic box, when it had arrived, and after pressing the fourth floor button, the doors closed automatically.

A few moments later, the lift doors opened

again onto a long corridor with dozens of brown wooden doors. Just outside the elevator, Harriet used a sign on the wall to direct her towards her room number. She walked down the almost silent corridor, looking for her room, and as is always typical, her room was the last one, at the far end of the corridor.

The key worked perfectly and shortly after, Harriet had placed her bag on the floor near the door and was now sitting on the edge of her hotel bed, alone and extremely full of remorse at what had transpired between her and Freda.

It was not only the fight that consumed her thoughts but she had just been made aware that Justin now knew everything. She pondered on what thoughts were playing on his mind. She contemplated on what he might have done when he got the news and what feelings he now held towards her. She did not expect him to be understanding about it all but she hoped he would forgive her at least. She wasn't going to hold it against him if he were to decide never to want anything to do with her again.

The other major issue for Harriet was that she didn't know what to do with Peter. He had come into her world, managed to turn her against everything she had going for her, only to leave her feeling like a fool. She didn't know how she was going to deal with it, or even how she would feel if she ever saw him again. She was confused; even after getting this bombshell from Freda, she still felt she wanted him, regardless of the fact that she felt angry and hurt. Surely there had to be an explanation, she thought; she was yet to hear his side of the story.

But then, the negative stories she had heard about him began to creep back into her mind. He had a terrible history with women and maybe this was a warning to move away, leave him before things got any deeper. She was even more angry with herself that she had allowed things to go as far as they had done. Now he was probably going to move on from her, having got what he wanted.

The hotel room was reasonable and comfortable, and she was grateful. The most important thing for her was that it was warm. She hated the cold. She had been lucky to come to the UK in spring. The weather had been warming up from the bitter British winter and besides some days when it just rained endlessly, most of it was bearable. She had expected far worse, having heard the stories of the unfriendly British weather but she had been pleasantly surprised at how warm it got some days.

She was by the small desk in the room, taking out a few clothes out of her bag, when her mobile phone went. She had turned it on in the cab on the way to the hotel, and when it rang she knew instantaniously who it was. Only one person had the number to this line. She picked it up from the side cupboard, where it had been charging and answered.

"Hello," she answered, her state of melancholy evident in her voice. He picked it up straight away.

"Hi," Peter responded. "You sound really low, are you OK?"

"I'm not," She replied truthfully, with a hint of hostility.

"What's going on?" He asked, puzzled by her tone.

"I don't know Peter, maybe you need to tell me. Its all coming out of the woodwork, people telling me things that YOU should have told me!"

"What things are you talking about?" He asked, unsure whether he knew what she was talking about.

"I bet you knew what you were doing, just wanted to use and abuse me, just like you did with Freda. She told me about you two, something you failed to do!"

"What did she say to you?" Peter asked, not in any way trying to deny that it had happened.

"Everything Peter, she told me everything. And you thought I wouldn't find out. How could you think that this is something I wouldn't want to know?"

"Harriet, listen, it's not how you think. This was nowhere near what me and you have, far from it... Where are you? Are you home? I want to see you?"

"No, Peter. I don't think I want to see you right now. My head's not in the right place. You don't know the stress and humiliation you've put me through."

"Harriet, please trust me, you got this all wrong. Let me come over and we can talk about it properly."

"It's not a good time right now, Peter. I need time."

There was silence from the other end. Peter did not know how he could convince Harriet otherwise. He realised she was in a very difficult position and there was nothing he could do or say to change her mind at that particular time. He thought it best to leave her be for now.

"Ok, I won't push. But we need to talk. Can I call and check up on you later? I am worried about you." He was trying his best to defuse the situation and reassure her. He blamed himself for not having been honest with her the first time round, but yet again telling her might have not been a great idea either.

"I'll think about it." She replied and cut the call.

The phone went dead and Harriet resumed unpacking her small bag, wondering what she was going to eat that night. She would have to ask at reception for local eateries or just do a quick wonder around the area.

Her thoughts also meandered to her conversation with Peter just, whether there might have been any truth in what he was saying. Was he truly being genuine about their relationship being different from what happened between him and Freda? She knew this issue wasn't going away until she had spoken to him face to face.

Chapter 16

Justin sat quietly at his desk the following Monday morning, and even with all the will in the world to get on with his work, he was struggling to focus. His mind was so foggy and clouded with the events of the weekend that he looked like an ill man. Some in his office had noticed how ailing he appeared but no one had approached him to ask.

He spent the first part of the morning closed off, trying to bury his head in his work, but this turned out not to be the remedy to his woes. He was so slumped in a state of deep dejection that he couldn't see a way out of it. He finally decided that he had given work a try, but this situation in his private life was weighing him down heavily. It had to be resolved first, if he was ever to be himself again.

He got up from his chair and began packing his laptop into its travel bag. He still needed to speak to Lawrence, his new boss, someone he was still trying to get his head around. It was not that he disliked the guy, but it was just that he did not agree with how he had got his job. Nepotism was still very much alive in Zimbabwe and Justin was a true victim of it.

As if by coincidence, he had just finished packing and straightening out his desk, when his phone rang. He let it ring whilst he zipped his bag and casually picked up the phone from its hook.

"Justin," he answered, his tone quite subdued. He knew it was an internal call from the intermittent ring he had been giving out.

"Justin, yes, can I see you in my office right away please?" It was Lawrence.

"Yes, sure. Meant to catch up with you too."

"Well, perfect timing then. You know where I am," came the usual pompous response.

Justin placed the phone down and shook his head. He truly loathed everything about this man. He was quite the chip off the same block his uncle was made of. Sonderai was exactly the same and far worse in parts. Justin had spend many years under him, taking it all in and wishing for the day he could be free of him. Now he had two of them to deal with. Justin knew it was only a matter of time before he lost it. He did not realise at that moment that this day was the very day that this was going to happen.

He picked up his laptop bag and slowly walked towards Lawrence's office; he was in no hurry; he can wait, he thought. He got to the far end of the cubicles on the same marketing floor and turned towards one of the end offices, the one which housed the Deputy Director of Marketing. He got to the door and knocked whilst simultaneously entering the room. He did not think he had to wait for a confirmation to enter. As he did so, Lawrence looked up at him, a little surprised and rather annoyed that Justin had just walk in, but he did not comment on it.

"Justin, come on in, sit," he said, waving to a chair next to his desk. Justin pulled the chair nearest to him back and sat down on it. "Right," Lawrence continued." I have a job that I would like you to do for me. I am sure you are going to like this."

Lawrence paused, adjusted his suit jacket and tie and leaned forward, resting both his elbows on the desk and interlocking his fingers in front of his face.

"I would like you to travel to Mutare for me. The Eastern Highlands departments have not been performing well and I need someone of your calibre to go down there and look into it for us. It's a great opportunity to move out of head office for a bit and see how the company works as a whole. All expenses will be covered as usual of course."

Justin's face registered some confusion, he had never been asked to do this before. He could not understand what Lawrence was trying to pull but he knew this was not a genuine offer of any advantage to him. The timing, above all, could not have been more wrong.

"Lawrence, I......," he tried to speak, but did not finish his sentence as Lawrence interrupted him.

"I know you might have not planned for

this, but consider it a great way to build up your career to the next level. Imagine this, you go to a struggling region, fix it up, help them get back into action and who knows what that will do for your CV."

"Lawrence, I don't think I can do that right now." Justin declined.

Lawrence looked at him intensely, perturbed by his response. He moved from resting his arms on the desk and sat back in his executive leather chair.

"And why not, might I ask?" Lawrence asked, suggesting that what he had said should not have been objected to really.

"Like I said on the phone, I wanted to see you even before you rang me. I need some personal time away, an emergency leave of absence. I have a few personal matters that need my urgent attention," Justin spoke, displaying how down and depressed he was with what was happening in his life at that time.

Lawrence did not speak for a moment, considering what Justin had just said. He sat forward again and rested his elbows on his desk, as he had been before.

"Well, this puts things in an awkward position. I understand that you might be going through some personal situations right now, Justin, but this is very short notice and I think your work should come first at this point, don't you?"

Justin could not believe what he was hearing. He could feel the anger starting to swell up inside him. How very dare this man to try and insinuate that work was more important than the lives of its employees. He was disgusted and knew he had to work hard to keep himself calm.

"I don't agree, Lawrence," he started, calmly." I have very serious issues that are stopping me from giving my undivided attention to the job right now. I can't work or be myself until I get it all sorted. I need time away to do this, at least 2 weeks. Are you telling me you are refusing me this?"

"Two weeks?!" Lawrence snapped." At such short notice? Come on Justin, I have a department to run here, and right now I need everyone on their post doing what needs to be done. This situation of yours will have to wait. You can apply for the leave and I will consider it for the near future but right now, I need you to be in the Eastern Highlands by tomorrow, and that's my final word."

Justin was usually understanding and had put work ahead of his personal life on many occasions. Usually he would have dropped everything and gone; he loved the challenge of problem solving within the organisation, as it increased his experience and knowledge, but this was different.

He sensed that not only was Lawrence trying to ship him out of Harare, for God knows how long, but he was clearly only doing it to throw his weight around. Justin knew from the moment that Lawrence took the job that he would be coming after him. Lawrence would have come into the job with knowledge of Justin's reputation at Glenson & Glenson, as a grafter, and surely his first mission would have been to get rid of him. Lawrence's mantra was; if you are going to be the brightest light in the room, then it is best to turn off all others.

Justin was now sweating from trying to keep his cool. He never liked this man from the moment he met him and he knew it would not have been long before they were at each other's throats. Justin's tolerance levels were very low on this day and he was already starting to disintegrate.

"I have sacrificed a lot of myself for this company, long before you showed up. Now you come out of nowhere, with help from your uncle and think you know how to run this place. You are out of your depth man, and I should be sitting where you are sitting right now. Now don't try and show off or else I will turn this whole place against you and we'll see what you do then!" Justin said, fuming, and feeling incandescent at the way he was being treated. He had lost all control and his frustrations had just taken over.

Lawrence got up from his seat, now also charged up."What did you say to me! What the hell did you say to me? Who do you think you are. Know your place, man. Now if you want to keep your job, I suggest you get out of my office and do as you are told; and that's me being very generous right now, on account of whatever it is that's going on with you!"

Lawrence expected Justin to muzzle up and obey, but today was certainly not the day.

"You know what," Justin said, as he got up from his chair, still blazing with anger," I am sick of you, sick of your uncle and I am sick of this place. You can keep your bloody job, but be warned, next time you hear of me, it's going to be a whole new ball game." He grabbed his bag and went for the door.

"Don't you threaten me!" Lawrence shouted after him." You don't get to quit! I decide when you go! YOU ARE FIRED! GET OUT! GET OUT!"

Justin was already outside the door and he

slammed it as he left, rousin the whole office floor. Everyone got up and looked in the direction of the back offices trying to work out what the commotion was all about. From that direction they saw a charged up Justin fly down the isle towards his cubicle. He got to it and did the unexpected! Like a bull in a pottery shop, he angrily swiped all the contents off his desk on to the floor, pushed over a filling cabinet and kicked his desk over, before casually walking towards the doors and exited the floor.

A couple of days later Justin's Nissan Sunny sedan raced from the city via the Seke Road towards Graniteside Industrial Area. It then took a couple of turns and was now heading towards the Harare International Airport. He was driving but was not alone in the vehicle. Ken sat next to him on the passenger seat and as always, Ken was chewing his ear off.

"Seriously bro, I can't believe she did this to you man. After all the years together, the time you gave her and everything you two have been through together. I just can't believe it."

Justin did not reply. His mind was on the journey ahead. He was already thinking about what he was going to do once he got to London and what Harriet would say once they were face to face. Well, he hoped she would want to see him; she owed him that at least.

"Now you are having to fly all that way after her. For what man? She made her bed, let her lie in it. You can find someone else, move on. You don't need her!" Ken added.

"Ken!" Justin shouted to get him to stop. "Leave it man. It's not your concern. I will sort it."

"Sort it? Sort it? Nothing to sort out here man. She is a two timing slug, a real …."

"Ken! Seriously man, you don't want to go there. Stay out of it!"

"I am on your side man. What're you getting all tangled for?" He was relentless.

"I don't need you calling her names." Justin defended Harriet." I don't care what has happened, I won't have anyone talk bad about her. There is a reason this is happening and I just need her to talk to me face to face."

Ken eased off for a bit. They were not far from the airport now. Justin had asked Ken to come to the airport, not only to see him off, but he wanted Ken to drive his car back to his flat. Parking at the airport was extortionate.

"She better be worth it, all this flying around you are doing for her. Hope she appreciates it."

"That's all I am hoping for," Justin replied, more calmly. "I just want a chance to talk to her."

"She has to talk to you. And that Peter Chuma, you need to punch that girlie face of his. Don't care who he is. He can't come in and take people's women just because he's loaded."

"Ken, you talk rubbish man! Just leave it. I don't think Harriet is that cheap. Give her some credit."

They arrived at the departures terminal and jumping out of the car, Justin opened the boot and grabbed a small travel bag. Ken had also got out and they gave each other a quick hug before Justin made a beeline for the terminal entrance.

"See you in a few days. I'll call you to pick me up," he shouted as he disappeared into the terminal.

Chapter 17

Freda's apartment door shook violently, threatening to come off its hinges, as it was subjected to some vigorous pounding from the outside. The perpetrator was determined to communicate urgency, deep frustration and lack of patience to the occupant of the house. The door mat on which the aggressor stood ironically had the words 'Welcome' inscribed on it, but this might have not been applicable to the visitor. It did not appear that whatever the issue was, it would end in a peaceful and civilised manner.

Freda unlocked and opened the door, packing a face that conveyed disapproval of her property being violated in this manner, but the visitor cared less about her feelings; that was the least of their concerns. With the door open, Peter stormed into the apartment, grabbed Freda by the throat with both hands and pushed her into the interior wall adjacent to the front door entrance.

"WHO THE HELL DO YOU THINK YOU ARE!" he bellowed into her face.

Freda froze in shear terror at Peter's aggressiveness. She had never seen him this angry.

"WHO... DO YOU THINK.... YOU ARE!" He barked at her, as he poked her on the forehead with his other hand.

"Peter! Stop, please!" Freda cried out, blanketed by pure dread. She wasn't sure how far he was willing to go and what he would do next. She knew why he was there and why he was so enraged.

"SHUT UP!" He screamed, kicking the front door to close it. He did not want to take the chance of a passerby witnessing what he had come to do. "Who gave you the right to get involved in my business? Huh? Why did you tell her? Why would you even talk about it to anyone? I told you never to speak of it, ever!"

"I'm sorry!" she said, crying. He had started to loosen his tight grip on her throat.

"Why did you do it? Especially when I specifically told you never to disclose this to anyone?" He was still standing right in front of her, trapping her.

"Why her!?"she screamed back. "How could you start seeing my friend from right under my nose? How did you think it would make me feel?"

"Why would me seeing Harriet be of any concern to you? You and me were never in any kind of relationship. I was never attracted to you and I told you."

"But you were attracted enough to sleep with me. WHY?! You just wanted to use me?" she challenged him.

"I didn't force you Freda! You were the one throwing yourself at me, desperate to be with me. I never loved you then, and I will never be in any kind of relationship with you."

He had now stepped back from her but still near the entrance.

"YOU BASTARD!" She screamed at him. "You horrible monster! You have no conscience. You think you can just use people and dump them like trash!"

"I don't owe you anything Freda. You knew what the score was but you kept coming. I did not make you do anything, you chose whatever happened to you." He said, his voice sounding so cold.

"Get out of my house, GET OUT NOW! If you don't leave, I'm calling the police and telling them you hit me, and attempted to rape me. I will ruin you with one phone call," she threatened.

"Ruin me? You? You've got to be kidding me. Just try it. Unless you want your life to be a living nightmare, just go ahead and do it. Go on, DO IT!"

She did not move but glared at him, wishing all manner of evil upon him. She knew she was powerless to do anything.

"You will pay for this. I promise you, you will! No one uses me and gets away with it. Everyone will know about this and everything you did to me."

"You are mad, properly screwed up. You are no different from the hundreds of groupies who line up to sleep with me. You had your fifteen minutes, now your time is up. And ye, one more thing, if you ever disclose my affair with you, I will sue you.

You think those expensive gifts were because I liked you?"

"That has nothing to do with anything. You were the one buying me gifts. I never asked for them, and now you want to sue me, sue me for what?"

"You signed a non-disclosure contract. If you ever mention this to anyone again, I will take all of this away from you." He said, gesturing to the apartment and her belongings.

"I never signed such a document! You have never asked me to sign anything like that. Are you going out of your mind?"

Peter laughed loudly. "You should really read things before signing them. Did you ever look closely at the delivery notes when you signed the gold necklace from the carrier. That was someone I hired to make you sign a non disclosure contract. He showed you the top sheet and made you sign the bottom."

Her eyes opened wide in shock and her jaw dropped. She was still trying to process how conniving he had been.

"You are sick!" She growled at him. "A sick, rabies infested dog! That's illegal and I will deny signing it."

"You can deny it all you like but I have 'witnesses'. You'll never win. Now I'm warning you again, if you ever disclose anything else to anyone, I'll pull you through the courts so fast that you'll only be left with the dress on your back, and that's if I choose to let you keep it."

He pulled out a copy of the falsified document from his jacket pocket and gave it to her, accompanied by another warning before making his exit.

"Now listen and you listen good," he said pointing aggressively at her, "I don't want to you anywhere near me, my house, anything with my name on it, and especially anywhere near Harriet. I don't care what you think we had, but never, EVER, interfere in my relationships again. Here's you copy, happy reading." He threw the contract onto the floor, turned towards the door and left the apartment.

Freda picked up the contract and flipped to the last page, and in clear black permanent ink, she saw what she instantly recognised as her signature. Reading it confirmed what he had told her. She ripped the document to shreds and threw it in the kitchen bin. She could not believe how he had been so vicious with her, with no regard for her feelings whatsoever. She blamed Harriet for this. Peter had always been nice to her before she showed up.

London was not as cold as Justin had thought it would be when he stepped out of Gatwick Airport arrivals terminal. He kept his thick coat on though; it was warm but not sub Saharan warm, weather he was used to. He was glad he had arrived safely as he had never been one for flying. He had been to London before, on Glenson & Glenson business, an exchange partnership program with another UK distributing firm. This was also the reason why his entry through customs had been swift. He was viewed as a genuine traveller, having gone back the first time, unlike others who came in as visitors and disappeared, never to return to their home countries.

He had made the impulsive decision to change the trajectory of his life, the very same day he had had the fiery exchange with his new boss; which incidentally was also the day he had decided he was done with Glenson & Glenson. His first task would be to get Harriet back and then return to Africa and establish what he should have started a long time ago, his own business empire. It would not be easy; he had a lot of catching up to do, but he was prepared for whatever it was going to take.

He had a relative living in London, a cousin from his mother's side, also a nurse and she had accepted to host him for the days he needed to track Harriet down. He had also spoken to Freda, who was clearly disinclined to get involved, but had only agreed to let him know when Harriet was coming by to pick up her remaining possessions. Freda was to call him when she knew, and let him know where to come.

He hailed a cab from Gatwick, which had taken him to his cousin's three bedded semi-detached house in Slough. He spent the next few days trying to get hold of Harriet, and hounded Freda on a daily basis to find out if she had heard anything. It took nearly 4 days before anything started to happen. It was Harriet who called Freda, partly to organise to collect her belongings but also to apologise as she felt awful about how they had parted.

"Freda, hi, it's me," she had started.

Freda thought about putting the phone down but she too wanted this whole business done with. She wanted Harriet to pick up her belongings and also for Justin to stop hounding her.

"Hi," Freda replied, unenthusiastically. "Are you calling to arrange to pick your stuff?" She said, cutting to the chase. She was not entertaining any pleasantries.

"Yes, but not just that. I wanted to also talk to you about what happened. I just wanted to say that I am really sorry things between us ended like that. I never planned for any of this to happen."

"But it did." Freda snapped at her.

"I know, and I feel terrible over it." Harriet replied, still trying to remain humble. "Can I come over tomorrow and pick up my things. I have found accommodation near the university. And I also thought it would be a great chance to mend fences."

Freda agreed after a moment of deliberation. She wondered whether she should tell Harriet that Justin was in town but she thought it best not to. She did not want Harriet to have a reason not to show up. Besides, she wanted to enjoy seeing her face when she saw Justin there.

"Ye, come tomorrow afternoon. I'll be here. Are you still seeing him?" Freda asked, blatantly fishing for information about Harriet and Peter's affair. She had to find out.

"I haven't spoken to him since I left," she lied. She did not want to start up another fight." I am staying clear of him," This part was true.

They finished the call with a solid appointment for a meet the following afternoon, a Friday, around three o'clock. Straight after speaking to Harriet, Freda called Peter's London number and told him the news he had been waiting all week to hear. She also told him how Harriet had not spoken to Peter since she left Freda's. This pleased Justin.

"You spoke to her? She's definitely, definitely coming?" He asked excitedly.

"Yes. She wants to talk as well. So be at mine at around 3:30 in the afternoon."

Justin thanked Freda wholeheartedly for her help and put the phone down.

Harriet's taxi pulled outside Freda's flat just after three o'clock, the afternoon of the next day. She still had a key but decided to knock first before entering. She felt that even though she had lived there for a while, it didn't seem appropriate after the fight, to just walk back in as if nothing had happened. She felt a little nervous about being there. She wasn't sure whether the incident had been resolved. Freda had not given her any indication that it was over.

Harriet knocked on the door and a few moments later Freda come downstairs and opened it. She knew it was Harriet, so she opened it quickly, muttered a quick 'Hi' and walked back into the living room. She wanted Harriet to realise that there was still a lot to put right before she could be welcomed back. Harriet got the message but replied in a more pleasant tone, doing all she could to show Freda that she did not harbour any more ill feelings about the other day. Harriet wanted this done and dusted as quickly and as peacefully as possible, and if they could still remain friends after this meeting, then that would be a bonus.

"How have you been?" Harriet began, still trying to stir this awkward visit in a more positive direction.

"Alright, thanks," came the nonchalant response.

Harriet was beginning to feel strangled, but she was not willing to give up yet."Oh great," she smiled. "Still on nights?" She said, thinking that a change of subject might ease the tension.

"Ye, still doing it," Freda replied, with yet another stony response. She clearly was not ready for things to move on. It was not that she did not want to forgive Harriet, she was just finding it hard to do so. Freda had stubbornness carved right within her DNA.

Harriet paused for a moment, working out how best to proceed. She decided to talk about the incident, hoping that if she showed how remorseful she was about what happened, maybe Freda might respond to that.

"Listen, Freda, like I said the other day on the phone, I never thought things would be like this between us, especially because of a guy. I wish we could just put it all behind us and move on."

Freda had gone into the kitchen and was drying up a few dishes by the sink, trying to appear busy. She was listening as Harriet spoke and replied.

"Ye, sure. Maybe that's for the best."
The response was not wholly reassuring.

Harriet decided she had done all she could but felt she was not getting anywhere. The only thing left to do now was go upstairs and put her belongings together.

"Alright if I go upstairs and sort my stuff out?" she asked.

"Ye sure. All your things are in the box room. I put them all together for you."

"Oh…," Harriet replied, a little puzzled expression across her face. She was not sure whether this had been done in good faith, or yet another veiled message telling her that she was no longer welcome. Either way, it wasn't going to matter much after today. It was up to Freda whether they would ever talk again. Before Harriet could get upstairs, Freda decided to inform her of the pending visitor.

"I didn't know whether to tell you before you came but you have someone coming to see you."

"Someone coming to see me?" Harriet asked, quite perplexed.

"Yes, he'll be here in a bit."

Harriet's thoughts went straight to Peter. There was a strong possibility that it was him. The only thing that puzzled her was why Freda would organise for Peter to come and see her. It did not make sense. Harriet's mind then shifted to Hector, whether it might have been him coming with a message from Peter. Now that was highly plausible, she thought to herself, but she was not sure whether to ask Freda more about it.

"Who is it?" she asked.

"He should be here now," Freda answered, continuing to be sketchy with details. She was not giving anything away.

Harriet could not work out what game Freda was playing, why she was being so elusive. Harriet walked casually towards the living room bay window and peered outside to see whether anyone was in the street or coming up to the flat door. There was no one. She turned to walk back into the room but as she did, from the corner of her eye, she caught a black cab pull up to the kerb. She turned again to look outside and waited for the passenger to step out. It seemed like a long while before the back door flew open and a figure emerged.

Harriet froze with shock when she realised who had just stepped out of the black cab. She had immediately recognised him, but her mind was struggling to comprehend that it was actually him she was seeing.

She could not believe that the man she was staring at was Justin, now walking up towards the door. Still overwhelmed by the myriad of thoughts and feelings, Harriet scrambled towards the door, opened it and stood there, with both hands covering her mouth, as she watched him walk up the steps.

"JUSTIN!" She screamed.

He just smiled, got to her and picked her up into the longest embrace they had probably ever had in the whole of their relationship, truly ecstatic at being reunited. Holding on to him tightly, Harriet could not believe this was actually happening. Somehow, him being there had made her forget everything that happening. She felt safe, and she had desperately needed to feel this way.

They let go of each other, and Harriet just stood there staring at him, words failing her. All she could master was a large grin and a shake of her head in disbelief.

"Oh my God! Justin! Where have you come from?"

He gave a quiet laugh, relieved at how pleased she was to see him. He had been quite apprehensive about it, his earlier thoughts drifting into a negative space where he thought that she may have moved on, moved on so far such that he might have not been able to reach her.

"How are you here, I mean... when?" Harriet said, hardly able to contain herself.

"Got my plane Sunday and flew in Monday morning," he replied.

Harriet registered confusion. Justin had been in London for nearly 4 days and she had known nothing about it.

"You've been here since Monday?" She asked, her voice sounding her bewilderment.

"Yes. Been staying with Alice." he confirmed.

Harriet knew of Justin's cousin but she had never made any contact with her since her arrival. She had never met Alice, even before she came over to the UK, and had never found any reason to. Justin had talked about Alice before Harriet left for England and even gave Harriet her contact details, just in case she ever needed them; the need never arose. Even when Harriet had had the fight with Freda, she preferred to pay for a hotel room rather than knock on yet another person's door.

They had eventually managed to make it into the house and Freda came to greet Justin. They had only spoken over the phone but had not actually met since his arrival. They too were also seeing each other after quite a considerable number of years. They spoke of how they had both changed and grown much older. The conversation between the three of them had seemed normal for a while but each would occasionally drift to the current predicament. It was tense and awkward from time to time, but they all tried to be civil about it.

Harriet felt that there would be no way she would be comfortable talking to Justin at Freda's. She had to get him to a space she had control over and then begin to address what had occurred between them. She was not looking forward to having this conversation though. He was here now, face to face, and she was going to have to tell him all about what had happened, coming directly from her, the way it was supposed to have been done the first time. She was going to have to explain why it had happened and why she had let someone else deliver the news. The prospect of that conversation drained her of all positivity.

But she still didn't know how she truly felt with everything the way it was. She couldn't convince herself of what she really wanted, or how she wanted things to be. She was not done with Peter yet; she had simply told him to give her time. Harriet had not counted on Justin coming in London, but he was here. She had to make up her mind, and make it up fast. What was she going to tell him? Was it over between them or was him being there, a game changer.

Harriet flicked the lights on, in the entrance hall of her student accommodation hostel, and pulled the key out of the door as they both entered the room. This was the university accommodation she had managed to secure, which housed 4 students, each with their own room but shared the lounge, kitchen and bathroom. As the next semester had not started, Harriet was the only one there, an arrangement she had negotiated with the university, after things rapidly changed in her living situation with Freda. The term was beginning in a few weeks and the other students would join her then.

She was grateful that the place was quiet especially with Justin being in town. They had quite a lot of issues to discuss and it seemed more appropriate for them to be alone. They had picked up another cab from Freda's and drove the half hour journey to Harriet's new home for the year.

They had not spoken much in the taxi but had only commented generally about the differences between life in the UK and life back home. Harriet told him how much she missed home and how she hoped to fly down at the end of her first year.

After putting Harriet's bags in her room, they both went downstairs to the kitchen and started to make plans of what they were going to eat that night. Although they were trying to be as normal as they could, there was a difference in how they were interacting with each other. There was an intimacy they used to share that seemed to have diminished a little. It was not that they had stopped caring for each other but it was as though they were being cautious not to add more strain to the situation between them.

Justin sat on one of the chairs by the dining

table whilst Harriet went through the cupboards and fridge to try and see if she could find ingredients to rustle up a meal for them. Harriet was doing all she could to keep busy, trying everything to defer from getting into the deeper conversation they were yet to have. She knew that he wanted answers and she was going to have to engage him at some point; he had not flown all this way for a vacation.

"You know what, I haven't even done any proper shopping since I got here," she confessed.

"Really?"he responded

"Ye. Just been busy trying to put things together for uni. I've been living on takeaway for the past week."

"That's got to be seriously unhealthy," he challenged her, laughing.

"Don't judge," she defended herself, turning towards him."You never cook either. Don't forget I know you too well."

He gave a half smile, quite evident that he still had a lot on his mind. The issue between them was yet to be mooted. Harriet got out a pack of diced beef and cracked open the plastic film on top of the packaging, before dropping all the contents into a sauce-pan. She placed the pan onto the gas hob and added a little bit of water, before covering the pan with its lid. She reached over the counter and picked up a half cut piece of whole onion she had discovered in the fridge, and stood by the chopping board dicing it.

Justin, who had been sitting quietly for a few minutes in deep thought, got up from his chair and walked towards her. He went behind her and gently slid his arms around her waist, and also placed his chin on her right shoulder. She froze!

They had done this so many times at his flat back home but for some reason in that moment, it felt strange. She did not flinch or move away, afraid that he might misread it as her not wanting him. It felt lovely to be held by him again; it was familiar and gentle, but now quite different. For the first time ever in their relationship, she felt as though she was being held by a stranger. She was confused.

She had stopped cutting the onion and stood there, as he started running his hands around her body and kissing her neck. She did not know whether to go with it or stop it. He was obviously trying to rekindle things between them, but she was not sure that this was the way to go about it.

With all those thoughts flying through her head, Harriet turned to face him and put her hand on his chest as if to block him.

"Justin, listen, I think we need to talk first." She said. She had never felt suffocated by him before.

He signed heavily and stepped back. He had anticipated that she might react this way, but he had hoped that seeing each other might have helped move things on, back to how they had always been. He felt slightly rejected by her actions.

"I'm really happy you are here," she continued. "That is the last thing I ever expected. Can't believe you flew all this way for me."

"What option did I have, Harriet? I really don't understand what is happening." There was heavy concern in his voice and on his face.

"Justin, please, I need you to understand that what happened to me was nothing to do with you and not something I purposely planned to happen. I got myself twisted in this situation and instead of reminding myself about us, I simply allowed myself to go with it. I truly don't know how to even explain it to you."

He did not respond but just kept his gaze on her. He wanted her to say something that would reassure him but he wasn't getting it. A major part of him had hoped that being there would have knocked some sense into her head but she seemed uncertain. He was not soothed to hear that she was unsure of how it had happened, and he was even more concerned that she wasn't talking about ending things with Peter.

"So what are you telling me then? We're engaged Harriet, remember? What does all this mean now?" he asked.

"I don't know!" She said, almost in tears. "Even I want to understand what is going on too. I don't like where I am and what is happening to us. Before I left home I was clear about where I was going and our future was clear in my head. Now I'm just all confused and I can't even work out why."

"You are confused about us?" He asked.

"No, not really. I'm just confused about where I am and what I want."

"Are you having doubts about us? Do you want it to be truly over between us?"

"I'm not saying that. I'm just confused at the moment. I just need time, just some time to work things out in my head."

Justin felt the door closing in on him, the feeling of being shut out. He had never heard Harriet talk like this before. Whatever had happened to her had really changed something very fundamental within her. He too was now very confused and unsure whether their relationship could ever be salvaged.

"You don't realise what this is doing to me Harriet. You don't even know how broken I was when Sandra told me about what you did. How could you betray me like that?"

She could not answer. The guilt ripped through her like a laser beam through soft matter. She could not look up at him.

"Please!" she begged him," Let's not talk about it."

"We need to," he insisted. "How else are we going to work out where we go from here?"

"I've told you already. I don't know what else to tell you." She said, genuinely getting quite distressed by the conversation now. Tears welled up in her eyes and began to flow down the side of her face.

Justin signed heavily again and turned away from her. He sat back by the table and buried his face in his hands. He had come all this way and he was not getting the answers he had hoped for. He could not understand how she was confused about them. They had been together for a long time and there had never been any doubt or even a shadow of a doubt about their future together. Now, thousands of miles away from home, they faced what could possibly be the final moments of their lives together.

Harriet dried her eyes and wiped her face with the sleeve of her blouse. She washed her hands and carried on preparing food; the silence between them continued. They both locked themselves in their thoughts for most of that evening and sometimes would delve back into conversation about their predicament, but the talk remained the same.

They eventually ate but even the food found it difficult to navigate down their throats, as it normally would. It was a surreal moment for the both of them.

After their dinner, they had both gone up to Harriet's bedroom to watch some television. She had managed to get a small 30 inch TV for her room, one of the few basic furnishings she had sourced. They both lay on top of the covers for a while, still fully dressed as they had been in the day, quietly fixated on the TV show they had stumbled upon. This seemed to ease the silence between them and gave them something else to focus on.

However, Harriet was not concentrating much on the show, and neither was Justin really. She was reviewing everything that had happened and how Justin had come to be lying next to her, a great sacrifice on his part and a huge sign that he truly loved her. She felt for him and again cursed herself for what she was doing to him. She turned slowly and looked at him. She wanted to remind herself of what had drawn her to him in the first place. She so wanted to find that spark that had pulled them together, that very first time she had laid eyes on him.

Justin noticed her looking at him and also turned to look at her. For a moment they just stared at each other, and even though no words were spoken, a lot was said. Harriet knew that it was now on her, her turn to try and make up; the next move was hers. He had made a serious gesture of his love for her by flying all this way. Now it needed her to do her bit and meet him halfway.

She sat up on the bed and kept her gaze on him. She knew what she had to do to make it up to him, but she was not sure how he was going to respond. Harriet made her move regardless and slowly began leaning towards him, then kissed him. Justin did not need asking twice, responding by hooking his arm around her and pulled her whole body on top of him.

They kissed, passionately, for a while longer after that, both trying to unlock the deep feelings they had always felt for each other. That night, they slept well. What had happened at the end of that evening seemed to be what they both needed, a chance to bond again. In the few days that followed, before Justin flew back, it had felt like everything had gone back to how it had always been.

Chapter 18

Justin felt the familiar sub-Saharan heat hit his face as he stepped out of the Boeing 747 and walked down the stairs to the airport tarmac. Zimbabwe International Airport did not have passenger tunnels that led from the aeroplane to the arrival terminal, so passengers had to take a little walk across the airport apron into the main terminal building. It was early morning and the Airport was not busy. Flights usually departed at night and this was when most people came to bid farewell to their loved ones, whilst others lingered and waited for arrivals.

He felt a little strange being back. He had had this feeling before, the first time he had been out of the country. Somehow being away in a foreign environment changed his perspective of his normal environment. For a brief moment after arrival, even the familiar felt different and it took him a while to get reoriented. He had only been away for a week and a half but that was still enough to still appreciate the differences of the two worlds. London was more grey and dull, whilst Harare felt more orange and cheerful. London was more structured and organised, everything constructed to be of convenience for its citizens, something that Harare and Zimbabwe as a whole lacked.

Moments later, after going through customs effortlessly, Justin had left the main arrivals terminal building and walked towards his car, where Ken was sitting and waiting as they had planned. It was the end of August and winter was clocking out, after having bitterly tormented people for months. He was glad to be home though.

"Hey London boy!" Ken said excitedly, as Justin jumped into the passenger seat.

"Hey!" Justin replied, he too excited, their hands came together in a high shake followed by a quick 'man hug'.

"How was the trip? Journey good? Got it all sorted?" Ken asked, as he negotiated the car out of the parking lot and onto the exit road.

"It was good, thanks. Saw her, we talked. We were together for the last 2 days. Ye, all went well." Justin said smiling. He was convinced that his trip had been a success.

"Serious? That's good then. At least you got it sorted."

"We did," he replied. Justin didn't want to give away too much. He was happy to have spent the last couple of days with Harriet and hoped that the past was now all water under the bridge. The only thing that still troubled him was that he had left her there. He would have wanted to bring her home; be somewhere where they could both function better. All he could do now was place his hopes and prayers on the next two years flying by quickly, and without another hitch, so that she could return to him.

"Man, you kicked up a storm at Glenson & Glenson. Everyone is still talking," Ken remarked, shaking his head.

"Really?" Justin turned excitedly to face his friend.

"Oh ye! You should have seen old Sonderai when he heard what you said to Lawrence," Ken said laughing. "He spent the whole day huffing and puffing. Some poor souls got tortured in your name that day."

They both laughed. Justin wasn't pleased to hear that some of his colleagues had suffered that day but he enjoyed hearing how Sonderai had lost his marbles over it.

"It's a good job you left when you did though, because there was a rumour that they were planning to destroy you, your reputation. This move to the Eastern Highlights would have been your downfall," Ken added.

"Seriously!" Justin asked, shocked.

"Yep. They were going to send you to a branch riddled with problems and blame you for every failure there after."

"No way! Serious? The sneaky bastards!" Justin responded, further unnerved by the extent at which Sonderai and Lawrence were willing to go. "Well, they ain't seen nothing yet. I am going to rip through that place, piece by piece. Sonderai should never forget I know all the shady dealings he has done in the past. If he tries to tarnish my name in any way, then he better be ready for battle." Justin's anger and disdain was evident as he spoke.

"So what are going to do now man. What's the plan."

Justin stared outside his passenger window at the buildings rushing past. He knew exactly what he wanted to do and how he was going to do it. He had never considered that he would ever resign from Glenson & Glenson. He had always been careful never to do anything to jeopardise his job. But it was done, his next move was clear and he knew what he needed to do. It had never been so clear before.

"Ken, it's now our turn to take over, buddy." he began, still looking out the window. "It's our turn now to take control and run this town. We are going out on our own and establishing one of the biggest distribution companies this country has ever seen. And you are coming with me all the way bro." He turned to face Ken at end, as if to look him in the eye to prove how serious he was.

"Really?" Ken asked, quite exhilarated at the prospect.

"Absolutely! Are you ready to come with me. Are you prepared to sacrifice everything for a chance to own a piece of this dream?"

Ken was struck by the confident manner in which Justin spoke. He believed in his friend's ability to deliver on his word and he had no reason to doubt him. This was going to be a big step, leaving a secure job for the unknown, but he was intrigued.

He did not hesitate with his response.

"Of course man. You know I've been waiting for this, for a very long time. Let's do it!"

Although Ken was still driving, they managed to shake on it, and the deal was sealed.

Justin had mapped it all out on his way back, as he had hours to kill on the plane. The thought of going back to Glenson & Glenson, begging for his job, had ceased to be an option now. He was done with all that, and wanted to show them how much of an asset they had actually lost.

A couple of months after his return, the formation stages of Justin's new company had gained significant ground, now registered and ready to start operating. He was pleased on his success with negotiations with his bank, how he had managed to win them over with his elaborate business plans. It was not just his plans they had been pleased with but it was also his confident manner and business references from his clients, that he had acquired and added to the pot.

He sat in his car, outside a vacant block of offices, waiting for the estate agent to come and show him around. He had seen the offices being advertised in the business section of the local paper, The Herald, and the pictures had captivated him. He could see this as being his headquarters, not too big for now but big enough to look like a business that knew where it was going.

The agent was late but it did not bother him much; it was only a few minutes past the agreed time. He picked up a brown envelope that was on the passenger seat and pulled out the letter within. It was from the Companies House, where new businesses registered.

He read the letter again, having read it earlier, this time taking more time to absorb more detail. He was pleased that the name he had chosen, his first choice on the list, had been available for use, Harstin Distribution LTD.

As he folded the letter and put it back into the envelope, there was a tap on the window next to him. He turned to look, and standing outside was a lanky white male, aged probably in his fifties, scruffy beard and an old tired beige suit. Justin got out of the vehicle.

"Mr Sangala?" The man said, stretching out to shake Justin's hand.

"Yes, that's right," Justin replied, as he accepted the hand shake.

"This way, please. I'll show you around the place. Are you alone today?"

"Thank you. My partner is a little late but he will be joining us soon, I hope," Justin replied.

"That's alright, we can always come back for him." The old man said.

They walked towards the glass entrance door, then the agent began fumbling through a large bunch of keys he had, to find the one he needed. He found it and unlocked the large doors. Once opened, the doors lead into a large open area which formed the first part of the office suite.

"This is a large open plan area, which you

can use as reception and can be partitioned into smaller offices," the elderly estate agent informed him.

Justin nodded, as he scanned the layout. "Yes, I can see that," he agreed.

They walked around somemore, as Justin tried and tested windows, fixtures and lighting. The estate agent just stood behind, observing.

"So you said you are looking for space with a lot of storage capacity in our conversation over the phone?" the old man asked.

"Yes, that's correct. I am starting a distribution company," Justin replied.

"Oh great! This place is definitely right for that type of business. Let's go round the back and I'll show you the loading bays and warehouse."

As they went round the back, Justin's phone rang.

"Excuse me," he said to the agent, who just nodded to confirm.

"Hi, I'm outside. Are you in already?" Came Ken's voice over the phone.

"Yes, you' re late. We will let you in," Justin laid into him, to make a point.

Justin informed the agent of his partner's arrival and the old man hobbled towards the front door and let Ken in. They returned to where Justin was and together they walked into the warehouse.

"Now, this is what I am talking about bro!" Ken whispered excitedly. "This is the beginning of an empire. By the time Harriet comes back, she will be so impressed with you bro."

"That's why I am doing all this, man. This is our future right here. Hey, I even got the name I wanted for it."

"They approved Harstin Distribution?"

"Yes, they did. They approved it. All checks went in and there was no other company with that name." Justin said, with a big grin on his face.

"That is so cool, man. It's all falling into place. Have you told Harriet yet, about everything?"

"No I haven't. Didn't want her to start worrying about me leaving Glenson & Glenson. Besides, I want all this to be a surprise for her when she comes back."

"She's going to be over the moon, bro. We are going to build this thing from the ground up, and take down a few giants along the way"

They both laughed and continued to wonder around the premises. They liked it. They even chose their offices, with Justin naturally securing the largest. This was his business but had given Ken the chance to own a small stake and help run it as partners. A few staff from Glenson & Glenson had also contacted them to defect and join their new venture. There was still one person Justin wanted to compliment his staff team and he was going to contact them straight after the viewing. The office space and warehouse were perfect, so Justin signed the lease agreement and immediately after, had made the call to secure the last person he needed to come on board.

"Hello Glenson & Glenson, can I help you?" came the familiar voice. It was Florence, the management personal assistant.

"Hi Flo, it's Justin. How are you?"

"Oh my God, Justin," she whispered, but pleased to hear his voice."How are you? We all miss you here so much,"

"I'm good thanks. How is old man

Sonderai? Has he been beside himself since I left him?"

She laughed quietly. "He hasn't stopped crying," she joked. "So you left, no proper goodbye to me. Where are you now and what are you up to?"

"I am so sorry my dear, it was rushed, as you probably heard, but I'm still in town. I called because I need you. This is a serious hush hush situation though, so please, if you are happy to come on board I'll be so chuffed. If not then I'm gonna ask you to keep this one to yourself. Are you ok with that?"

"A-ah Justin, you know me, we have been friends for a long time. I can definitely keep a secret. What's on your mind?"

"Oh good," he said, smiling. "Flo I want you to come and join my new team. I'm starting my own distribution company. We just signed the lease to our new offices and we are ready to go."

"Oh my God, really?" Florence answered, a little surprised. She hadn't expected that he would start his own rival company, especially this soon after leaving. She was pleased though that he would even consider her to join him. There was a lot she had to think about, as this meant leaving a very secure job, a job she had kept for years.

"I know it is a big step Flo, but I promise you this is a great opportunity. I want you to come lead my admin team, and I know it will grow. As the company grows, you'll also rise and in a few years, you'll be doing more management work. I have seen you work Flo and I know you hold all those top bosses together. You know far more than they do. They rely on you for everything, but I also know they don't value you as much as I will."

Justin was playing a very strong hand. He knew if he secured Florence, he would have tapped into the minds of the top Glenson & Glenson bosses. She was invaluable and she would bring in a lot of expertise to his new company.

"Justin…," she said, and paused as if she were about to drop a bomb on him."I have been waiting for an opportunity to bring this house down. For all the years I have given them, what have I got to show for it. You can count me in. When do you need me?"

Justin beamed with joy and banged his dashboard with excitement. "That's what I'm talking about," he exclaimed. "OK, right, now listen, don't leave just yet. Put in your notice but don't tell them where you are going. Over the next few months, just gather as much information as you can that you can bring with you. Every detail, and also the full G&G client list. I don't need to say much."

"OK. I know what to do. Leave it with me."

They finished their conversation and Justin turned to Ken, who sat on the passenger seat of his car.

"It's done bro!" he said, with the biggest grin spread across his face."Another vital piece secured."

"It's done!" Ken reciprocated, raising his hand for a 'high five'. They 'high fived' and Ken left Justin's car straight after.

They would meet several times more in the coming days to finalise the launch date and start knocking on client doors. Justin was so confident about the success of his new venture.

He had brought quite a considerable number

of customers to Glenson & Glenson, clients who believed in his abilities and were ready to do business with him, no matter where he ended up. He was going to start with those and once he had secured that client list, he would then set his eyes on more of Glenson & Glenson's client base.

Chapter 19

Harriet turned the shower tap off and the whooshing sound of the water hitting the shower floor came to a sudden stop. She grabbed handfuls of her long black hair extensions and squeezed out all the excess water, before untangling it again. She reached out for a long towel through the gap between the shower curtain and the wall, and dried the rest of her body.

She stepped out of the shower, towel now covering her from the top of her breasts to the middle of her thighs, and stood by the sink facing the small mirror above it. She scanned her face looking for any blemishes, spots or blackheads. Satisfied that there was none to worry about, she picked another mid sized towel, which she used to further dry her hair before wrapping the towel tightly on her head, like some type of middle eastern cultural head gear.

She walked from the shared bathroom into her bedroom and went to sit at the foot of the bed. She grabbed a bottle of cocoa butter lotion, which she had placed on the bed earlier, and spent the next few minutes applying the lotion all over her body. In the corner of the room, the TV was switched on and tuned to the news channel. She was not particularly focusing on it but was able to pick up bits here and there.

'And now we move to the sports desk, where Jason Brown will take us through the highlights of the day' the anchor announced.

'Thanks Mark' came in the sports presenter. 'It was quite an eventful day at Old Trafford yesterday when the two giants Chelsea and Manchester United clashed in a friendly match. This has been something the fans have been waiting for. We caught up with their foreign striker, Peter Chuma, after the match, to get his views'.

The television transitioned to another clip and Peter's face appeared on the screen. Harriet was stunned seeing his face on her television that her heart stopped beating, just for second or two. As Peter spoke to the reporter, Harriet became transfixed to the screen as though she had gone into a trance. Like someone under a voodoo spell she couldn't disengage herself from it. Seeing him and hearing him talk, took her back to that place she was trying to run away from.

She watched the interview as it progressed. He was even more poised and professional on TV, confident in manner; a confidence that impressed her. Even just looking at his jaw line as he spoke, sent pleasant sensations through her body.

As if to gain her control back, she picked up

the remote and switched the TV off. The room went silent and also a little dark. The TV had been helping to improve the lighting in the room. It was early morning and although the sun was out, she had not opened the curtains all the way as yet.

She got up, still wrapped in her towels and picked up her mobile phone from the dresser. There had been eight calls to her phone that she hadn't picked up and they had all originated from the same person, Peter. She looked at his name on her screen and contemplated her next step. She was going to have to talk to him at some point; but what would she say?

Justin flying out to see her had been such a welcome and pleasant surprise, but it had not made the situation any easier for her. She had already started to develop entirely new feelings for another man, Peter, something she had never considered would be a possibility. It had happened and now she had to make a choice; a choice between what was comfortable and familiar, or something new and possibly exciting. Yes, there was still the issue that Peter had not disclosed having slept with Freda, but Harriet had concluded that this had happened way before her time. Peter and Freda had never been together formally as a couple, so what if he slept with her? Harriet surmised that it might have been Freda who had made all the moves on him, all in an effort to get him to like her. And if it had worked and he liked her back, then they would have been together right now.

All these thoughts circled through Harriet's mind. She was further worried that Justin had flown back home thinking that everything was resolved between them. She had done her best to make him welcome and not to feel as though his journey had been a waste. She owed him that at least, but she also knew she had not been wholly truthful to him or to herself.

It was not that her feelings for Justin had completely vanished, and neither was she ready to jump back straight into Peter's arms, but she couldn't decide what she really wanted.

Without allowing time to talk herself out of it, Harriet pressed Peter's name on her phone and it dialled him instantly. Three rings went by and it seemed as though he was unavailable to pick up. She grew more nervous, she wanted to talk to him, but was also anxious about going into it all with him. There was a click that interrupted the ringing sound and Peter's voice came through.

"Hey," He answered, a feeling of relief in his voice.

"Hi," she replied, but found nowhere else to take the conversation.

"Are you OK?" He asked

"Ye, ye I'm fine. You?"

"I'm OK now. I have been trying you for days."

"I know," she cut him off. "I had some things to sort out."

"I know," he replied.

"You do?" She asked surprised, not knowing how much he actually knew.

"I mean, I know you had to deal with your fiancé. I heard that he came over."

Harriet did not have to ask how he knew. If Freda knew, then that meant Hector also knew about it, and if Hector knew, Peter would have eventually found out.

She had not thought about it for some reason. She wondered whether it was worth being upset about it. He seemed to have her under his radar all the time and part of her did not like this. She decided that this was a lesser battle to fight, considering the bigger issue at hand.

Peter sensed that she might have not appreciated him knowing that part of her business, but he still decided to ask her about it. He had a vested interest in this deal.

"Did it go OK?" He asked.

"What do you mean?"

"How did things end between you? What's the situation now?"

Peter was so desperate to hear Harriet say that it was over with Justin and that she was now totally ready to be with him. Harriet decided to delay answering his question and make him sweat a little.

"Peter, why do you like me? What is it about me that you really find you can't get anywhere else?" she asked, bluntly.

Peter was stunned by the question. He had not anticipated that she would ask him that.

"Well," he began, pausing to make sure he had the right words. "Truth is Harriet, if I told you I knew what draws me to you, I would be lying. I don't know what it is about you, but all I know is that I want to be with you. I have never felt this way for any woman, ever!"

"How do I know all this is true? What if this is something I will regret for the rest of my life?" She continued, with a firm, unperturbed voice. This was her future she had to consider; she was not about to let anyone mess with that.

"I wish I could convince you of my true feelings for you, Harriet. I wish if only you could see whats in my heart. I have never wanted anyone so badly." He sounded so sincere that she could not tell if there was any deception in it at all.

She wanted to believe him and a large part of her did, but there was a nagging feeling at the back of her head that seemed to pull her back. There was a possibility that she might have been judging him too harshly, she thought to herself. Was it the fact that he was wealthy that caused her insecurities; the fact that this made him a target for most women. She did not want to be hurt later on, if she could avoid it.

Yet again, he sensed the conflict within her and made a suggestion. "Harriet, let me send a car for you. Come down to mine and we can talk, face to face. What do you say?"

Harriet thought for a minute. She wanted to see him too but her sensible self was in charge, and that side of her was much harder to convince. However, Harriet also thought that this might be the only chance she might be able to find out, unequivocally, how she really felt about him. She accepted his invitation to go over to the mansion that evening and he had sent a car out for her as promised.

It was around 6 o'clock that evening when Peter's Range Rover Sport drove through the Surrey streets towards the mansion. A car and driver had been sent to Harriet's student residence to pick her up, as they had arranged over the phone. It was the same driver who had always come to pick her up, the same one who seemed to not like her for some unknown reason, Tau.

He had not spoken to her that much since picking her up except the usual greeting. Harriet could not work out what she had ever done to this man to deserve such a frozen attitude all the time. On this evening though, she was in a different state of mind, more confrontational than she usually was. She decided to put him to task over it.

"Excuse me, Tau", she began, breaking the silence in the car. He did not respond but just looked at her through the rear view mirror, his forehead creased in wonder as to what she was about to ask him. She went straight in for the jugular.

"Why do you hate me? What have I ever done to you that you can't even speak to me like a normal human being. Please tell me, because if I have ever said or done anything to upset you, I would like an opportunity to apologise."

Tau was dumbstruck. He had not anticipated this fire bellowing from her. He kept his eyes on the road for a while, before further infuriating her by giving a very limited response.

"You haven't done anything," he replied, still quite unmoved. Harriet was not having it.

"I must have," she accosted him. "You look down on me and you hardly say anything pleasant to me. It's as if I am some kind of pest to you. What is your problem?"

"I have never said anything like that to you," he snarled and refuted her claims.

Harriet was now even more flabbergasted by his callousness. He was a cold, hard hearted individual.

"I don't think you are a very nice person. That's all I am going to say. It's a shame Peter surrounds himself with people like you. I don't know what he sees in you."

By the time she made that statement, they had pulled up by the main gates. Tau rolled down his window and swiped his security pass on the intercom, automatically opening the gates. He drove the sports utility vehicle through the gates and up the drive to the main front doors. Harriet grabbed her bag and was getting ready to exit the vehicle when he turned to her in the back seat.

"Listen, I don't hate you. I don't hate anyone, but I have seen many women come and go in Peter's life. Most have come with bad intentions and ended up hurting him. Now I am very sceptical about anyone hanging around him. He needs me like this to protect him."

She was surprised at how he had had a change of heart and opened up to her. In many ways she understood what he was saying. He had probably met many shady characters and become untrusting over the years. She did not discuss the matter further with him but left the vehicle and went into the house.

The first thing she noticed and remembered as she entered the main hall was that the mansion felt clean, bright, warm and inviting. She had admired it from the first time she had been. This time though, as she walked through, she tried to imagine how it would feel to actually live there. She visualised herself walking in from a shopping spree, walking back into all that comfort. She knew this could be a reality if she wanted, well, he had made it clear that he wanted her in his life, so it was more than possible.

As she took off her jacket and put it on the hook in the hallway, Tau walked in through the same door she had used.

"He's in the dining room," he informed her, as he closed and locked the door.

"Thanks," she replied and went through the doors into the dining room.

Peter wasn't in there when she walked in but the dining table had been laid out for two. There was a display of plate and cutlery settings and two long candles lit in the middle. The light in the room was dimly lit, creating a very romantic atmosphere. She smiled to herself; Peter always knew how to get to her, she thought.

Almost immediately, he had walked into the room holding two small plates of starters, to what would be an exquisite three course dinner. He was dressed in formal grey trousers, black leather shoes and a cotton casual scotch shirt, with the cuffs rolled up.

She felt a little under dressed in her jeans, a sweat shirt and trainers. She had not made much of an effort, as she did not think that they would be going anywhere, with the situation as it was between them.

"Hey!" He said excitedly, as he placed the two small plates down. He went across to her and hugged her. "Good timing, food's done."

Harriet was a bit perplexed to see him serving. He usually had his cook do that.

"What's going on?" She asked. "What's the occasion?"

"You," he smiled back at her. "Thought I'd make you dinner. You didn't know I could cook, did you?"

She smiled back and shook her head in disbelief at how he had put in the effort. She was pleased he had though. There was something special and incredibly romantic about it.

"Where is your cook tonight?" She asked, as she sat down by the table.

"Gave him the night off," he replied, as he sat down too.

She looked down at the small plate with the starter in front of her and was impressed to see that it was a scrumptious mixture of tiny white melon cubes, Parma ham and wild rocket, draped in a tangy mint sauce.

"Oh wow," she murmured. "This looks nice. Did you seriously make this yourself?" She asked, looking up at him.

"Of course I did. Don't you trust me?"

She just smiled; his response had come just as she was making a start on the food. As she chewed and her taste senses picked up the fusion of the ham, wild rocket and mint sauce, she could only think how ironic his question on trust was. She wanted to trust him, but he had already unnerved her through his actions. There was too much about him and his world that she was not quite clear about yet.

However, as the evening progressed, she began to remember why she had fallen for him the first time. They ate, talked and laughed throughout. They had finished their starters and he had again wowed her with the main course of lasagne and a side salad. The finale was a serving of dark chocolate cake with vanilla ice cream and a dollop of whip cream. She still could not believe that he had gone all this way to do this for her.

That night she stayed over. He had managed to convince her to stay. They had relaxed on his porch after dinner, overlooking the back gardens, where she remembered the party being held. The patio was as cosy as the inside, with large cushioned outdoor loungers and outdoor gas burners to keep them warm. The gardens were well lit at night, making quite a pleasing view under the dark sky.

Harriet had not been able to go into anything involving Freda. She just could not find the most convenient opportunity to do it; the night had been too perfect to ruin. Harriet was happy she had come, she was having such a wonderful time, just the two of them alone again. It was the first time they had spent time together like this, relaxed and not rushed.

"Are you OK over there? Come and sit with me over here?" Peter asked. He was sitting on a three seater outdoor settee and she was on the single next to it.

Harriet hesitated for a second, before getting up and planting herself next to him. She sat in a closed posture with her arms and legs crossed, looking out at the garden. Although she was warming to him, she was still not going to make it easy.

"Do you like it here?" He asked, softly, his gaze also transfixed at the garden in front of them.

"I do, it's lovely." Harriet replied. Although

she was still trying to project a hard front, she had an abundance of pleasant emotions that she was feeling, just being there with him. It would have been even more enhanced if she was all cuddled up to him but she was not going to make the first move. As if he had just read her mind, her put his arm around her shoulders and pulled her into him.

"Come here," he said softly, and with arms still folded, Harriet allowed herself to be pulled into him.

"Are you OK?" He whispered down at her, her head now resting on his chest.

"Yes,"she whispered back. She undid her arms and for the first time since seeing him again, she relaxed and wrapped her arms around him.

They stayed out there for a while without saying much to each other. They were both absorbing the moment of just being back in each other's arms again, both happy to be together again.

Harriet opened her eyes and took a minute to adjust to the light that had filtered through the window into the bedroom she had slept in. There was a comfortable quietness to the room's ambience, which was so relaxing; with not even a hum or a hiss anywhere.

She was wrapped well under a silk covered duvet, lying on smooth silk sheets. She even loved how the texture of the pillow felt against the side of her face, like the soft touch of a chick's feathers.

She lay there for a while, thoughts of the

previous night circling in her head. It had all been different from how she had thought the night would end. She had not anticipated that she would end up having such a pleasant evening with Peter, let alone staying over. She wanted to chastise herself for being so gullible, but she was glad it had happened. She was surprised at how a big part of her had wanted it.

She lay there, still reminiscing, and from the contact of her body with the bedding, she remembered she was naked all the way down to her panties. She had slept in the same bed as him and he had been gentleman enough not to go any further. She had wanted the contact but was glad that she had not allowed things to go too far. In a way, it had been a test to see whether it was her he truly wanted, and not only just after one thing.

She threw the covers aside and sat on the edge of the bed, trying to give her head time to catch up. She looked towards an armchair near the window and realised that is where her clothes had ended up. She stumbled to her feet, still a little drowsy, and staggered towards the armchair.

She stood near the armchair for the next couple of minutes, putting her clothes on, as she took in the magnificent views of the gardens again. She couldn't get enough of the beauty of this place.

After getting her bra and jumper on, she sat down on the armchair to get her jeans over her legs first, before standing up again and yanking them all the way up. It took a bit of breathing in to fasten the single button that held the waist band together and clicked her tongue in annoyance at how she seemed to have gained a little weight.

She opened the bedroom door and staggered

cutely towards the stairway. It was eerily quiet on the top floor as no-one else was up there. She knew she had to travel downstairs to find company. As she neared the bottom of the stairs onto the ground level main hallway, she began to hear voices from the kitchen, two males talking. She walked towards them and it became apparent, as she draw closer, that Peter was conversing with someone she had never met. She could not make out the voice.

"There she is," Peter said, as she walked into the kitchen.

Harriet just smiled back, a little shy. The unknown male sat on one of the high kitchen stools by the island, whilst Peter stood the other side. She walked towards him.

"Sam, this is Harriet, the girl I can't stop talking about. Harriet, this is Mr Sam Fuller, my manager."

"Nice to meet you, Harriet. We finally meet," Sam said

"Likewise," Harriet replied, "Pleasure to meet you too." Her voice still slow and groggy.

She wondered whether this was one of the people Peter had mentioned, the team he was answerable to and could not make any decisions without their involvement. She wondered how much influence they had in his private life and whether she had actually been a subject of discussion herself.

"Tea, coffee?" Peter offered her.

"Coffee, please," she replied.

He opened a cupboard under the island and pulled out a coffee mug. He reached out for the coffee maker on top of the island and poured some black coffee.

"Sugar? Milk?" He checked.

She nodded. "Two please."

As he went on to do this, the visitor decided his business had been concluded with Peter and made it known that he was departing.

"Peter, I best be on my way," he said.

"Ye, OK, sure Sam. Let's catch up next week. I will come down to your office."

Sam bid Harriet farewell and left. Peter walked towards her, coffee mug in hand and passed it to her.

"Did you sleep well?" He asked.

"Yes thanks," she replied and took a sip of her drink.

He took the coffee mug back from her, which took her by surprise, and he placed it on the island counter. He moved closer into her until their bodies touched, and put his arms around her waist.

"I would love to make coffee for you every day. What do you say to that?" he said, looking down at her with his signature cheeky smile.

She smiled sheepishly and answered softly," That would be lovely. And breakfast too?" She added, reciprocating his cheekiness.

"Oh course," he laughed.

As he held her, her face dropped and she put both her hands on his chest, as if she were trying to stop him. She wanted to get something off her chest before she could allow this to go even further.

"Peter, I still need to know what happened between you and Freda?" She let out, hoping that he would not over react but just give her an honest answer.

He stood there for a few moments, still holding her and staring down into her eyes.

"OK, I will tell you what happened," he said softly, "Harriet, I really need you to believe me when I tell you that nothing, and I mean nothing, ever developed between Freda and me. She came with Hector to one of my parties and she did everything to gain my attention. I admit that I went with it but that's all it was, and I truly regret it. I realised straight away that I didn't feel anything for her, and not wanting to waste her time, I ended it. And that's the God honest truth."

She believed him; this was how she had imagined it happening. She had made up her mind already but she wanted to hear the words coming out of his mouth. Now that he had said it, and he sounded sincere enough, she was now ready to move on. As she finalised her thoughts, Peter decided that he too had a few things he needed guarantees about.

"So... what happened with your fiancé? Did you guys end it? Is that totally done with now?" He asked.

She hesitated. She was not sure whether she was ready to answer that question, but she had to give him something. If there was a moment to decide and put an end to this saga, this was it. Whatever she was about to say in that moment, was going to be the final seal. Her life was either going to go back to how it had always been, or it was going to change for good.

She hesitated again, before giving in and said, "Yes, it's over between me and Justin. I am all yours now."

Her neck and throat tightened as she uttered the words, not quite believing she had just done it. A big smile materialised on his face and then he moved down and gave her a long kiss.

Chapter 20

By September things had moved on significantly for Harriet and Peter's relationship. Peter was so thrilled to have her in his life that he wanted her even closer. He asked Harriet to move in with him and she had moved out of university accommodation and joined him at the mansion. She had also begun her studies at the university and Peter had arranged for her to be driven and picked up daily. Even Harriet's relationship with Tau, the driver, improved as he was the one who drove her around the most.

Life for Harriet had taken a complete transformation. Since coming to England she had often had sleepless nights wondering how she would cope financially if her finances dried up. The loan from her father would have only managed to last her so far. She would have had to think about looking for a part time job. Now that she was with Peter, she did not have to think about any of that anymore. He was very generously and had offered to take care of everything she needed.

Some of the aspects of this new lifestyle came as a surprise and shock for Harriet. Most things she knew and was accustomed to, but some things were a steep learning curve. Firstly she had to get used to attending numerous official gatherings and parties, and learn to mingle with wealthy folk. She realised quickly that rich people had the incessant need to throw a party every chance they could get. The social circles were not very big so the parties seemed to have pretty much the same people all the time; it was the same party that just changed venues and themes after every few days or weeks.

Harriet met and was introduced to many celebrities, many she had only seen on the big screen, or on television, both in the UK and back home. Most TV shows that aired in Zimbabwe were very similar to those screened in the UK. She never thought she would be sharing the same space with them in real life, or even mingle and chat to them. Most were football lovers that adored Peter but the admiration would spill over to whoever he had arrived with. Harriet was not completely comfortable being in this situation but she did her best to cope. Peter always wanted her to go with him. Something had changed about him. He was happy to tell all his colleagues, friends and business acquaintances about her. He now came across as someone serious about wanting this relationship to go further, ready to commit and make it permanent.

Harriet enjoyed quite a lot of things about her new lifestyle. She loved shopping and every party was an excuse to go on yet another shopping spree. Attending the first few parties had quickly schooled Harriet to the fact that she needed to step up when it came to looking good.

She had attended the first one in what she thought was a decent outfit but had soon realised that she needed to bring her game up a few more levels. Most of the ladies attending were immaculately well put together, probably by their teams of people, whose only purpose was to ensure that every bit of whatever they wore had a reason to be there. Harriet did not have those kind of resources straightaway, so she had to learn to do it herself.

She often became so busy trying to keep up with all these new engagements that she feared her studies would suffer. She had been to some functions that had been held midweek and had lasted till very late. This in turn usually affected her the next day at uni, causing her to lose focus and unable to concentrate. She tried though, to keep up with it all, as she did not want to disappoint Peter, especially in the first few months of their relationship.

One thing she knew she was going to struggle with from the onset, was making new friends within these circles. Most of the other footballers wives and girlfriends were very different from her. Even though she was not bad looking, by most standards, she did not picture herself like the others. Most were or had been models at some point in their life. It seemed like this was the standard mould when it came to choosing a partner for footballers. She was from a different mould entirely, of pure African built, with curves everywhere; which she carried admirably. It did not bother her being different but she wondered if it would ever bother Peter. If not now, then maybe eventually, she thought.

On the way to uni one morning, she had spoken to Tau about it. He had been with Peter for a considerable number of years and if anyone knew much about Peter, it was most definitely Tau. Besides, he had opened up to her about the other women who had been in Peter's life, so it was natural that she now wanted to know more. It worried her though, what she might hear, but she had her own insecurities that she needed help with.

"So, what were the other women like, you know, the ones he has been with?" She had asked him.

Tau had sighed a little, not eager to engage with this topic. He feared saying something she might not like and causing further upset. Besides, there surely had to be some ethical consideration around keeping his bosses historical shenanigans confidential.

"What do want me to say? Yes, of course he has dated other women," he had replied evasively.

She kissed her teeth, hinting at her frustration with him; he wasn't playing ball. She was frustrated but she also understood that he had to keep his boss's secrets too.

"I know that, but what were they like? Were they ever like me, and did he get on really well with anyone in particular?"

"They were most definitely not like you," he had answered diplomatically, with a smirk on his face, still trying to avoid delving deeper into the matter.

"What do you mean they were most definitely not like me. Were they better?" She asked.

"No. No, I don't mean that they were any better, just different. You come from a different background, different upbringing than most of them. You seem more grounded and I have already seen a change in him since you came."

"Really? A change?" She perked up in her seat. She was pleased to hear that she was coming across as a positive influence for him.

"Yes, definitely," Tau continued. "He spoke to me about it. He talks differently about you. His other relationships seemed to just be a fun kinda thing, but with you he talks different, more about future plans with you. I think he has finally grown up and finds you to be the lady he wants to settle with and probably even raise a family with."

"Really?" She had said smiling. She was intrigued

"I think so," he replied

She had found a lot of reassurance from their conversation and she hoped that all of it was true. Her feelings for Peter had grown since they had started again and she was hoping that somewhere in his mind, he had serious thoughts of settling with her. They were now together, living together and that seemed to be going in the right direction.

She had been thinking lately about how her parents would have been so disapproving of this situation, if they knew that she had moved in with a man they did not know about, and no dowry ever been exchanged. She was going to have to make sure that they did not know anything about it until she was ready.

That evening though, she could not wait for him to get home. She wanted to see him and tell him how much she wanted him, how much he meant to her and made her feel. She was in the lounge and TV room when he walked into the house. She got up and went to meet him in the hallway.

He had on his team 'off pitch' kit, which was a navy hoodie and sweat bottoms, both with the Chelsea emblem embroidered on. He was also wearing his sponsored Nike trainers, that had his name inscribed on the side. He dropped his gym bag at the door as he entered and walked towards her. She was also in a hoody of her own; small, tight and pink in colour; faded skinny blue jeans and no shoes. She wore a big smile as she walked into his arms.

"Hey babe," he said, putting his arms around her, and planting a kiss on her lips.

"Hi," she answered softly, in between the kiss.

"I missed you so much today," he added, still trying to keep his lips on her.

She absorbed the kiss for a minute more, before pulling away a little and answering.

"Me too. I couldn't wait for you to get home."

"Really?" He asked, still holding her.

"Ye," she smiled up at him.

The connection between them had intensified significantly since they had decided to put everything to one side and move on with their relationship. Harriet, especially, had to put a lot of her past behind her to make things work. She had never gathered the courage to tell Justin that it was truly over, preferring to simply stop all communication with him and give him a chance to move on.

Soon after leaving London, Justin had called Harriet on several occasions, in an attempt to keep communication channels open, but she would always use her studies as an excuse for not engaging. Justin, not wanted to give her any pressure, had agreed to minimise contact, until she was settled. He hoped that things would gather momentum after a few months or so. He also secretly hoped that keeping her head buried in her books might help Harriet to forget this man who had almost ruined their future.

After dinner, Harriet and Peter got comfortable in the lounge and watched a movie. He sat leaning all the way back into the reclining three seater and she sat next to him, her feet on the sofa and her head buried in his chest. He had his arm around her and would often move down to kiss the top of her head. She loved the way he was affectionate and how he cared for her. She now felt even more connected to him, both on a physical and very high emotional level. Her old life had all but disappeared; Justin now a thought in recesses of her mind.

At Hastin Distribution, phones were ringing and computer keyboards tapping away, three weeks in after their official opening. The office space on the ground floor was now populated by desks, topped with computer screens. Other areas had been partitioned to make smaller offices for more senior members of the staff team. What was once a vacant lot, was now a hive of serious business activity.

Justin stood on the balcony outside his office, which was located at the back, overlooking the open plan office space below, and from there he watched as his empire took shape. He smiled with pride at his new team, and to himself, for getting everything off the ground to a flying start. He was pleased many had jumped ship with him from Glenson & Glenson, and he wondered whether he was going to get a call, or a visit, from his old bosses.

Pleased as he was with what was happening, there was one person on his mind as he surveyed his new project. He had done all this with her in mind and he knew she would be proud to hear of all the developments. He was not sure whether to tell her now or just wait to surprise her when she got back. Justin could not wait for Harriet to be part of it.

He turned and walked back into his office. As he sat down behind his desk, Ken came up the stairs and into his office holding a magazine in one hand. His face was a picture and Justin wondered what had struck his friend to that extent. Ken walked towards Justin and stood there staring at him as if he was waiting to be summoned to speak.

"You ok," Justin asked, puzzled by his partner's expression. He sat back in his chair.

Without as much as a word, Ken opened the magazine to a page he had been holding with his finger. He spread the magazine across the table in front of Justin and pointed at an article with a few pictures accompanying it. Ken's face was now ablaze with fury and Justin leaned forward to find out what had made him this irate.

Justin's face could have dropped off when he looked at the article and realised who it was about. He could not believe what he was seeing. In clear high definition images, he saw Harriet and Peter walking arm in arm somewhere in London, with the title 'ZIM INTERNATIONAL STRIKER FINDS LOVE AGAIN' above it. There was no mistaking it, the two people in the article were very much in some type of close personal relationship.

Justin picked up the magazine from the table and sank back into his chair with it. He read quietly, horrified by what he was seeing. He thought his journey to London and the days he had spent with Harriet had settled things between them. He could not believe what he was reading. Hardly two months since his return, here she was, hand in hand with him again. It tore him apart so much. What was worse was that she seemed happy and comfortable in the company of the man she was supposed to have dumped and forgotten about.

"It's over man, done!" Ken spoke. "You need to cut her out now and put an end to this bullshit. She has made up her mind."

Justin put the magazine on the desk again and towered over it, still looking through it as if the story was going to change miraculously. The article detailed how the two had been spotted several times in London, shopping, and also out on social engagements. The reporter had gone further to find out who Harriet was, where she was from in Harare, and even the schools she had gone to. What they failed to pick up was that she was still engaged to another man.

Justin eventually moved away from the magazine and sat back in his chair again, his head tilted upwards and his eye shut. He took a deep sign. This time he felt a much deeper pain, and for some reason he wasn't angry, just heartbroken. He realised in that moment that all he had planned and hoped for was now gone. Everything he had visualised and set out to do, all for her, was now never to happen. He felt empty and destroyed.

"Are you alright bro?" Ken asked, realised his friend was not doing well with the news.

"I'm fine." Justin replied, calmly. He sounded defeated.

"I'm here man, talk to me." Ken offered.

Justin stared forward briefly, a blank expression on his face, then said again," I will be fine mate. Thanks for the offer."

He got up from his chair and grabbed his laptop bag from the side of his desk. He did not feel like being there anymore. Ironically, this space he had created for them, was now strangling him. It felt small, suffocating, and all he wanted to do was breathe. He grabbed his suit jacket from the back of his chair and threw it on quickly.

"I've got to go. Can you look after things here?" he said to Ken.

"Hey, sure bro. Take all the time you need. I will keep things ticking over here."

Justin picked up his bag and left the office. He walked downstairs and made effort not to make eye contact with anyone. He got outside onto the car park and before he got into his car, he looked back at his office building. He looked up at his new sign, which read 'Hastin Distribution LTD'. Somehow it all seemed pointless now.

Chapter 21

It was a Saturday, a couple of months on since Harriet moved into the mansion. She sat on the edge of the bed having just woken up, contemplating whether her body was up to leaving the bedroom. Peter was still fast asleep next to her and she knew he would not be up any time soon. He had been out most of the night at the Chelsea club bar, drinking, and had to be picked up by Tau around 2am. He had been in no state to drive so they had left his new toy, his Lamborghini Gallardo, parked at the club.

Harriet was not feeling like herself that morning, and she had not been well in the last few days either. She wondered whether she was coming down with something. She hated being ill. She dragged herself up and walked into the bathroom. As she stepped in, the automatic lights lit up the room and she had to squint her eyes to acclimatise.

The light in the bathroom needed adjusting. It was too bright and annoying, especially in the morning after you just got up.

She undressed and walked into the glass shower cubicle. She turned the tap on and several shower heads fired clear warm water at her simultaneous from all directions, including from directly above her. She spend the next few moments in there but did not stay for too long, as the steam was not helping. It was making her feel faint and out of breath. She quickly dried herself off and walked out of the bathroom. Several minutes more later, she was downstairs, fully dressed up and ready to go out.

She walked into the kitchen and found Tau sat by the table reading the morning paper, a plate of half eaten breakfast in front of him. James, the chef, was in there too, preparing more eggs and bacon. He was a tall thin Caucasian male dressed in chef whites and a small white chef's cap.

"Morning ma-am," James said, as he was the first to see Harriet walk in.

"Morning James," she replied.

Tau pulled down the paper to look towards the door and before he could speak she had already got to him.

"Morning Tau. Can you please give me a lift to Dr Dugus? I have an appointment at 10:30."

"Yes, sure," Tau replied, putting his newspaper down and finishing his breakfast hurriedly.

"Are you having breakfast before you go ma-am?" James asked.

"No thanks James. I don't feel like food right now. Maybe when I come back. Peter will be up in a bit though, so please have something ready for him."

"Yes ma-am," he nodded and took his attention back to his pots and pans on the hob.

Tau drove Harriet to Stourbridge Surgery where Harriet spend the next ten minutes waiting for her turn to see the doctor. Her name was called out and she went through into Dr Dugus's office. Dr Dugus was Peter's doctor and Harriet had registered with him when she moved in. He was an elderly gentleman with years of doctoral experience up his sleeve and was very fond of Peter.

"Harriet, come on in my lovely, come on in?" He said, gesturing her into his office, with a large reassuring grin as he waved to one of the visitor seats.

"Thank you Dr Dugus," Harriet replied and accepted his offer for a seat.

"How are you and how is my favourite footballer?" he asked as he sat down in his usual seat.

"Peter is fine, thank you."

"Good, good. That's what I like to hear." He said. "So…, now, how about you my darling, how have you been?"

"I'm not too bad Dr Dugus, but I have not been myself lately. I booked the appointment so that you might help me find out what is happening to me."

"Oh, alright. Describe for me what you've been feeling?"

"Well, I feel it mostly when I wake up. I am very lethargic and I sometimes don't want to up in the morning. My appetite is very poor and I am struggling to keep my energy levels high."

"OK. Alright." He replied, deliberating on what she had just told him. "Do you have fevers, cold sweats, some kind of temperature fluctuations?" He continued.

"Not really, but I do get very hot sometimes and my face feels very puffy at times as well."

"OK," he said, rolling his chair towards her and picked up his stethoscope. "I'm just going to do a few checks, just routine BP, temperature and pulse, that sort of thing."

Harriet offered herself and Dr Dugus went through his routine. He recorded the findings in his file and rolled his chair back into its normal position.

"OK. All your obs are perfectly fine. You do have a slight elevation in your temperature and a low blood pressure, but nothing to worry about. However, I have to ask you this, are you sure you are not pregnant? Have you thought of that?"

Harriet's heart skipped a beat. Of all the things that it could have been, she had not stopped to think that she might have been pregnant. She had been worried about the irregularity of her periods but this was not something new. Her periods were awkward. She had been having pain in her stomach too, but she thought it was just period pain. Now she had a strong suspicion that Dr Dugus might be right.

"I... I don't know. I haven't tested myself," she managed to answer.

"Well, I suggest we do it right now to eliminate things. Just give me a minute."

Dr Dugus got up and stepped out, returning moments later with a sealed pregnancy test.

"Take this and use one of our bathrooms to

do the test. Instructions are here on the side. This is a quick test but we can also get a urine sample sent out for a more concrete result. Go, take it and come back to me after."

Harriet took the pregnancy test from Dr Dugus and left the room. She walked back in moments later and gave him the test back. His eyes lit up when he saw the result and looked up at her.

Harriet walked through the front door of the mansion and placed her hand bag on a small table near the door, which had a large Areca palm tree on top of it. She was slow in her walk as if someone ailing, but it was more what was on her mind that weighed her down. She did not hear any activity downstairs so she gathered that Peter was still upstairs in the bedroom, or maybe he had gone out already.

She entered the bedroom and had immediately deduced that he was in the shower. She could hear the water splattering onto the shower floor and his awful rendition of the song 'Freak Me' by the boy band Another Level. He had carried on singing, adding more of his style to the song and further desecrating the reputation of one of the best baby making songs of the 90s. It was only after he stepped out of the bathroom, large towel wrapped around his waist, and back into the bedroom that he had realised he was not alone.

"Oh, hi sweetie. I didn't know you were back." He said, a tiny bit embarrassed that she might have heard it all.

"Ye. I've been back for a WHILE," She said, emphasising the fact that she had been in the bedroom for just the right amount of time to hear him serenade the shower head and destroy a classic. She had a tiny smirk on her face.

He smiled sheepishly and made his way to the dressing table to lotion up.

"What did the doctor say?" he asked, as he squeezed the body lotion into his palm and rubbed his hands together before applying the mixture on his arms.

She did not reply straight away; she was trying to find the words. He noticed her pause and turned to look at her. She was sitting on the single armchair that lived near the window, still wearing what she had gone out in, minus the shoes she had kicked off. She had a look of worry.

"What's wrong sweetie? Is everything OK?" He said walking towards her. He knelt beside her and put his hand on her thigh." What did the doctor say?"

"Nothing. Nothing to worry about," she reassured him, but her demeanour was still concerning. She knew she had to tell him what had happened but she was still processing it herself. She looked down at him as he knelt next to her, "I have something I need to tell you. I'm not quite sure how you're going to take it." She signed, then continued, "I'm pregnant."

"What?" He said quietly, shocked and surprised.

"Yes, Dr Dugus had me take a test. I may be about 3-4 months pregnant."

"What!?" Came an even more perplexed

response. "How can you be? But I thought...?" Peter did not finish. He was now even more confused about what he was hearing. They had obviously been sleeping together but he thought they had taken enough preventative measures to stop pregnancy, at least for now.

"I know!" She agreed with him. "I thought we were safe too. Apparently not."

Peter got up and paced a little. He was not sure whether to be pleased or not. Surely this was good news, how could it not be. It may have not come at the time when they both expected it but it was still something that both of them would have wanted to happen, eventually.

"Wow," he muttered to himself. "Didn't see that one coming... But hey..." He went back to kneel next to her. "This is a good thing. I'm OK with this." He said, smiling excessively, over compensating, all to try and put her at easy.

"You think so?" She asked, still registering concern.

It was not that she did not want to have a baby with Peter but she was just worried that this might have happened a little too soon and could jeopardise a few things. They had just got together. Were they ready for such a big next step? Besides, this was not going to sit well with her parents. A baby out of wedlock was still a serious taboo, even in modern Africa. She would have wanted first to get them used to the fact that she was now with Peter, but now she had the additional task of informing them that they were about to become grandparents as well.

Another thought that crossed her mind since learning of this new situation was what Justin would think and feel upon hearing this. She did not know why he came into her thoughts but it was probably an ounce of guilt she still harboured. It had been barely three months since she left him and now he was going to find out that she was expecting. Harriet knew that this was going to break him apart even more.

"Yes babe. This is good news! It was going to happen to us sooner or later, so why should now be any different." Peter said, now a little more excitable.

He was coping well with the news and this was helping to reassure Harriet massively. She had been so consumed with fear on the way back from the doctor's, not knowing what his reaction would be. She never envisioned fear as part of the experience if ever she found out that she was having a baby. She had always visualise her and Justin together in a doctor's office getting the news, how they would hug each other after and hold hands all the way home; in some kind of fairy tale type scenario. It was not to say that her life now wasn't a 'fairy tale' in itself, it was just that she had never thought it would be quite like this.

Harriet was smiling a lot more now, pleased that Peter had handled it much more calmer than she had anticipated. Unbeknown to her, he had not finished.

"I think we need to do the right thing," he said. He stood up again. He was still not dressed yet, but just the towel around his mid section covering his delicates.

"Do the right thing?" She asked

"Yes," he replied. "We need to make this official. We have to go to Zimbabwe and I have to see your family. We have to do what needs to be done."

Harriet was pleasantly surprised. She had not seen this side of Peter, and she was pleased to see him this excited. His 'no panic' and 'take charge' attitude to the whole thing had truly impressed her. She was not afraid anymore. It was all going to work out.

"I think that would be a really good idea, honey. When do you think we should do this?" Harriet asked.

"I'll have to talk to coach and get some days between training and matches. But very soon though."

The premiership season had just started and Peter knew that getting time to travel abroad was going to be difficult. He wanted to do the right thing though, especially now that they were expecting. He knew they would have to face severe criticism for things happening the wrong way round but he was confident he could convince her family to accept him and the situation.

It took her days to gather the courage to pick up the phone and dial the international prefix +263 before adding her parents home telephone number. Peter had urged Harriet to get in contact with her parents and inform them that they would be coming to make official introductions, and make the required contributions to her dowry.

Peter wanted to formally introduce himself and ask Harriet's parents for her hand in marriage. He could have sent his family, who were back in Zimbabwe, to go and do the initial meet with her family, as was the way it was usually done in Zimbabwean culture, but he wanted to move things forward quicker.

Harriet and Peter had spoken in great detail a few days earlier about how things had moved much faster than they had both expected but they were both happy and were willing to move with the new schedule. Peter was eager to get the ball rolling because he did not want his child to be born out of wedlock. Even though a few corners had already been cut and their relationship starting in a different order to what their culture would have otherwise dictated, Peter was determined to make sure it ended well.

They debated whether it was wise to let her parents know that she was pregnant. This would obviously add more strain to the proceedings but there was no way they were going to get away without saying. The timeline of whenever the meeting would be set and arrival of the baby a few months later would have definitely revealed some inconsistencies. They decided that it was better to come clean and face the dragon's flame.

Harriet sat by the dining table in one of the meal rooms in the mansion and stared at the phone in front of her. She knew she had to make the call but she had never dreaded doing anything this much before. She knew how the conversation was going to go even before she spoke to her parents; she had lived with them all her life and she knew how they reacted to situations.

Peter was away on training week and she wished he was there to give her moral support. She needed it. She gathered a little more courage, then picked up the phone. She entered the country code and telephone number. The phone dialling tone came first and then the ringing tone. She waited. She wondered who was going to pick up the call and prayed that it would be Beatrice first. She had to suss out the situation first. Her prayers were answered.

"Hello," Beatrice's unenthused voice came on the line.

"Oh my God, wake up little sis. Were you asleep?" Harriet nagged her.

"Oh, hi Harriet. *Ye*, I just got up. I was at a party last night and came back very late, well it finished at 3am this morning."

"And mum and dad allowed you to stay out that long? They never used to let me stay out till early hours of the morning." She berated her further. Harriet was genuinely shocked at how her little sister could get away with something like this. She would have been dragged through red hot coal ashes in her day if she turned up at three in the morning from a party. How things had changed. "Anyway, are they home, mum and dad?"

"Yes, they are still in the bedroom but awake."

"OK, I need to speak to mum. Please call her to the phone but before you do, what mood are they in today?"

"I don't know, I haven't seen them yet," Beatrice replied.

Sensing that she was not going to get the

preparatory information she was hoping for, Harriet just asked for her mum to come to the phone. A few minutes went by before her mum's voice came through her receiver.

"Hello?"

"Hello mum, how are you?"

"Harriet, how are you my daughter? How are you over there?" She enquired.

"I'm well mum. How's dad?"

"He's well, much better these days."

"Oh good." Harriet replied. She did not want to waste time so she went straight into the reason for a call. "Mum I have something rather important to talk to you about."

"OK, is everything OK? I have to say, we were expecting to hear from you as well."

"Were you?" Harriet asked. She knew instantly though that the only thing they could have possibly wanted to talk to her about was to do with Peter and Justin.

"Yes, my dear, but I will let you go first."

"Oh OK." Harriet said, thrown off her course a little. "Mum, I want you to know that everything is fine over here for me so I don't want you to worry at all. It's more than fine actually. I know this is not the way to discuss an issue this delicate, over the phone. If I were near I would have come in person."

"Its OK my dear, out with it."

Harriet gathered her thoughts for a second or two then proceeded.

"Mum, I wanted you and dad to know that I broke the engagement with Justin. We are no longer together."

"Oh Harriet, my child, why would you do

this! Justin came and informed us. We couldn't
believe it. He has always been there for you, from a
very long time and he did everything the right way,
coming to ask for your hand in marriage. Now you
want to disgrace us in front of everyone that
gathered to see you get engaged to him."

Harriet sensed that this was going to be
much harder than she expected. This was only her
mother she was talking to, and she was the sensible
one.

"Mum, things change."

"But you don't throw away a sure thing for
someone you don't even know. Is it because of that
football boy we heard about?"

"His name is Peter mum, and yes, we are
together now."

"Oh my God Harriet, how can you do this to
Justin? He is a good man and he would have done
everything for you."

"I know mum. You know I loved Justin but
things change, people change and I fell in love with
someone else."

There was a brief silence and a sigh from
her mum, before she continued,"Well I'm not the
one you need to convince. Your father is already
upset about it. He feels you disgraced the family."

"Mum, how can I be said to have disgraced
the family, we were not married yet. This was just
an engagement."

"It had gone further than that! You don't
even know. When Justin came back from London
he came and spoke to your father to organise a date
to come and give his dowry. He did not want to
wait".

"What!?" Harriet asked shocked.

"Yes, your father had given his family a date and also informed your uncles so that they could all come to hear you getting married. Then a few days ago Justin came to show us this magazine you were in, walking around with this boy of yours. Your father is beside himself with anger."

Harriet was dumbfound. She had not seen or heard of a magazine publication of her and Peter. She also could not believe the amount of planning that had happened without her even knowing. Here she was, living her life thousands of miles away, and on the other side of the continent her life was being mapped out without her knowledge.

"What the heck mum! Why didn't anybody think to tell me. Everyone just planning out my life without me?" She screamed at her mother down the phone. She was even more angry with Justin for moving ahead with all these elaborate plans, without even as much as a call to her, and above all, going to her parents to show them this magazine.

"No-one could get you on the phone. You have not rang us for a while now and besides your father thought this was all agreed since Justin had just come from there. But need I remind you Harriet, you were already engaged to the man, you had agreed to marry him and this was the next stage to it."

As her mother finished these words Harriet heard her father in the background, his voice drawing closer.

"Is that Harriet?" She heard him ask her mother.

"Yes baba," the reply came. There was a shuffling sound as the phone on the other side exchanged hands. Harriet knew her father was coming on the line and she braced herself. Her father was a 'no nonsense ' man with a fire tongue that could ignite anything it came into contact with.

"Hello," came the almost aggressive greeting.

"Hello daddy, how are you?" Harried replied humbly. She always feared and respected her father.

"I am not doing very well Harriet. Would you kindly explain to me what the hell you think you are doing? You go over there and you change into something I don't recognise. What do you think you are doing?"

"Daddy, please understand. I did not plan to come up here and just decide to leave Justin. This just happened."

"Things don't just happen, Harriet. You decided to allow things to happen. Now you have disgraced me and your mother in front of all our family and his family. I am seriously upset with you young lady."

Harriet decided it was best to just let him rant. Once he was on the go there was no interrupting him. She had had it all when she was living at home. Her father was so much about keeping the family image clean that anyone who dared put any blemish on his good name was definitely in for a strong dressing down.

"I don't want to hear this nonsense anymore about another boy over there. You have to do what is right by this young man over here. He has done a lot for this family and you."

Harriet knew she had to bring her father up to speed about the current situation, even though she knew it was like pouring a pale of lighter fluid over

an open flame.

"Daddy, I cannot do what you are asking. Things have moved on considerably between me and Peter."

This angered her father even further as she had anticipated. "What do you mean you can't do what I am telling you. You are the one who brought Justin to us, and now you're telling us we have to start accepting someone else."

Harriet always felt her father seemed to forget that she was now much older and able to make decisions for herself. Usually when he was upset about something he always regressed her to a teenager all over again.

"Dad there is more that I need to tell you and mum. Even if I could do what you are asking, it's now much more complicated. Peter and I are now together and we are expecting."

The line went quiet, neither of them spoke for a minute. She could hear her father breathing furiously on the other side. He came back, voice calmer but still carrying anger and said, "Well you have gone and done it now. Bringing more shame on this family. How could you be so stupid? Getting pregnant from a man who hasn't married you or even met your parents. Do you know how disgraceful this is to our whole family? Well I hope you're happy now. Just don't bring any of it here to us."

"Daddy please!" She begged her father. She could not understand how this was being viewed so negatively.

She understood partially that in their culture having a child out of wedlock was a serious affair

Olive Tree Restaurant

199 Midsummer Boulevard,
Milton Keynes MK9 1EA
01908691414
olivetreerestaurants.co.uk

Order#: 13174

07/08/2021 12:53 Restaurant   Tkt#: 26935
Table #. 100

Hummus	5.50
Complimentary Bread	0.00
2 @ 0.00 each	
Mediterranean Breeze	5.95
Complimentary Bread	0.00
2 @ 0.00 each	
Falafel Starter	6.25

TOTAL: **£17.70**

Change   0.00

VAT RECEIPT SUMMARY
VAT No.: 324028045

--<COO>VAT No.:

You were served by

Olive Tree Restaurant

100 Midsummer Boulevard,
Milton Keynes MK9 1EA
01908591114
olivetreerestaurants.co.uk

Order# : 13174

07/06/2022 12:53 Restaurant P:14 955.23
Table #: 70

Hummus	5.50
Complimentary Bread	0.00
2 @ 0.10 each	
Med Halloumi Cheese	9.7
Complimentary Bread	
2 @ 0.00 each	
Falafel Starter	6.2

Total	£17.70
Change	0.00

VAT RECEIPT SUMMARY
VAT No: 2 4996012

COPY# : No 1

You were served by

but times had changed. It seemed her father had not. They never got to finish that conversation. Her father cut the call and left Harriet hanging. She stared at the receiver and could not believe he had just done that. She dialled the number again but this time no one picked it up. She knew instantly that they had all been told not to communicate with her.

Her day had instantaneously morphed into a nightmare. She cried much more than she had ever done before, tortured by a whirlwind of emotions turbulent in her thoughts. She felt lost and rejected, ostracised by the very people she had always thought would be there for her no matter the circumstances. She had never felt so isolated and alone.

Chapter 22

Harriet was in agony as she lay on the bed in the side room at St Giles Private hospital. She was not due for another 4 weeks but she had started to experience some complications with the pregnancy. Peter had not been around to take her there personally as he was still at the club training that afternoon, but he had instructed one of the drivers to rush her down.

St Giles Hospital was not too far from their Surrey mansion, accessed through a string of narrow roads in the English countryside; it was isolated from anywhere. The hospital had been purposely built in that location by the Wellesley group, a private equity establishment that targeted its facilities for people of a certain calibre and status. This usually meant people with so much money that they did not know what to do with it.

Peter had insisted that this was where he was going to have his son born, no matter the cost, even after Harriet had tried to convince him that there was nothing wrong with a nearby public National Health Service hospital.

"I won't have my son brought into this world in an NHS hospital." He had said, some months earlier, when choosing where their son was to be born. They had attended appointments for routine scans and they now knew the gender of their anticipated new born.

"Do you know how under invested and poorly staffed the NHS is now. I won't let that happen. I would rather pay a million pounds to ensure my son gets the best," he had said.

Harriet knew that he would not go as far as paying a million pounds just to have his child brought into the world but she knew Peter wanted the best for them both, the child and her. He had shown a lot of maturity throughout the whole situation and he was preparing himself to be a great dad. She had no doubt that he would be.

"The NHS is not that bad," she had tried to convince him, "There are many hospitals that have received excellent reviews from that organisation that rates hospitals, you know, CQ something. I don't really mind as long as the place is clean."

"Well, be that as it may, we are going to look for a place we can pay to make sure its clean," he had concluded, refusing stubbornly to be swayed.

Harriet had just smiled and shook her head, intrigued by his determination to ensure nothing went wrong. They had explored a lot of Surrey the following weeks, visiting private hospitals and collecting brochures. After further weeks of analysing each and every hospital, they had settled on St Giles. It was not too far and appeared to offer exceptional service. Above all, it was important that Peter approved and was pleased with it.

Back in the side room, Harriet was restless, sweating profusely, and occasionally screaming from the pain. She could not understand what was going on and was very worried. She did not want to lose her baby, especially as she was so near to the end. Everything had been going well and there hadn't been any issues in the last eight months. Why now? What was happening to her unborn child?

The side room door burst open suddenly and a doctor walked in, trailed by 3 nurses. The doctor, female, was distinctly dressed in her white coat and cream formal trousers, with a stethoscope dangling around her neck. The nurses were in surgical type theatre uniforms which composed of a loose blue top, matching blue loose trousers and white clogs on their feet. The nurses dispersed around the room and started operating various machines whilst the doctor advanced to Harriet's bedside and began speaking to her.

"Afternoon Miss Sande, my name is Dr Cartwright. Do you know where you are?" She asked, in a commanding yet reassuring voice.

"Yes…., St Giles." Harriet replied, in between the groaning and grimacing from the pain.

"That's right, thank you," the doctor continued. "Right, Miss Sande, or can I call you Harriet? We are going to need to do an emergency C-section as we believe the baby is struggling and needs to come out right away. I am going to need your permission to get this going. This needs to happen as quickly as possible."

This worried Harriet even more. Now she knew something was definitely not right.

"Peter?" She groaned.

"Yes, your next of kin has been notified and he's on his way, but unfortunately we cannot wait. The theatre is being prepped as we speak and we need to get you in now. Do I have your consent, Harriet?"

Harriet nodded.

"OK," the doctor said and turned to summon her support crew of nurses. "Lets get Miss Sande to theatre ladies!"

Like an army pre-rehearsed drill, the nurses swamped around Harriet taking readings and sticking things into her, before transferring her onto a gurney and wheeling her to the surgery suite. Although Harriet was in pain, her mind was on her unborn baby and Peter. She wished he were there. It was all happening so fast and she wanted him there to tell her it was all going to be alright.

They wheeled her into the operating theatre and transferred her from the gurney. This time they placed her onto a theatre bed that had a host of lights above it beaming down at her. There were now even more people in this room, all prepped for surgery, in navy bandanas, face masks and latex gloves on their hands. It was all ready to go.

As she lay there, watching the hype of activity around her, Harriet remembered that she had never been operated on before, never in her life. The thought that they were just about to be sedate and cut her open, overcame her and did little to help with all the anxieties she was already feeling.

She reached out and touched one of the nurse's arm, as if she wanted to tell them to stop, but she just ended up starring up at her. The nurse knew straight away that Harriet was struggling, she had seen this many times in her experience as a theatre nurse and so she reassured her.

"Don't worry darling," she smiled down at her." It's going to be all over soon. Your baby will be here in a few moments."

On hearing of her baby's imminent arrival, Harriet relaxed and for a moment forgot her pain. She had not stopped to think that in less than an hour she would be holding her baby boy in her arms. Only the night before she had been counting down the weeks, having been pulled down by the thought that there were still four to go. Barely a day later, he was going to be here, it did not seem real.

Harriet was still in her thoughts when the theatre suite door opened again and yet another surgical professional walked in. How many more people, she thought, but no sooner had that thought crossed her mind that she realised it was not another medical personal. Pulling down the surgical mask they had put on him on top of all the theatre apparel, Peter smiled at her and walked towards her. Harriet smiled back at him between the pain but so pleased that he had made it.

They did not even have a moment to talk, when Dr Cartwright walked up next to the bed.

"OK Harriet, we are going to start now. In a few minutes it won't just be the two of you any more. Happy with that?" she said, smiling at them both.

Harriet could only manage a smile back and in the moments that followed, she just lay there felt it as they tagged and pulled around her mid region. She was awake through it all and was grateful for the regional anaesthesia they had given her, which had help ease the pain.

Hours later they were back in their delivery suite, the operation having been a success. Harriet lay on her bed, awake, still in pain but this time the pain was more from her surgical procedure. They had put her on morphine and that was helping.

Peter was on the other side of the room looking down at their son, who lay in an incubator in just his nappy, with a few tubes running from his body. Due to his premature birth and the complications earlier, he was now connected to various monitoring machines and receiving a blood transfusion. Harriet and Peter had opted for direct blood transfusion which meant that their baby could only receive blood from either of them. This had been facilitated and that had made them feel even more connected to him.

"Aww, he is so tiny, but very handsome indeed, just like his daddy," Peter commented, smiling proudly.

"Why wouldn't he be?" Harriet croaked back, looking in the direction of the two most important people in her life. She was still quite drowsy from all the medication.

Peter moved over to her bed and sat on the edge, facing her.

"You did well," he whispered, taking her

hand into his.

"You did too," she reciprocated. He leaned down towards her and kissed her gently on the lips.

As he sat back up, there was a light knock on the door and it swung open. Dr Cartwright walked in, sporting her usual confident smile and advanced towards them.

"How are my new parents doing this afternoon?" she asked.

"Good, thank you," they both answered "Happy," Harriet added, her voice still spent.

"Very good. Good to hear."

Dr Cartwright picked up Harriet's notes at the foot of the bed and scanned them for a few seconds before continuing. She began by explaining what had happened and the rationale for the caesarian section.

"OK, so that was a bit of a rush wasn't it, earlier on." They both smiled and nodded in agreement. "Well, what we know is that, Harriet, from your bloods you are what we call rhesus negative and we now also know that your son is rhesus positive. What then happened, which is quite common really, is that the baby had a little bleed inside the womb, blood which came into contact with mum's blood. At that point mum's body would have perceived the baby as a threat and would have naturally started to develop antibodies. The complications you had were the baby fighting for his life."

"But how can that be," Peter asked, puzzled, "Doesn't that usually happen in a second pregnancy, this rhesus thing?"

Harriet did not speak. Besides being surprised at his knowledge on the subject, there was more that now occupied her mind.

"You are absolutely right," Dr Cartwright agreed with him, and then turned towards Harriet. She was counting on Harriet to come in at this point and fill in the blanks.

Harriet quickly realised that it was now all on her to bring sense to the issue. There was definitely something she had failed to mention to Peter, which she had hoped would have never seen the light of day. She had never wanted Peter to ever know about this, although Justin had been aware of it. He had been there for her through it all and the recollection of that made Harriet feel even worse, considering what she had done to him. She was not sure how this was going to affect things between Peter and her, but this was part of her history she wished was buried, gone and never to be spoken of again.

Peter was also looking at her, now seriously confused. Why had she not mentioned anything to him and what was so difficult that Harriet found it difficult to say?

"Sweetie, have you been pregnant before?" he asked softly, partly hoping she was going to say no. Even if she had been, he did not see that bothering him too much. It was just another thing they would have had to deal with.

Harriet, who was in a semi-seated position in bed with three pillows behind her, closed her eyes and tears began to stream down the side of her face.

"Sweetie, what's the matter?" he asked, now even more concerned.

Harriet's lips quivered as the emotions flooded her. She seemed to be reliving some distressing event. She eventually managed to speak.

"I was pregnant before,.... and I lost it."

Peter just looked at her helpless, not sure how to comfort her. He could understand how losing a baby would have been traumatic for her but he could not work out why she was taking this so hard, especially that it was all the way in her past. Dr Cartwright just stood there patiently and waited for the couple to go through this emotive moment.

"Hey, don't cry, it happened, it's in the past and there is nothing you could have done about it." Peter said, doing his best to console her.

"I didn't want to you to know about it, it was awful," Harriet cried.

"Hey, stop crying. Losing a baby is awful I know but no need to be hard on yourself," he said.

"No, you don't understand!" she whimpered.

Peter was puzzled and wondered what else could have happened.

"What do you mean sweetie? What else happened?" he asked.

Dr Cartwright sensed that this probably needed to be a private moment, so she made a statement to leave. "I think you two have a lot to talk about. I will give you a moment."

She exited the room and left a stumped Peter looking down at Harriet, not quite sure what else was to come, and whether he was prepared to hear it.

"Talk to me, what happened that was so terrible. When were you pregnant, before?" He was handing her tissues from the personal box on top of the hospital drawers as he spoke.

Harriet took her time wiping her face.

"I was 15 and still in high school," she continued.

"What?" Peter asked, shocked.

Harriet snivelled and wiped more tears away.

"When I was 15, my mother's brother came to live with us for a while. He was 24 and going to college. My parents went away for a few days, left him in charge of my sister and me and that's when he raped me…. I was so traumatised it took me a while to get over it; my own uncle. I was never the same again after that."

Peter signed heavily, words failing him.

"I told my parents and my dad ran him away from the house. My dad wanted to kill him!"

"And so he should have!" Peter agreed. "I hope you got the bastard arrested!"

"He ran away before my dad reported him and we never saw him for years. My mum was destroyed." Harriet said.

"I can imagine," Peter said. He was still sat on the bed facing her, holding her hand as she spoke. "That must have been awful, at 15?"

"You don't know the half of it. It was the worst time of my life. To make matters worse, I found out later that I was pregnant, a few months after. I was horrified. I wanted to get rid of it but my parents, being religious and all, talked me out of it. I carried the baby for nearly 20 weeks and then I miscarried. I won't lie to you, I was not sad about it. I was glad I had nothing else left of that monster!" Harriet's tone had intensified into pure hatred.

"Hey, it's OK now. It's in the past and no one will ever hurt you again."

She smiled at him, happy that he was there

with her.

As they sat there, Peter's phone went. He took it out of his pocket and looked at the screen.

"It's Sam. I need to take this. We need to go through a contract today. I'll go grab a coffee down in the cafe whilst I'm at it. Shall I get you anything?"

Harriet shock her head.

"OK, back in a sec," he said, and left the room speaking into the phone as he walked out.

The room went quiet except for the beeps and humming from the machines they were both connected to. Harriet turned and looked towards her son. She had a lot to process. She was happy their baby was here but she was also sad that her parents did not want anything to do with them. She wondered how or if ever they would speak to her again. Surely they would have to come round at some point, she thought.

Harriet had also been trying to put someone else at the back of her mind, but even with all the effort in the world, Justin kept coming back into her thoughts from time to time. The present now seemed so different from the future she had always conceptualised. The life she had visualised with Justin had all but faded away. She could not see them together any more and she wondered how he had moved on from her.

She was still engrossed in her thoughts when Dr Cartwright walked back into the room. Harriet wondered why she was back but thought she was probably checking on her after how upset she had been earlier.

"Harriet, how are you feeling now my love," she said, walking towards the bed.

"Better now, thank you doctor," Harriet replied quietly.

"Good, good… OK, I know you have been through a lot today and I wouldn't want to add more to your plate but I wouldn't be doing my duty if I didn't notify you of a few more things. I am glad I have just you in the room because I wanted you to have a chance to process this on your own and then maybe, when you are ready, you can inform your partner."

Harriet's face dropped. What more could this day bring surely, she thought.

"Is everything OK doctor? Is the baby OK?" Harriet said, as she sat up in her bed, forgetting the pain she was in.

"Baby is fine. He will be OK. This is more about you, the parents," Dr Cartwright said, "Well, I don't know how to put it to you but when we tested your partner's blood this afternoon for compatibility for the transfusion, something did not seem right to us. You are blood type A and the baby is blood type AB, but your partner is blood type O."

Harriet stared at the doctor, not quite believing what she had just heard. "What does this mean doctor?!" She said, eyes still fixed on the doctor. She knew though, what this meant.

"I'm afraid there is no possible way Peter could be the father of your child," the doctor informed her, "I know this is the last thing you wanted to hear today but I'm obligated to tell you as the mother of the child. We can do a detailed DNA test if you prefer, but from these blood results we can tell for certain, Peter is not the father."

Harriet fell back into her pillows, repeating the word 'NO' over and over again to herself, as the tears returned to her eyes. She could not believe how the best day of her life had suddenly turned into an epic nightmare. How could Peter not be the father? How was she even going to tell him?

As Dr Cartwright concluded and walked out of the room, Peter was walking back in. Everything appeared as though it were in slow motion for Harriet as she watched the doctor leave and Peter walk in. They exchanged a few words by the door and as they did, Harriet hurriedly wiped the tears from her face and eyes. Peter walked to her bed side and smiled down at her.

"Everything OK babe?" he asked, innocently.

"Yes, everything is fine. Everything is just fine," she said, smiling back at him.

The End
Volume 1

TORN

Volume 2

Coming out soon!

Hope you enjoyed the story so far! Join us on Facebook and let us know you views. Our Facebook Username is **@tornbookseries**.
You can also visit the series website:
www.tornbookseries.com.

Please tell us what you are hoping to find in volume 2.
Our website & Facebook page is also where you will get updates of the release of Volume 2 and many more publications to come.

See you soon!

Printed in Great Britain
by Amazon